THRICE

THRICE

A Needle and Leaf Novel

ANDREW D MEREDITH

Games Afoot, LLC

To Tricia

My heartsong

My soulwell

My shieldmaiden

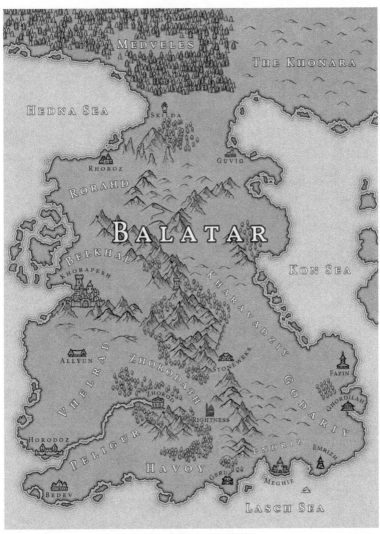

Map by Andrew D Meredith

PROLOGUE

"Do not stop!"

She looked back down the road. Their protector held a torch in his hand, his horse spinning in excitement as the fourth rider galloped hard after them in pursuit.

"Do not stop!" the blonde girl repeated.

She faced forward. The long lead from her horse's bridle to the other rider's went taut and the palfrey lurched forward beneath her, just as another pain shot through her body.

She placed a hand to her belly and huffed out several breaths.

"Not until we reach the safety of the town," the blonde girl called. "Do not let them come just yet."

She turned to look back again, but her horse faltered for a moment and pressed on, jerking her attention to the town ahead.

"Where are we going?" she asked.

"To complete what we started," the blonde girl said. "Do you not remember?"

"No," she offered blankly.

She couldn't remember the blonde girl's name. She wasn't even sure of her own anymore.

The gate ahead stood open. A few people stood watching them as they rode into the small town.

"We need a physician!" the blonde girl called.

Another wave of pain rolled over her, and she held her belly, wincing. She felt strong arms take hold of her, pulling her to the ground to sit.

"What is this?" asked an older lady standing over her.

"She is to give birth this night," the blonde girl answered for her. "We had hoped to arrive well before, but it has started much sooner. The stress of the trip was too much."

The pain was too much. It was too much.

"What on earth possessed you to travel with her as she is?"

"The father was very angry. He pursues us now. He is not far behind."

"You, needlesmith," the old lady called to whoever had laid her down on the street. "Go back down the road and keep watch."

The low voice of the man answered simply, "Yes, Lady Windro."

"Let us see if we can get her someplace safe."

The arms of several men took her up, and carried her she knew not how far.

"A message needs to be sent to Kallidova," her companion said.

"We haven't seen her here in some time," said the older woman.

"Then she needs to be found."

"I shall see it done," Lady Windro said.

They laid her down on a table. Pillows and blankets were brought to make her comfortable.

"What is happening?" she asked weakly.

"You are to give birth," someone said.

"I am? I can't remember."

"She is very, very full with child. The shock of the birth, or the ride, is causing her a great trauma," Lady Windro said.

"She has been through more than you know."

She cried out in pain from the table.

"There is no time to get the physician," the old woman said. "We start this now."

The old lady took hold of her belly and felt around.

"Do you know what you're doing?" the blonde girl asked.

"Well enough. I've not done it myself, but I've saved several mares from a difficult foaling. Now listen to me, girl," Lady Windro said, her eyes piercing through the fog and the pain for an instant. "Do as I say: push once!"

She bore down. Her body knew the way.

The blonde girl braced her from behind.

She took panicked breaths.

"A second time!" the old woman said, and she once more bore down around the pain, the old lady guiding from atop her belly.

The pain was dizzying. She could not recall where she was, as though her memories had been given up to create the life within her.

"Empty yourself and trust that all will be all right," whispered the girl next to her ear. "I'll provide a bit of strength. I've a bit left to feed the well and the means to it."

A surge of energy flowed around the numbing pain, caressing her with strength. And there was another feeling, of a power and the word that carried it, that flowed into her, past her, and into the life within. She felt it take hold of the last of her true memories, leaving only her will to live, and the need to complete the work. She lay on the table with people around her she did not know. There was only pain.

"Thrice!" the old lady shouted over her own scream.

And she pushed, and felt a shuddering release.

CHAPTER 1 — GERUZ

There was a satisfying crunch as Jovan's fist met the other man's nose. Red spattered across his knuckles, adding color to an otherwise gray-washed world. The man lying on his back roared up in frustration, spitting his own blood into Jovan's face. The sound barely registered in Jovan's mind. All that mattered was drawing more blood from the man he straddled. He rained his fists down until the man ceased raging up at him. Now he just lay there, taking the beating without opposition. Pain wracked Jovan's chest as his heart pounded within and the long, deep breaths stretched his lungs with a matching fire.

"Jovan!" a voice broke through.

Amisc.

He wondered how he could hear the man's voice from ten shops away. His tired fists fell to his sides and he took another deep, controlled breath. The bloodied victim did not move until long, shuddering breaths came out of him.

"Jovan," Amisc said calmly. "Let's get you off him."

Jovan stood and looked around. His surroundings confused him. The red door of Amisc's shop stood not far from him, telling him he now sat in the dust out front of the cooperage. He vaguely recalled chasing the man he'd pummeled down the street.

"Jovan," Amisc said. "Are you good?"

He took another breath and nodded.

A crowd had gathered, keeping away from the middle of the cobbled street and against the sides of the stores that lined the thoroughfare in the small coastal town of Geruz.

He reached up and wiped spittle and flecks of blood that had beaded on his full beard. The smear that it left on his palm told him he must appear like a vengeful creature come from the underworld. A small roll of leather fell from his shirt and hit the ground. Jovan reached down and tucked it back into his belt.

A single guard stood between the people and Jovan. He held two ends of shackles, uncertain if he could approach or not.

"Go ahead, Gostis," Jovan said, holding his arms in front of him.

The guard approached warily. "Lord Valle-Brons will want to see you after this."

"I know," Jovan replied.

Gostis continued, though it was clear he still feared Jovan might suddenly lash out with a renewed fury.

"No need to be afraid, Gostis," Jovan said. "I didn't hurt you when we were younger and I won't change that now."

"I...I know," Gostis said. "But I also know your word means nothing when you're hot behind the ears."

"I'm...not anymore. I'm fine."

One shackle finished screwing down on his wrist. Gostis struggled to twist the other one on.

"Here," Jovan said, "let me. You're threading the key."

Jovan gave the key a twist and it popped into the ramp.

"Now try."

The shackle key turned and they were on their way.

They passed by the glazier, who nodded with a smile, as though thanking Jovan for not bringing his fight near his goods. A series of panes sat out in the sun, leaning against the side of his shop. Jovan's reflection was clear in one.

His chest-length beard hung stiffer than usual, flecked in blood. A red misting had dried across his shaved scalp. Two feelings battled within: passion for violence that crept toward the front of his consciousness, and a deep shame that sought to pull him down into himself. If either won, the rage would take control of the bridle once more.

He shook his fists toward the ground and grunted. Gostis startled and took a step away from him, still holding the chain, which jerked Jovan forward. Gostis froze and stared at him in fright. The sparse whiskers on his chin made him look ten years younger than Jovan, despite their both being born in the same month thirty-five years earlier.

"I didn't mean...," Gostis said.

"It's not you," Jovan said.

Gostis took a deep breath and turned, continuing the walk through the town. They passed Jovan's shop. The boy would be watching from the window. Jovan did not want to look up. The shame would only double.

He glanced up, regardless. Ice blue eyes inquisitively met his through the window, framed by gentle white skin and hair the color of burnished gold. The small four-year-old boy smiled and waved, seemingly uncomprehending of what had transpired. He wore the long white tunic of a boy, belt-less, yet clean.

Jovan looked away.

Five other guards came rushing down from the gate. Gostis guided Jovan to the side as they rushed past. They held the pieces of a collapsed litter.

"We should move a little faster," Gostis said, "so you're already sequestered away before they return with...what was his name?"

"Ilon Das."

"An itinerant leather worker, I think?"

"Yes."

"A bit well-dressed."

"Works mostly for nobility. Saddle adornment and such."

"Hrm," Gostis said. "He can't be getting much work here."

"No. I don't think he did."

"Why did you...?" Gostis stopped and looked sheepishly back up the road. "Not my place to ask, I suppose."

They came to the gate. The soldiers above joked with one another, paying little attention to the two men walking underneath.

The motte rose and the road to the main gate with it, circling to the right, though they turned in the opposite direction, following the outer wall around to where the stone bailey sat sagging on the hill like a large man stuck in his chair. Wild herbs, picked bare in places by the kitchen, sprawled across the slope.

The scent of sprigherb filled Jovan's nostrils as they passed the row of sharp-leafed bushes. A break in the row marked their destination, a stone archway leading into a dark entrance. Jovan had been in there before and did not relish entering again.

Gostis disappeared into the pitch black, the darkness eating the chain. A spark exploded and ignited the wicking in Gostis's hand. A candle took the light and illuminated, however dimly, the space within. A tug on the chain told Jovan he was to enter. He stepped forward, ducking under the lintel. He could not stand up straight as he shuffled forward and into the first cell.

"Go ahead and turn around," Gostis said, though Jovan had already started to. The guard worked the shackles off his wrists and then closed the bars.

"I need to go up to Gull Stone—report that you're here and what I saw."

"No need to tell me your business, Gostis," Jovan said. "It's yours, not mine."

"Right. I'll return for you later."

He almost took the candle with him. He probably did with other prisoners—drunks that needed to sober up in darkness, and the few cutpurses who made the mistake of choosing the small town of Geruz as their mark.

A mild autumn storm was blowing in off the water, spattering outside, but did not blow cold in the cramped prison house.

After a few minutes, the guards passed, a stretcher now between them. The town medicae followed and then a young girl. Her head was shaved, marking her as a virgin-healer. Jovan did not envy the short life she lived, fulfilling an ancient role that no longer had the backing of society, nor even less the crown.

He sat down on the bedding and stretched his back. It had been over three years since he had last been sitting in this cell, awaiting the mercy—the undeserved mercy—of a far-too-kindly lord.

A small figure blocked the little light from the doorway as the boy slipped in and came to stand at the bars. His quaint smile paired with his thoughtful eyes and delicate features.

"Leaf," Jovan said.

"Papa Jov?"

"Why are you here?"

"I wanted to make sure you were well," the young boy said. The boy always seemed wise beyond his years, yet at the same time always his age.

"I am fine."

"Why did they take you away?"

"I beat that man." Jovan reached up and tugged at his right ear several times. Ilon Das's dried blood flaked off onto his fingers. He worried that his violence might rub off on the boy. What words would they have when he had to reprimand him for doing what his papa did? Though in their three years together, the young boy had never so much as harmed a mouse nor kicked a dog.

"I'm sorry you have to see me like this," he said, looking at the flakes of blood on his hands.

"Why? We pay our debts."

The boy's discernment once more exceeded his own and filled Jovan with shame.

"I want you to go home, boy. Pack my things."

"Will you return soon?"

"I hope so. Pray to the gods the man I harmed does not die. Or else you might be on your own."

"No. I don't think that will happen. I'll prepare your things, though. Where are we going?"

"Road north maybe."

The boy's smile lit up. "To the market town? You've never taken me before."

"You've never been old enough. Regardless, you get everything packed. If I don't return, you must go north to the city of Rightness. Ask for Mamm Kallidova."

Leaf pushed on the bars and the door clicked open. Jovan frowned.

"Close the door, boy. No need to embarrass Gostis if he left the door unlocked."

"I opened it," Leaf said matter-of-factly. "So you can come home."

"No," Jovan said. "Gostis left it unlocked."

"Yes, Papa Jov," he said as he pushed it closed again with a click.

The boy turned to leave.

"Leaf," Jovan said. The boy stopped and turned, smiling.

Jovan stared for a time at the little boy he had come to love as his own.

"Yes, Papa Jov?"

"There are two pairs of socks with no holes, but pack all your socks. We'll fix the others on the road."

The boy grinned. "Do you want me to pack your bench roll?"

Jovan nodded.

"I'm sorry you have to see me like this," Jovan repeated.

"You're a good papa," Leaf said. "And Lord Valle-Brons is good."

"I think you're good. And you see the good in everyone else," Jovan muttered.

Leaf beamed.

A shadow filled the doorway and Leaf turned.

"Hello, Leaf," Gostis said.

"Hello, Gostis," the boy said. "Papa and I were just talking."

"You need to run home now."

Leaf turned to look at Jovan, seeking his agreement. Jovan nodded. Leaf smiled and scampered off.

"You have a good little boy," Gostis said. "If...anything happens, Sereh and I will take care of him."

Jovan grunted. "If anything happens, he'll disappear. But if he doesn't..."

"We'll take care of him."

"You see he gets to Rightness. He knows who he needs to find."

Gostis nodded. "It's time, Jovan. Lord Valle-Brons wants to see you."

Jovan stood back and let Gostis quietly do his work. Once the shackles were on him, they walked out into the wind as rain began to fall. After a few short steps it fell in waves.

"I was hoping to beat this inside," Gostis shouted over the downpour.

Jovan followed the man up to the gate. After knocking three times, the door opened more abruptly than usual and Gostis shoved his way in, pulling Jovan with him. The door closed behind them and two soldiers dropped the bar back into place with a *thud*—pierced by a girl's scream.

Gostis froze, then led them through the gate room and into the fire-lit and very crowded hall. The elderly medicae knelt over the form of the bald girl collapsed on the ground by the hearth. He stood, nodded, and then checked the patient laid out across the table. The guards and the other attendants crowded around.

"It worked. The fracture is set." As he turned, he stopped and considered Jovan, dripping rain water on the hay spread across the stone.

"You did a right messy job on him, Jovan," he said, wiping blood from his hands. "But he'll live. For that you're lucky."

Jovan grunted.

"You're right," the medicae said. "You're not so lucky, are you? If you live past this, that man will probably do what he can to ruin you."

"I can't take back what I did," Jovan said.

"Doesn't mean you can't pay the bills owed for my services rendered," the old man said. "And the healer: she set the broken jaw right. It'll cost her more of her soul to fix his eye once she rouses."

"You'll get your money," Jovan growled. "Whether it be from me or the lord or from the man on the table. Don't be taking a surplus from my carcass when the meat's not even been hung."

The medicae scoffed and turned to Gostis. "You can tell Lord Valle-Brons that this man, one Ilon Das, had his nose so severely broken I had to dig out the bones so they didn't infect or go up into his head." He held up several fingers, and began counting them off. "Nose broken. Jaw cracked. One eye mangled. And his wrist almost snapped in two."

"That's the extent?"

"That's the worst of it," the man said. "There was more, but nothing worth noting."

"And the man will live?"

"Yes. So the charge is doubled."

Jovan laughed.

"What makes you laugh, boy?" the old man said as he turned and looked up at Jovan with disdain.

"You would steal for saving that which you are charged to do."

"The lord here and I have an understanding. I charge what is fair."

"What people can barely afford," Jovan muttered.

"Your sister died of infection. No one could have possibly saved her. She was dead before anyone arrived and no healer could give enough to bring her back."

"You could have saved her. But you wouldn't."

"I will not sacrifice a piece of soul—just as you would not make a needle of gold—without full payment first." The medicae turned and walked away, muttering incoherently.

"Don't mind him," Gostis said.

He turned toward the stairs, but stopped as the door to the castle burst open and three men shoved their way through into the hall. Two of them wore rich blacks of the capital. Chains covered their upper arms, and on their belts hung beaked axes. The third wore the brown leather chaps and canvas of the Kharavadziy. Strapped across his chest and on each of his hips sat broad-bladed knives. He wore the furs of a hunter and let the other two men push forward while he took the room in calmly.

The two black-clad men shoved their way through servants and city guards to stand over the broken form of Ilon Das.

"I told you we ought not to have traveled on to Godariy," one muttered angrily.

"He told us to," the other said. "And you know what happens when we fall out of favor."

The first looked up, scanning the room, frowning as his eyes fell on the medicae. "You. Who did this to him?"

Jovan sighed and felt Gostis tensing next to him as all eyes turned toward the two of them. The first man circled the table and touched the axe at his side.

"Who is he?" the second man asked the room.

"A needle smith," someone replied.

"No blood to speak of, then?"

The first man walked cautiously forward. Jovan tensed and prepared for the worst.

"This man has been requested by Lord Valle-Brons." Gostis stepped forward, his hand still on the chain on Jovan's wrists. "He is safe from any harm you would do to him until the lord has his way."

"We're Khorapeshi Blackguards, charged with the protection of nobles from the capital. Your capital. If this smith has harmed someone under our watch, then his life is forfeit to us."

"I understand the laws," Gostis said, "but Lord Valle-Brons is kin to the king and his rule outweighs yours. Now stand down and let me deliver my charge to our lord."

Gostis turned and tugged on the chain, leading Jovan up the stairs along the wall without a backward glance.

"Looks like you chose the wrong man to bloody, Jovan," Gostis muttered.

Jovan grunted his acknowledgement.

They came to the door at the top.

"I was told to leave you here. You'll go in on your own."

Jovan nodded and walked up to the door, lifting both bound hands to knock. Then he rested his head against his hands, leaned on the door and awaited the lord's man to come and open the portal to his judgment.

CHAPTER 2 — ACCOUNT

There was silence in the open room down below as those huddling close to the blazing hearths watched. Jovan heard the steward shuffle to the door and dropped his hands in front of him as it opened. The man looked up at Jovan, startled by his closeness.

"This way," he said, turning around.

The fire in the hearth roared, though the room was still cold. A large oak table sat in the center, Lord Verth Valle-Brons behind it in a high-backed chair. He was leaning on one fist, watching Jovan enter. Verth wore a simple black tunic, lined with a short white fleece. His dark-blonde hair hung in two forced ringlets next to his full red beard. The rest of his hair was tied back rigidly, slicked with resin.

Verth indicated the chair opposite him. "It's the least hospitality I can offer as a goodbye."

"Thank you for not circling your prey," Jovan said, taking the seat. "I'm to leave then?"

"That was what we agreed upon last time," Verth said. "I've heard everyone else's story, but I'd like the peace of mind hearing yours. I think we've come to respect each other enough to give each other that decency."

"Of course. I'm sorry to have to leave."

"Was it worth it?" Verth asked.

"I...hope so?"

"You broke his nose so thoroughly, I don't expect him to win any awards from the womenfolk at the summer market."

Jovan chuckled. "Good."

"Tell me your side," Verth said.

"Very well," Jovan said. "It's simple: he insulted Lady Windro."

"Elaborate. I need to have a reason not to charge you with more—to not give your life over to that man."

Jovan sighed and tugged at his ear.

"Ilon Das came into my shop over a week ago. He ordered a set of tools, to be delivered tomorrow. Lady Windro came in at the same time. She ordered a set of needles. It was a simple transaction. Although Ilon had placed his order earlier, he waited around until she left and then became pushy—asking me whether I'd be making her order first. I told him to mind his business, and he'd get his order when he asked for it."

"What had Ilon ordered?"

"A set of heavier leather working awls. I already had the material I needed to make Lady Windro's, so it would be no trouble to prepare hers. The week proceeded. One evening at The Boar I came in later than usual. Ilon was sitting at the bar, eyeing the bones table, and looking put-off. I assumed he had just lost some money and was nursing his wounds. He saw me and began to belittle me—wondering why I was out drinking instead of working. I had the mind to realize he was hoping to insult me enough that I'd quit his job and return the payment he had already made for the needles. I didn't give in."

"Until today."

"Yes. Today. When he saw Lady Windro enter my shop to gather her order he came storming in, accusing me of working on her order first, and then began to suggest the two of us were bedding one another."

The lord burst out laughing.

"I asked him to leave. He refused. I came around to push him out of my shop, keeping Lady Windro behind me. Ilon swung wildly, and I think he hit me across the jaw."

"And now we're here," Verth said, sitting back, and wiping a tear from his eye.

"Now we're here."

Verth sat quiet, fighting back chuckles. "Old Lady Windro?" After a time, the chuckles subsided, and the lord took a deep breath and sat up. "I warned you last time that we couldn't have any more violence from you."

"I know."

"My cousin made me promise that I'd take care of the problem when you broke his boy's legs. He thinks I had you executed."

"I understand."

"He never bothered to listen to my explanation of your actions."

"So you've said."

"I don't appreciate Ilon Das's audacity. Lady Windro may be a low-ranking noble, but he has no pedigree besides his skill, so she still out-ranks him. The insult shows he out-stepped his bounds."

"As you say," Jovan said.

Jovan pulled a leather wrap from his belt and placed it down on the table.

"What is this?"

"After I have left town, will you give this to Ilon Das?"

Verth picked the wrap up and opened it, and then laughed.

"You finished his work a day early."

"I always do. If he had given me a moment to speak, I would have told him."

"Does he owe you anything?"

"I took it from him in blood, I think," Jovan said. "I promise to be gone by morning."

"I'll have Gostis unshackle you once the sun has set. Can you pack your things by cover of night?"

Jovan nodded and approached the door.

"Give my best to Sephaly," Jovan said.

"You're welcome to give it to her yourself." The lord walked to a curtain and pulled it back.

A young blonde woman sat on a seat overlooking the sea. She turned and smiled faintly.

"Hello, protector," she said.

Jovan bowed his head.

"The boy is well?" she asked.

"He is better than well."

"Then keep him safe," she said.

"I wouldn't have it any other way," Jovan replied.

"Please be careful; do not let your anger take you too far down a black road," she said. "Where will you go now?"

"I'll make my way toward Rightness, I think. I know someone there who will help me."

"Kallidova." Sephaly nodded. "Fitting."

"Sephaly," Verth cautioned.

"You may have your own reason not to trust her, Father, but you know I have every reason."

Lord Valle-Brons took a step back, his head dropping in shame.

"I...should go," Jovan said.

As he closed the door behind him, Jovan could see the lord closing the girl off with the curtain once more, paying no heed to Jovan as he left.

Jovan followed Gostis back to the prison as the sun dropped below the horizon.

He rubbed his wrists after the shackles came off. Gostis tossed them onto the table.

"Sorry to see you go," Gostis said.

"Have your wife go into my garden and uproot what she wants. I don't suppose whoever takes up the tenancy will care for it."

"I will. Where will you go?"

"Wherever I want. It's not turned too cold to stay out of doors. Perhaps we'll start by going to Miller's Hollow. I've been promising for a while to take the boy there."

"Do you have enough for the road?"

"More than enough," Jovan said.

"I'm supposed to walk you to your door."

"That's fine. I'd rather get there sooner than later."

CHAPTER 3 — UNWANTED GUESTS

Gostis held a lantern and walked behind Jovan down into town. A few candles still stood in windows. The tavern had a group of carousers within, singing together. They passed by and came to the front of Jovan's shop, a single candle flickering inside. He pressed his hand to the door, turned, and nodded at Gostis, who returned the gesture and left.

He pushed in and closed the door before turning. "Is the boy abed?"

The figure sat in the chair, shadows concealing them from view.

"He is," the figure said. It was older and educated. The edge of her voice was tempered with a fondness that had never been there before. "He was most courteous and saw to my needs. I pray you don't mind my sitting here in the shadows. After today, imagine what people might think, wondering if that fool's coarse and ribald insult might be true."

"Those that know me, Lady Windro, and more importantly, those that know you, would know it wasn't."

"I was comely in my younger years," she said. "I might have considered the possibility then."

"I would not. You are above my station."

They said nothing for a long while.

"You wonder why I am here?" she asked.

"I do."

"You honored me today."

"I did what any man who calls himself a man would do."

"My late husband would never have done what you did." She sighed. "Nonetheless, I thank you for doing what you did. No one has showed me respect the way you have since my husband left me old and childless, with lands that will revert to the king when I die."

"Very well, then I say, 'you are welcome.'"

"Fah... I've heard how difficult you can be. I should like to give you a gift for your trouble, as I suppose you'll be leaving town?"

"Yes. I will be leaving town. And I will not accept a gift."

"I expected you would say so. I've given the little purse of silver to the boy already. It's for his well-being more than anything."

Jovan scoffed. "You're as shrewd as we all call you."

The woman laughed. "I'll let myself out once you blow out that candle and go upstairs. The boy has already packed your bags. I saw to it that he did it well. He's a very good little boy."

"He is."

"Goodbye, Jovan Nedeller."

"And to you, Lady Windro."

He walked over to the candle and stopped.

"I will leave the candle lit on the counter. So you're not fumbling around in the dark."

"A kindness after a kindness. Thank you again."

Jovan climbed the ladder-stairs to the room above and paused to listen as the old lady left. He crossed the small room to the window and loosened the rope knotted around a hook, lowering the rope through the hole in the floor, which would drop a thick wooden slat into place, barring the door below from the safety of the room above.

The little boy, lying on the bedroll in the corner, started and turned over, looking up with a smile.

"You came back, Papa Jov."

Jovan nodded.

"I packed the bags," he said, rubbing his eyes.

"I heard."

"Did the lady tell you?"

"Yes."

"And did she tell you of the gift she gave me?"

"I have not seen it, but yes."

"I'm not supposed to show you until later. She thought we ought to go to Miller's Hollow."

"She knows us better than she lets on," Jovan muttered. He touched the boy's small bag, a bit heavy for the lad, but Leaf lifted the pack onto his back. "What did you pack?"

"What you told me, and a wheel of cheese."

"Good lad."

Jovan lifted his. It was heavier than he would have liked.

"What did you put in mine?"

"I traded Baker Jonn. He gave me travel tack for the other wheel of cheese."

"And he took your request seriously?"

"He said he saw what you did and it wasn't fair, but fair enough. He paid me two silver a wheel for the rest."

"You sold our cellar?"

"I figured you would want me to."

Jovan stood beaming. "Yes. I would want you to. But I didn't expect you to."

The boy smiled up at him.

"You are wise beyond your years," Jovan said.

"You've never taken me to the Hollow," Leaf said.

"You haven't been old enough."

"But I am now?"

"The way you sold our belongings and packed our bags? Any four-year-old boy that can do that is old enough to know not to fall into the dark, cold waters at the Hollow."

"Three men came by looking for you," Leaf said.

"They came into the shop?"

"No," the boy replied. "They stood across the street and just watched. Because it was evening, I was able to stay where they couldn't see me. One of them left, and then right before the lady came, the other two disappeared."

"And you haven't seen them since?"

"I went to bed after that."

A sound trickled up from the shop below.

"Someone is trying to pick the lock," said Jovan.

"I thought the keyhole wasn't real."

"It's not. They don't know about the bar. Stay here."

Jovan walked to the side of the window, and then peaked down below. Two men stood in the shadow cast by the shop. While one crouched before the door, the other kept watch.

"I'm going to go downstairs," Jovan said. "Leaf, come and stand by the bar rope. When I say, I want you to pull on the rope."

"But then they'll come in," the little boy said.

"It's the only way we can leave."

Jovan moved softly down the stairs, then circled the small front room of the shop, avoiding the places he knew would squeak, and came behind where the door would swing open.

"Come on," one man whispered hoarsely.

"It's not working?" the other said.

"We'll have to kick it in. We'll still have taken him by surprise."

"We could wait for the nomad."

"He said he was going to wait outside of town, in case they get past us."

"And if they go out the back way?"

"It's a solid wall."

"Then move."

The man crouching before the door grunted as he rose.

"Now, Leaf," Jovan muttered as he looked up to see the boy's eyes pressed down against the rope hole in the ceiling.

The wooden bar rose and settled into place above the door.

The man outside rushed at the door, slamming it open and cracking it against the doorstop by Jovan's feet. He tumbled into the room and cracked his head against the counter. The second man stepped in, laughing.

"So much for surprise," he said, helping the other man to his feet.

"No one is moving upstairs," the other replied, rubbing at his sore head. "Did we miss them?"

"You didn't," Jovan said from behind the door. He kicked it closed and rushed toward the men. He kicked the first man in the knee and he fell again, howling.

Jovan reached up and caught the axe handle as the second man brought the blade down on him. The man tried to pull the axe back and Jovan let it go, the man crashing backwards into the shelves behind him.

"Where did you come from?" the man shouted, pushing himself off the wall, brandishing the heavy axe in his hand. "How long were you behind that door?"

"You were making so much noise, it was easy enough. Why are you in my home?"

"You attacked Ilon Das. Maybe that means you're who he's been looking for."

"Looking for?"

The man shrugged and threw himself forward. His axe swung up and Jovan took hold of the haft below the head and shoved. The blade veered sideways and into the lintel of the door. The second man, still rubbing his head, lurched forward, pulling a knife from his belt and slashing too wildly.

Jovan backed against the wall and a flash of light suddenly lit the room. The two attackers yelped and backed away. Jovan felt an odd sensation and realized he could see better than before.

"His eyes!" one of the men shouted.

"Tov-Ol's eyes," the other hissed.

One made for the door and pulled on the handle. Jovan kicked the door with his boot as the man tried to slink through the opening he had made. He screamed as the door smashed his hand.

The other man made to rush toward the back of the small shop. Jovan grabbed the man's collar and pulled him backward.

"Legggo!" he shouted. Jovan pulled him into the man now holding his wrist. They both slid down the wall, the one with the axe holding it limply until Jovan grabbed it and tossed it aside.

"Don't look at me!" the man said, covering his eyes.

"Why not?" Jovan asked. "What's wrong with my eyes?"

"They burn with a fire," man holding his wrist said.

"What did Ilon Das want with me?" Jovan asked.

Both said nothing.

"Answer me!" Jovan yelled, pulling the first man threateningly toward him.

"He came looking for some man and his boy," the man stuttered out in fear. "I don't know why. We're just bodyguards."

Jovan lifted him to his feet and then took hold of the broken wrist of the second man, who squealed in response. He pulled them both behind the counter and motioned for the first to pull open the trap door to the cellar.

"Get down there," Jovan said.

The man did as he was told, and then from below helped the second, who dropped more than descended.

Jovan closed the door and shoved the pin through the latch, locking it.

Leaf came out from a shadow made by a shelf.

"Boy," Jovan said, "why can I see in the dark now?"

As though in response, the room suddenly plunged into darkness.

"I can't see your eyes," Leaf said innocently.

"Get your bag." Jovan sighed.

"Yes, Papa Jov."

The boy lifted his bag onto his shoulders and walked to the door.

"Leaf," Jovan said, "don't do that again."

"All right," the boy responded.

They walked together down the street toward the open gate. Gostis stood beside it, a torch in his hand.

"Come to see us off?" Jovan asked. "Or to make sure I leave?"

"The first," Gostis said. "The boys at the tavern wanted to make sure you got your winnings."

"Winnings?"

Gostis chuckled.

"The day after Ilon Das came to town, Old Magg said Ilon'd get beaten before he left. Everyone started a little bet at the bar. No one but Camen, and I'll admit, myself, thought you'd be the one to do it. Halfway through your little beating, Old Magg placed another bet that you'd kill the man. Camen doubled down his bet and said you wouldn't. Just about broke the old man's purse. He wanted to make sure you got some of the winnings."

Gostis held out a satchel that jingled with coin. It wasn't light.

"Tell Camen thank you, and that I'm sorry for the beating I gave him when we were younger."

"That's why he said he owed the winnings to you. Said he owed you for the lesson you taught him."

They passed through the gates. No more words were spoken as Jovan walked, the little boy alongside him, shifting his own pack every few yards to settle it on his untried shoulders.

CHAPTER 4 — FOREST ROAD

The boy was stepping up over fallen logs, swiping at dead branches with the stick he had found. It was the fifth he had picked up since they left Miller's Hollow. They had split the cheese wheel from the boy's pack, and the remainders had gone into Jovan's. Walking lighter, the little boy danced and moved in the wood naturally, like a sprite.

Jovan held a bow up in the fresh light of day. It had been stashed in the cottage by someone, likely a poacher, still strung. It had been left long enough that the string was worn, and likely would not last more than a few shots. The woods leading up the hill from the Hollow were thick, but not impassible.

"Which way?" Leaf asked from twenty yards ahead.

"Whichever way you like, boy. It will be a pleasant three weeks before the early winter storms begin. We can survive in the woods."

"Like the brigand king Norrun?"

"If you'd like."

"Do you think we'll see a dragon?"

"There are no dragons in these woods," Jovan said.

The boy's shoulders drooped.

"But there are goblins," Jovan said, hiding a smile.

Leaf looked up, and then looked around, suddenly alert.

"They can be seen hunting the wild wyrms."

"I want to find a wyrm and hunt it!"

The boy dropped the stick in his hand in exclamation as he reached for another one. It was a walking staff, carved from a sapling, but left long ago.

"I found a Sword of Danger!"

"I've never heard of that one," Jovan said, walking alongside the boy as he swung it with both arms against a tree with a *crack*. The staff took the hit well.

"That's because I made it up," the boy said. "It will tell me where danger is."

"I'm sure it will."

The boy charged ahead into the woods, attacking invisible goblins, wyrms, and brigands. The trees were just starting to show a change. It would be a cold night, but if they found a decent hole to shelter in, they wouldn't notice.

The sun crested above their heads and began its long descent. The boy had tired of charging headlong and walked now only a few steps in front. They found a woodsman's path and followed it along a wooded valley.

Leaf stopped in his track, his "Sword of Danger" standing straight on the ground.

"Danger," the boy whispered hoarsely.

Jovan rolled his eyes and sniffed, and then smelled wood and meat burning. He stopped and put a hand on the boy's shoulder.

"Good boy. Where?"

"I don't know," he said. "But I don't wanna go any further. Let's go home."

Jovan sighed and crouched beside him.

"There is no going home, Leaf."

The boy threw his arms around Jovan's neck and whispered, "I want to go home."

"I know. You are a brave, wise little boy. You know we can't go home."

Jovan stood and looked down the path. He could make out a waft of smoke across the path ahead. Someone camped alongside it.

"But we don't have to continue down this path. Come with me."

Leaf followed right behind Jovan, bumping into him to stay close. Jovan walked back the way they came, then left the path, and began to circle up a small hillock with a cropping of rocks at the top. It was steep enough to discourage anyone from camping atop it. Jovan noticed that it would make a fine shelter for the two of them, if it came down to it. They scrambled up the rocks. Jovan looked back at the little boy who had eyes full of fear.

"This cropping of rock?" Jovan said. "It's where Norrun stayed when he courted Fair Nella."

The boy's eyes sparkled in awe and he seemed to forget his fear.

"Now you stay here, out of sight."

Jovan dropped his pack, took the bow and three arrows, and began to creep down the other side of the hill. The going that side was steep, and he slipped twice, almost swearing out loud.

Two men sat around a fire. One wore the full furs of a trapper, the other wore a long robe of roughly knit brown-and-green-dyed wool. A rabbit had been stuck on a spit over the frugal fire between them.

"Which way will you go?" the man in green asked the trapper.

"Time to head up to my mountain home. The critters will start turning their winter colors. You?"

"I should be able to take down a few fat bears before they find their caves."

"And if they're too scarce?"

"I'll probably do what I always do and revert to the old trade," the hunter said. "If the rich are foolish enough to travel the paths that stay clear in winter, I'll take advantage of the situation. After all, the rich have no problem stealing through taxes."

"When you get to be my age," the old trapper said, "you'll find it harder and harder to fall back on that. Too risky. Life is too short to give up years in a cold cell if they catch you."

"If they don't hang you."

"Then I'd get north, and stay away from Geruz here on the southern coast. The lord there is none too kind to the likes of thieves."

Jovan's foot slipped. With luck, he fell silently, though he stared with wide eyes at the trapper, who looked at him vacantly, doing nothing.

"Will you stay and share the camp with me?" the hunter asked.

"No," the trapper said. "I have a place I'll go. I travel as well by night as by day in my old age. It'll be a nice night to do so."

The hunter nodded and took the rabbit from the spit, placed it on a log, and then cut it in two with a swift swing of his large hunting knife. Jovan watched them eat in silence. The trapper ate more fiercely, quickly devouring his half, and then rose.

"It has been a pleasure trading stories and goods. That little satchel of smoke root will do me nice this winter. I wish I could have bargained more from you."

"I'm sorry I couldn't. I need a bit for myself, you know."

"I know," the old man said. He picked up his staff, pulled his small pack over his back, and turned toward the forest. He moved slowly, and the hunter watched him, sharpening his own knife by the light of the setting sun. As the old trapper neared the point where Jovan wouldn't be able to follow his movement, the hunter rose and kicked the fire's embers. He muttered something about the old man having gotten the bargain. Then he set off along the way of the trapper, knife held menacingly at the ready.

A sinking feeling settled in Jovan's gut. He felt something press him forward. He could not sneak after the hunter, but he had a good guess as to what the man's intentions were. He stood and tramped up to the smoldering fire.

"Good man!" Jovan shouted.

The hunter froze and turned.

"How did you come up upon me?" the man asked.

Jovan recognized him now. He had been in the tavern a few times over the years, though he did not know his name.

"I saw the smoke of your fire, and thought to speak with you. I...have something to trade, if you're willing."

"I'm always willing to do some trading," the man said, though he moved cautiously.

"I thought I smelled some meat," Jovan said. "I haven't had fresh meat in a while."

"It's all gone now," the man said. "Sorry."

"What were you and the old man talking about?"

"None of your business."

"He was a bit blind, wasn't he?" Jovan asked.

"So what if he was?"

"He shouldn't be walking around in the dark. Something bad might happen to him."

"And you should mind your own business and move along."

Jovan held his hands up. "I'm just looking to do some trading."

The hunter glanced over his shoulder toward where the old trapper had gone. He sighed.

"You look like a quarry is escaping you," Jovan said.

"And you seem to know my business better than you should," the man said, his fist tightening around the knife in his hand.

"Perhaps I do," Jovan said. "Perhaps you should rethink your business."

The man suddenly lunged forward over the ashes. Jovan stepped to the side and kicked the log that had served as the man's seat while he'd eaten. The man made to step up on the log that was no longer there. He stepped down hard as Jovan swung with the old bow on the man's back. It did nothing, but it angered the man enough.

Jovan caught a movement over the man's shoulders. Leaf was back on the path, reaching for something.

Jovan let out a controlled fist, which met the man's shoulder. He dropped the knife and then threw himself to the ground to grab it from the forest floor, but Jovan kicked it into a bush.

"You son of a bitch," the man said.

Jovan shook his head. "My father and mother were well wed before I came."

The man took hold of a small stick and tried to use it as a knife, stabbing into Jovan's thigh. It met the heavy leather that lay there under his pants.

"I use needles all day long. Keeps me from bleeding while I work."

The man looked up, scoffing. "Why are you protecting the old man? We could go after him together. Split the profits."

Jovan glanced up. Leaf had disappeared again.

"I protect him because he is an old man looking to be left alone, not killed by an outlaw like you."

The man sneered. "What are you going to do to me?"

"I'll let you go. The Miller's Hollow? Know it?"

The man nodded.

"Someone stashed a very nice hunter's bow there. I wasn't sure, but I think the chest that was stashed with it had a wad of giftmel wrapped up in it."

The man's eyes brightened. "That's worth a lot of money," the man said with greed. He held out a hand. "Bygones?"

Jovan took the man's hand in his and shook firmly.

The man turned to pick up his belongings, but Jovan's grip tightened. He looked up in shock as Jovan's other hand came across and struck him up the side of the head with a rock. He fell limp to the ground.

Jovan crouched down next to him. He breathed shallowly, but he was not dead.

He turned to the woods and called, "Leaf! Come down, and bring me the rope."

Jovan moved the man to a tree and sat him up against it.

"Bring it here, boy," Jovan said as Leaf returned and handed him the rope.

Jovan began to wrap it around the man and tree.

"Why were you down on the road?" Jovan asked.

Leaf looked up, startled. He said nothing.

"I asked you to stay out of sight."

"I know," the boy murmured. "But I had left my Sword of Danger behind."

"It's a stick," Jovan retorted.

"I'm sorry," the boy said in an even smaller voice.

Jovan shook his head. "Next time, do as I say."

"Yes, Papa Jov."

"You're a good man," a voice boomed, almost next to Jovan. He lurched away, taking Leaf up in his arms. In the twilight, the old trapper stood not far away.

"Oh, I'm not as blind as I let on," the old man said. "Thank you for leaving him alive."

Jovan didn't say anything.

"I'm not going to kill him, mind you. But I knew he was going to come after me. Now I can take his belongings and be on my way. He'll probably think it was you." The old man chuckled to himself. "We can split what he has, if you'd like."

Jovan shook his head.

"Rules of the forest," the old man said. "You know them?"

Jovan grunted.

"Only talk when you got something to say, huh?"

"I prefer to be a good listener."

"Wise words. And respectful, too." The old man began riffling through the hunter's belongings. "The first rule is to leave no trace that you have been here. The second is that if you share something, you get something in return. I shared a meal with this man and he broke the trust. If he wants to take advantage of an old man, he will get treatment in kind."

The old man took the other man's leather satchel and placed it on the dying coals.

"This," he said, "I'm just doing to be vindictive. It won't set it alight, but it'll ruin it, nonetheless."

Jovan continued to watch him go about his business.

"Last bit of advice? Since you're such a good listener. This man here spent most of his time suspiciously blaming everyone around him for his folly. Assumed everyone was out to steal from him. The thing a man complains about most is likely the sin he metes out on everyone else. If someone assumes everyone else is a liar, I expect the man is a liar himself."

"What does that say about me if I think everyone talks too much?"

The old man stopped and looked at Jovan. Then he barked out a laugh.

"I'll admit. I do get to yammering, don't I?"

"No more than most," Jovan said.

"You get in a fight recently?" the man asked. "Your knuckles look a little raw."

"I recognized the hunter from Geruz. You there, too?"

The old man said nothing.

"I'd ask you not to mention my passing through here," Jovan said. "I'll have enough trouble if this man decides to come after me."

"When I finish here," the old man said, "I'll step over that ridge. After I do that, I won't be seen again until the frost breaks. If I get a bit drunk in a tavern come spring and spill my guts, I imagine by then the news I spread won't matter, will it?"

"No. I don't think it will."

CHAPTER 5 — SILENT WOODS

Jovan opened his eyes with a start and rolled over. Leaf was fast asleep on a bed of moss near Jovan's head. He sat up and wiped his eyes. The wall of roots and intertwined rocks they'd sought shelter under cast deep shadows from the light of dawn. A single bird flitted from tree to tree, giving tight warbles of warning to others. He stretched as he stood, and peered out over the lip of the hole.

The sun had not yet appeared over the surrounding hills, but the forest was lit by a ruddy red. A deer moved through the dense trees climbing the nearby hill. Jovan watched it begin its ascent to the upper meadows.

It froze in its tracks, ears whipping about as it watched something to the north, and then it bolted up the hill and out of sight.

After a little while watching for what scared the creature, Jovan lowered himself down, and started to roll up his blanket. Leaf woke up yawning, and reached for his Sword of Danger stick.

"I'm hungry," he said.

"We'll find that brook you heard and boil some water for the tack."

"I like tack."

"You're the only one I know who does," Jovan said.

He lifted Leaf out of the hole, and then pulled himself up. Leaf was already walking down the easy slope toward the silver water that was much more visible in the morning light than it had been the night before. The boy gathered dry sticks as he walked, and had a nice bundle as he reached a flat rock next to the water's edge.

Jovan joined the boy and filled his pot with water, setting it on the rocks. Together they built the sticks into form, and Jovan started the work of lighting the kindling.

Jovan stirred some salt in with the rock-hard tack, which softened quickly in the soon boiling water. Then he poured the gruel out into their wooden bowls, washed the pan, and set more water to boil to fill their jugs.

"Papa Jov?" Leaf asked as Jovan fed the fire and tended the water. "Where are the birds?"

"What do you mean?" Jovan asked.

"I don't hear any."

"We probably scared them off by being here."

"They haven't flown away before."

Jovan listened. Leaf was right. There had never been quite this level of heavy silence. He looked down at the water, which hadn't even started showing signs of warming. Jovan picked up his bowl of gruel, swallowed the rest, and then leaned down to rinse their bowls, dipping the pot into the water to cool before placing it back in his satchel.

"Let's move away from the stream, to where we can hear better."

Leaf smiled at Jovan. They followed the stream down to a log that crossed the water, balancing their way across it, and then up the other side. There was a small ridge, which Jovan and Leaf went over, to a small footpath that hid sight of the stream.

Just as Jovan came down the path, he heard the shuffle of rocks tumbling across the other side of the valley. The ridge blocked most of the sound of the brook, but there were still no birds.

He took Leaf's hand and they walked faster down the path, coming to a pair of boulders.

"Let's take a rest," Jovan said. He pointed to the crevice between the two boulders.

"We just started," Leaf laughed.

"I'd like to sit and listen for birds," Jovan said.

Leaf nodded, and climbed up to a little ledge only a boy or a squirrel might sit on. Jovan dropped his pack, and then sat still, one eye on the path, watching for movement.

It reminded Jovan of waking before even bakers rose and the deafening silence held him in his bed. Every once in a while the sound of the stream could be heard, but there were no creatures moving, and as Leaf pointed out, no birds calling.

Then, the trill of a songbird lit up the forest, and Jovan sighed in relief.

"My Sword of Danger says we can go now," Leaf said.

"All right, boy."

They stood and walked down the path together for a time. The brook came alongside them and Jovan took up a pot of water. At an old fire circle, they set the water to boiling while they chewed on dried meat. Jovan saw a family of rabbits stick their head up out of a hole.

"I know we didn't make it far today, but let's set up camp and see if we can't catch those rabbits."

Leaf's eyes grew bright. "Can I keep one?"

"I'm afraid not, boy. These will be for food."

Jovan looked around for green wood to set a trap, and a good place to set their things where they wouldn't be covered in dew by morning. He took out his extra rope, and laid out a tripwire near the log they'd settle down next to, then prepared his spring trap for the rabbits just out of their hole.

Leaf was traipsing about the woods, having finally settled on a Sword of Danger stick he liked. He was poking at various rocks and soon found a snail making its way across a log, and squatted down to watch it.

The twang of the green stick, pinned between two rocks, suddenly jerked, and the bow string Jovan had used for the snare whipped tight around the leg of a rabbit as it tried to dart out of the way. It kicked and fought, but Jovan easily took it by the scruff of the neck and lifted it up to consider it.

"We've not been out here so long that you'd be a bad idea to eat," Jovan said.

The fur sitting atop the green moss was the first thing he saw before he realized he was in a hare's snare himself. Two eyes peered out from under the fur cap, watching Jovan intensely.

Jovan reached for the knife at his belt slowly. It wouldn't matter. They had locked eyes. The man was twenty yards away, and had come up on them in silence. He stood suddenly, covered in tight deerskin leathers. He was tall and lean. The unmistakable features of a Kharavadziy nomad, a huge knife in each hand, sent a shiver of fear to match the struggling rabbit in his hand. Jovan chucked the animal at the face of the advancing hunter—the third bodyguard of Ilon Das.

The rabbit scrabbled and twisted in the air toward the attacker, who with a swingle swipe cut the creature down.

He flew across the forest floor at Jovan, who struggled to turn and run. He heard the man gasp and fall to the ground, finding the tripwire Jovan had set. Jovan saw Leaf stand up to consider the two men chasing after one another. As the Kharavadziy struggled to stand, Jovan motioned for Leaf to get down. The boy understood the command and disappeared.

Jovan threw himself over a log, took a rock off the ground, and turned to throw it, but the Kharavadziy had disappeared again.

"I am sorry for what happened to your master," Jovan called.

The bodyguard came out from behind a tree and charged at Jovan faster than he could track, suddenly on top of him, one knife lost in his tumble with the tripwire, the other grasped firmly.

The two of them fell to the ground together. Jovan took hold of the man's knife hand, but the man moved the knife into his other hand.

"I could care less what you did to that man," the Kharavadziy said in his thick accent. "I am here to complete our mission."

He shoved down on the knife, meant to find purchase in Jovan's rib cage. Jovan struggled to keep it from inching closer.

"I'll not die easily."

"You will die easily. And the boy is young enough, I should have no trouble taking him back, even if I have to stick him in a sack and carry him there."

Jovan roared and shoved the man up and off him. The other man flew back like a rag doll.

The rage in Jovan snapped into control of his actions and he lunged toward the other man. But the hunter was faster. He rolled away and was suddenly on Jovan's back, his arm around the bigger man's throat. It was sudden and overwhelming. The rage that coursed through his blood caught like a waft of smoke in a breeze and disappeared. Blackness replaced the gray tones of a world washed by the anger coursing through him.

All feeling melted away.

There was the sound of his own heart thundering in his head.

The numbness in his arms returned and he rolled over.

The Kharavadziy man stared down at Jovan, his arms held back by some unseen thing. Then, up through the leathers of his clothes, hundreds of little mossy vines crept up, encasing his body and holding him in place. Jovan struggled to his feet, taking deep breaths and looking around. Behind the Kharavadziy stood Leaf, his hands outstretched toward the man. A verdant carpet of moss crawled across the ground from the boy toward the man.

"How are you doing this?" the Kharavadziy said, staring at Jovan. "Are you vedmak?"

Jovan shook his head. He found the man's knife nearby. "Who sent you after me and the boy?"

"I will not say," the Kharavadziy said.

"Even at knife point?"

"My family's debts are paid if I succeed or if I die. That is all that matters. If you are vedmak, then I doubt any will succeed."

"Leaf, go to the path and wait for me there."

Leaf looked up at Jovan and nodded. As he turned to leave, the moss at his feet melted to the earth, its disappearance slowly creeping toward the man now nearly encased.

"Do it quickly," the man said. "Or else I'll pursue you from here to Nal."

Jovan nodded and turned the knife in his hand.

When he joined Leaf on the road, the boy walked next to him in silence.

"I've asked you not to do that," Jovan said softly.

"You were dying," Leaf said.

"So this time, I am grateful. But you know that if you continue to do that, one day you will die."

"Why?"

"I don't know," Jovan said. "But all the stories say a vedmak dies young. You must not do that."

"All right, Papa Jov."

"What does your Sword of Danger say now?"

Leaf looked up and smiled. "It says that nothing can hurt me if you're here."

Jovan gave a wan smile at the boy and tousled his hair. "I won't let anything happen to you."

CHAPTER 6 — WAYSTOP INN

The game path was easy to follow despite the frost that stayed upon it the whole of the day. Jovan let Leaf lead the way. They saw no game, though the broken twigs and hoof prints that sunk deep where water sat close to the surface told them that they were always just far enough ahead to stay out of view. The dense forest began to give way to more light, and Jovan could see telltale signs of civilization—from stumps with no moss grown on them, to a few clearings that showed signs of woodsman camps. The boy did not seem to notice and Jovan felt no ill ease, so they continued on.

They came to a long straightaway with fallow grass filling a pasture to the right.

"Boy," Jovan said, tugging on his ear.

Leaf spun and looked at the large, bearded man.

"Look to your right. What do you see?"

Leaf turned. "Grass."

Jovan strode forward and picked him up onto his shoulders.

"Oh!" the boy said. "Is that smoke?"

"Shall we go look? You've been gone from civilization long enough."

"I do not mind," Leaf said.

"I'd like to see where we are," Jovan said.

They stepped out into the field and pushed through the tall grass. Ahead, a roof rose out of the back edge of the field, though there was no building underneath it, simply a sharply steeped roof with only the barest wisps of smoke rising out of the top. They moved past a run of apple trees with only wrinkled fruit hanging from the branches.

"I think this is Borevez," Jovan muttered.

"What's Borevez?" Leaf asked.

"It's a small little waystop. We're probably a day's walk on the road to Rightness."

"A 'waystop' means an inn?"

"Yes. A warm one, too."

They came to the roof. A small, cobbled square stood below and before them. The grass berm they stood on stopped abruptly.

"To the left there, boy. We can step down over there."

They walked along the edge. The grass descended to the level of the yard near an animal trough. Leaf gasped as he realized they were standing on top of an inn. The front of the tavern had a tall roof, but the rest of the building spread out along the berm. The windows were small, set where single stones had not been placed.

"Where is everyone?" Leaf asked.

"Inside. And not everyone, just one. The waystop is owned by one man. Come along."

Jovan walked toward the door. As he reached for it, it opened. A man as tall as Jovan, but with arms twice as strong, pushed his way out. His blonde beard and hair had been tamed together in a single braid that ran half way down his chest.

"I was starting to wonder who was walking overhead," the man said.

"Borev."

"Jovan." The man looked down at Leaf. "This boy yours?"

"My charge, yes. Can we stay the night?"

"I'll not turn down good silver, and perhaps the replacement of a few of my needles."

"I'll have a look," Jovan said. "Food and ale first, though."

"Of course. I have a fine cider-ale just come ready."

"That'll be fine. Something thinned down for the lad," Jovan said.

"Of course."

They stood in an inner room that ran the length of the front. It was shallow and not meant for staying in. Jovan dropped his pack in an alcove along the wall and then walked toward the door at the end of the hall. It led back and turned the corner toward the common room. The ceiling was low and there were only three small tables with chairs that did not match each other. To the right stood the small bar with no stools up against it, and a single barrel tap behind it. Borev had two tankards out and had filled them from a tall stoneware bottle. He came out from behind the bar, a fresh apron around his middle, and stood watching the two of them.

Leaf looked around in awe. It was a small place and while the furniture was garishly mismatched, the woodwork that covered the room was immaculately carved.

"My father built this place," the huge man said. "I've done a poor-man's job of caring for it, but it's mine," he said, winking at the little boy.

"You've done wonderfully," Leaf said.

"Where will you take your seat?" Borev asked.

Leaf tapped a finger to his chin and then chose the table farthest back in the room. He pulled himself onto the chair. It gave a wobble, a single leg slightly shorter than the others.

"Maybe we find you a chair that doesn't teeter," Borev said.

"I like it," Leaf said. He rocked a few more times, and then the chair seemed to sit firm.

Borev lifted an eyebrow.

"He's got a knack for balance," Jovan said.

Borev nodded and put the tankards down in front of them. "I'll be back with the bread and soup."

"Thank you, Borev. We can discuss a room later?"

"Of course. And the needles I mentioned."

"What type?"

"My darning needles. If you've got a spare sail pin, I could use one. I've got some canvas to mend."

"I'll see what I have once we unpack."

Borev turned suddenly, as though he heard a sound, wiped his hands, and then walked toward the door, muttering something to the effect of "two guests in a day..."

"Don't drink too fast," Jovan said.

"I won't, Papa Jov," Leaf responded.

Borev came back in, talking back over his shoulder to another traveler behind him. This man had no hair on his head, though he had a tight little mustache and beard. He wore a loose blouse with sweat stains across the shoulders, still damp from the pack he had no doubt left in the vestibule.

"You're welcome to any table. Those travelers over there just arrived, as well. Just as road worn as you, I'm sure."

The man glanced over at Jovan, then away, to find his own table. He had a small and meager coin purse that hung heavily from his belt. He took out a cloth and wiped down the sweat that clung to him.

Borev brought bread and two bowls to Jovan's table, and then went back to grab some for the other traveler. Leaf took his time eating, selecting each bite before putting it carefully in his mouth.

"Your boy is a quiet eater for his age," the other traveler said.

Jovan almost jumped. He had not seen the man twist out of his own alcove to sit where he could see the two of them. He leaned forward and breathed through his mouth between bites.

"He's a quiet lad," Jovan said.

"Which way are you traveling?"

"Why do you ask?"

"I'm headed north myself. Toward Rightness. Wasn't sure if you knew what the road held."

"I couldn't say."

"North then, too?"

Jovan took a bite from his bread and considered his words. "No. South."

"But you didn't come from the north?"

"We were setting traps out in the woods west of here," Jovan lied. "This was the first time I've taken the boy. I needed to see if he was ready to be taken out during the mink season."

"Ah. I see. Trappers then."

"Only in the winter."

"I'm a wool trader myself," the man said. "Stergis Wooliz."

"The gods grant you health," Jovan said with little emotion.

"They do," the man said. "And I think I'll go see my animal now. And see about a room."

Wooliz rose and left.

"Not every day you see a wool trader without an ounce of wool on him," Jovan said to no one.

"You mean he's not a wooler?" Leaf asked.

Jovan nodded. "Eat your food."

Jovan leaned forward with his hands on his knees, awaiting the return of the little bald man.

After a time, two men stepped into the room. The first was nearly as big as Borev, with a deep, fur-lined hood that hid his face. He wore a full-length tunic of yellows and greens of the capital, but it had faded almost completely from years of use. He had no emotions on his face, and looked around the room with sleepy eyes.

The second man also wore a full-length tunic, though his was of the deepest black and lined with matching fur. The tunic brushed the top of his mud-encrusted boots. Borev looked the two of them up and down and scowled at the muddy boots flaking off dirt onto his floor with every step.

"Two chairs?" Borev offered. "Long ride?"

"We walked," the man in black said in a nasally voice. "Just two beers and a loaf of bread."

He slid into a seat without a sound. The other man, though, dropped his hood and grabbed a chair, dragging it audibly across the floor toward the table his companion had taken. His face was closely shaved and his head was covered in old scars. His ears looked swollen from years of fighting.

Jovan turned to the little boy next to him. The boy looked over at the two men with a sense of awe.

"Keep your eyes on your food, Leaf," Jovan said.

The boy nodded and returned to his bread, now picking at it slower.

"Leaf," the man in black said. He was standing next to the table. Jovan almost jumped again, but this time he'd caught the man beginning to move before he'd turned to tell the boy to mind his business.

"That's a nice name for your son," the man said. Though his voice was high-pitched and had a hint of gravel in it, he sounded educated. "You don't often see hair that pale and wispy on one his age. They usually grow out of it before they can wean."

"He kept all of his."

"You want to see a trick?" the man asked Leaf. His mustache twitched again.

"I was just about to take him up to bed," Jovan said. "We have a long road tomorrow."

"Ah, you must be headed to Righteousness."

"Rightness. Yes, we should make it in time to find an inn tomorrow."

"I don't doubt it. My friend Zvediz and I are headed there ourselves. It's been a while since we've seen home."

"We ought to head up," Jovan said to Leaf, standing.

"I didn't introduce myself," the man said. "I am called Slant." He held out a hand. His fingers twitched and stood out in awkwardness, as though he wasn't quite sure what to do with them.

"Nice to meet you," Jovan said, though he did not shake the man's hand.

"You look like an able tradesman," Slant said.

"Able enough."

"Are you headed to Righteousness for work?"

"You keep calling it that. It's Rightness."

The man gave a sly chuckle. "Yes. My own private joke. I laugh at the town with my little jest."

"I am not going that way for work. Work will find me. I know enough people there."

"Ah?"

Jovan squared off to the man. Zvediz began to rise from his chair at the movement. Jovan just made out Slant's hand motioning for him to sit still.

"I don't know you, Slant, but I feel like you have something to say and you intend to direct it at me. Say your piece so I can take my boy upstairs. It's getting far past his bedtime."

Slant held up his hands in defense. "I apologize, friend. I was only making small talk. You're the only one here to talk to."

"But there's more."

"I like you," Slant said, glancing back at the big man behind him. "You see through others' sheep pat. My friend and I are headed to town, same as you. We just finished a circuit down the coast and we're headed back toward the capital. Righteousness first. We could use another companion or two to travel with—help us legitimize our entering town."

"What do you do that would keep you from entering the town on your own?"

"My friend Zvediz here? He's a bear wrestler. I'm a smoothsayer."

"Bear wrestler? I've heard of bear baiters, but not bear wrestlers."

"The man is intrigued," Slant said over his shoulder to no one.

"I don't want fortunes told in front of my boy."

"Bah. I'm not like that," Slant said. "But to answer your first inquiry, sure, Zved has wrestled a few bears. More than anything, he can beat any physical con. You know most bear baiters are a falsehood? I see through their sheep pat and give Zved the hint that he needs to stack the table back on the other. Me? That's my gift. Seeing through the pat. I can out-con a cup game. I can hang out a priest's undergarments for his mistress to see."

"Which is why you aren't welcome in Rightness. The priests there don't like you."

"No one does! I've broken up a few cells of swindlers here and there. But none more so than in Righteousness."

"Why go through there then?"

"I have to. My poor mother is there. She can't leave town and she has a few baubles of mine I need to get. I wondered if you were headed into town and maybe through, and we could join you."

"Awful trusting, aren't you?"

"Like I said. I can spot a con and call it. But you? I think you're an honest—if not a bit world-worn—man."

"I'll think on it," Jovan said. "For now, I'm going to sleep."

The boy followed him up the stairs to their room.

"I wanted to see a trick," Leaf said.

"I know, boy. I know."

The room only had one bed. Borev had obviously assumed the boy would sleep on the floor. Jovan lifted the little four-year-old onto the bed and tucked him under the meager blankets. He took the extra blanket off the stool and laid it down on the ground for himself in front of the door.

"Papa Jov?"

"Yes, boy?"

"What is Rightyness?"

"Right-ness," Jovan corrected. "I need to visit a friend of mine."

"Why is it called Right...ness?"

"It's a very long city built on a single straight road. They say it was built 'right.'"

"Then why did that man say it wrong?"

"I think he thought he was funny."

"I thought he was funny. Why did you tell Slant and the wooler two different places we were going?"

"Go to sleep, boy."

Jovan settled himself down in front of the door and leaned up against it. It would be a long, restless night.

"What did you do with him?" he heard the dimmed voice of Slant asking his companion as they walked down the hall.

"He won't leave the outhouse."

"Good. Let's see if we can get them to leave with us early tomorrow morning. I don't want any more complications."

The door down the hall closed and all fell silent. It would be a long, restless, sleepless night.

CHAPTER 7 — RIGHTNESS

Jovan left the room as light began to show over the horizon. The outhouse was set across the yard. He opened it slowly and saw nothing. He heard a snore and almost startled. Circling the house, he found the wooler tied up with several horse blankets over him. The knots were tighter than even Jovan could manage.

Jovan touched the man's face and gave him a prompt slap. Wooliz woke and looked up groggily. "Whu uh gih meh?" he asked. His mouth sounded like it was full of cotton. "We affer the same man."

"He probably gave you goat-nag," Jovan said as he pulled at his beard with one hand while touching his ear with the other.

The man's eyes popped from his head when he realized it was not the large Zvediz who crouched before him.

"Why are you after me?" Jovan asked.

The man shut his mouth tight.

"Now you can't talk? He was kind enough to leave you alive and behind the outhouse. Maybe you'd prefer to go into the outhouse. It's hard to breathe upside-down and stuck in the muck."

The man growled.

"Talk fast, Wooliz. I don't have much patience."

"I won't," he said.

"So you fear your master more than I? That leaves me with much to think on. Do you fear me enough to heed a warning?"

The man nodded slowly.

"If I see you again, you'll wish I had put you head first in the hole."

Jovan rose and returned to his room. He took up the small roll of needles he had prepared for Borev over the course of the long night—he'd had plenty of darning needles and sail pins prepared, as always—and placed it on the small side table for their host to find. He sat on the edge of the bed and touched Leaf.

Leaf roused and said, "Where did you go?"

"Just out to relieve myself."

Leaf sat up. "Is it morning?"

"Close enough. We should be going."

Leaf yawned as he pulled on his small boots. Jovan had to correct him to put them on the right feet, and then turned the shirt Leaf had pulled on backward.

"Do you think you can walk long and fast today?" Jovan asked as he pushed the second boot on.

Leaf nodded.

"Good. Then let's go."

Jovan shouldered his pack and they walked out of the inn. The man dressed in black, Slant, was coming out of the outhouse himself. He looked up in surprise and then smiled.

"Good man! Up and out early?"

Jovan kept walking.

"We'd still like to join you," Slant said.

Jovan spun on his heel. Slant ran face first into his chest. He sputtered as Jovan's beard dragged across his mouth.

"Why are you following me?" Jovan asked. "Why were you seeking me out?"

Slant looked up, an eyebrow cocked sharply.

"And why is a man tightly bound behind the outhouse?"

"Ah," Slant said.

"Ah," Jovan parroted.

"Zved and I were sent by a mutual friend to find you and bring you north."

"And what does that have to do with the man behind the building?"

"I don't know. But when we were arriving, he was sharpening his knife, and preparing to head back into the tavern. We decided to stow him away and ask questions later. As it turned out, you were inside the tavern, and everything fell into place."

"Care to elaborate?"

"On the road I would," Slant said.

"No. I don't trust you."

"Fair enough. Mamm Kall asked us to find you. We've been up and down the road between Righteousness and Geruz several times the past ten days looking for signs of you.

And as it turns out, several others were, as well." He indicated toward the outhouse.

"You know Kallidova?"

"Who doesn't?" Slant winked.

"You'll have to do better than that."

"What do you mean?"

"You drop a name I know and expect me to allow you to travel with us."

"Very well. It was raining and the herring came a week early," he quoted.

Jovan growled and then tugged at his ear several times. It was a code for the day he first met Kallidova and Leaf was given to him to care for.

Zvediz came out of the inn carrying both of their bags over his shoulders.

"You'll give me any weapons you have until we arrive at Kallidova's."

Slant nodded, taking a pair of knives from his belt and handing them to Jovan. "It'll be hard to take Zved's arms from him, though."

Jovan couldn't help suppressing a chuckle. He turned and started walking. Leaf looked up at him.

"They'll be coming with us," Jovan said. "Maybe you'll get to see that trick he promised after all."

As the sun began its long and final decent over the western plains, the trees gave way to the valley below, showing a long straight city that stretched on for several miles toward the Red Mountains farther north.

"Oh!" Leaf exclaimed.

The boy climbed up onto a stump. He had another branch in his hand that the lumbering Zvediz had cleaned of twigs and given him. It was the seventh the boy had brought to the big man that day.

"You see how the city gets wider at the far end?" Slant pointed out to the little boy.

"Uh huh!"

"That's the Temple of Negligent Assurance. The priests there wear white robes, so you know they are sure of themselves."

The boy's eyes widened.

"Don't go planting bad apples in the boy's orchard," Jovan scoffed. "Leaf, it's called the Temple of Neligyne's Assembly."

Leaf scrunched his brow in confusion.

"Slant thinks he's funny. Remember?"

The boy hopped down and began running down the hill, off the road, and through the tall grass.

"Where did you pick the boy up?" Slant asked.

"What do you mean?" Jovan asked. "He's mine."

"I don't believe that for a second," Slant said. "He looks nothing like you."

"He looks like his mother."

"Of course he does. We all do. You should see how ugly Zved's mom is."

Zvediz turned and grinned stupidly.

"Where did you get Zvediz?"

"No turning the question on me," Slant said. "I asked you first."

"I've had him since he was a baby," Jovan said. "And I'd like to leave the facts there."

"That's just fine. I can respect that."

"Anywhere we need to avoid?" Jovan asked. "You mentioned you weren't welcome."

"Hard to avoid anything," Slant said. "It's all one street." They walked another hundred yards in silence. "I'd like to keep away from Red Run. But I need to get to Tinker Alley."

"That'll be difficult," Jovan said. "The Alley is on the other side of Red Run."

"Unless you can bring Tinker Alley to me."

"I don't see that happening. We'll need to go straight to Kallidova's. You'll just have to hope."

"I expected as much," Slant said.

"Does nothing bother you?"

"Not much. Except lies. I don't like lies."

"Yet you lied to me," Jovan said. "And I don't like being lied to, either."

"That's fine. I don't like lying. I prefer uncovering them."

"You're a terrible liar," Jovan said.

"Zved's a better liar."

"He never says much, anyway."

"All the better," Slant said.

They were nearing the city gate where a lone guard had watched their half-mile approach.

"Why did she send you?" Jovan asked.

"I don't know. But if I had to wager a guess, I'd say word travels fast. Mamm Kall was very quick to hunt me down and practically kick me out of town to look for you. By the time

I arrived in your little town the whole place was abuzz with the story of how a needle-maker beat a customer within an inch of his life."

"What's your business in Rightness?" the guard called down to them.

Zvediz had stopped ahead of them and only a hundred yards off from the gate. He held Leaf's hand so he wouldn't wander any farther. Jovan and Slant picked up their pace and came up next to the big man.

"What's your business?" the guard repeated.

"My simple friend here doesn't know his own business," Slant said, indicating toward Zvediz.

"Then you can answer for him," the guard said.

"I'm a nedeller," Jovan said, stepping out front. "I'm looking for a place to set up a new shop after my old one burned down. My friends here assist in the day-to-day affairs."

"I never saw a needle-maker need more than a single desk to ply his trade. Why do you need two grown men and an apprentice boy to do so?"

"Perhaps you might simply direct me toward the guild hall? I could inquire if your town has a needle-maker."

"We have plenty of tailors," the guard said.

"I'm not a tailor," Jovan said. "I make needles.

For woolers and tailors.

For fishers and sailors."

"Well, I doubt we'll need you here," the guard said.

"Nonetheless," Jovan said. "I'll need to try before moving on. And I can't move on unless I move through."

The guard didn't seem impressed.

"Naturally, I'll also need to show my regards to the temple," Jovan added.

This seemed to be what the guard hoped to hear. He disappeared from the wall and soon the gate was open.

"Is it always this hard to get in?" Leaf asked. "You never brought me when you went to market."

"On market days, the gates remain open. Now look lively, before they close them again."

The boy ran ahead of the three men, only to stop right inside the gate, staring in awe at his first view of a large city.

Though the street ran straight, the people who lived there did what they could to break the lines, jutting their windows out over the street as far as they could, like trees in a forest fighting for their share of the light. The people bustled under the eaves, all seeming to avoid the light in the center, as though it might burn them.

A few Havats wore signs of their hereditary beliefs openly, with orange shirts under vests, while others wore small orange ribbons in their hair. Even this got lost in the over-inundation of colors that surrounded them. Vendors had embroidered the canvas of their market tents set up in the front of wheeled carts. Customers wearing their finest clothes moved from stall to stall.

A pair of guards monitored the moving of one disgruntled merchant. The goods on his cart, little wooden trinkets, jostled around. He tried to put them in place as he pushed the cart with one free hand, as though people passing him while he was not stationary might see what he had to offer and follow him to the new spot. He sidled up against a wall, the guards talking to each other. One of them turned to him and held out a hand. The merchant handed them a handful of coins. A single silver dropped into the pocket of the guard, while the rest went into a box on the other's hip. The merchant shook his head as he turned and began to set up his wares again.

"You have this spot until the end of the day," the guard said. "Make sure you have the proper paperwork next time."

They turned and pointed at a woman selling flowers across the street and walked toward her. She held up her hands defensively, a paper in hand. They guffawed as they looked the paper over and turned to find another victim to bully.

"Come on, boy." Jovan put his hand on Leaf's shoulder. "The best thing in this town is to keep moving."

"Sound advice," Zvediz spoke.

The three looked up at the big man. But Zvediz said nothing more, and they continued to shuffle forward.

"Do you see how one side of the street the buildings are made of black stones and the other side is gray?" Slant asked Leaf.

"Oh! Yes! Why?"

"They say it was here that Vhezin and Tov-Ol, the fifth and sixth gods, were riven from one another."

"Don't speak of Luck and Bad Luck," Jovan said.

"What is riven?" Leaf asked.

"Those two," Slant said, "that I'm told by your papa I'm not allowed to speak of, used to be one. Together they were Fate. But the gods split Fate into two and they became the twins: the Sable of Luck and the Black Fox of Death, or Bad Luck as you said, Jovan."

"I don't understand," Leaf said.

"That is because it's just a story," Jovan said. "You can't split a soul in two."

Slant sucked in a breath, hissing. "I mean, it might be possible. But it's not recommended. Who can say what good and evil might come of it? And a mortal split in two would cause irrevocable damage."

"Let us not talk of such dark magics," Zvediz said, halting the conversation.

The city street narrowed around them and twilight settled in. Candles sat in windows, and a few odd drunks stumbled along, already well into their night of carousing.

A man shouldered his way into Jovan, almost splitting Leaf from his firm grip. Jovan lifted the boy up by his arm, to get him free from the street. He rested the other hand on the drunk's shoulder.

"Watch where you push," Jovan said.

"You watch it!" he shouted up at him. He reached for his knife, but Slant was behind him, pulling the sheathed blade from his belt before he could find it.

"No need for that, friend," Slant said, wagging the knife at him.

"You were in my way," the man drawled. Jovan smelled a little beer on his breath, but the drawl was almost too deep. "I should kill you. Don't you know who I am?"

"Brother Gelivic, I think," Slant said, putting his arm over the drunk's shoulders like a friend. The drunk flinched and straightened his back, a little too fast.

"I thought so," Slant continued. "What does the Patriarch have you up to now?"

The man shoved an elbow into Slant's side, but he deftly stepped away. He indicated toward the man and Zvediz took hold of the drunk's arms. He almost lifted him off the ground as he set him in an alcove that served as an alley.

"Who is this?" Jovan asked Slant.

"This is Gelivic. He's sort of an honorary monk at the temple."

"Honorary?"

"Yes. The way the Patriarch there treats him, I imagine his pedigree disqualifies him from taking the robe. Acting as the Patriarch's errand boy seems to be enough for him."

"You were keeping an eye out for me, weren't you?" Jovan asked.

Gelivic grunted.

Jovan put a strong hand on the man's shoulder like a claw. Gelivic yelped.

"Why is everyone looking for me?" Jovan asked through clenched teeth.

"I don't know!" Gelivic shouted.

"Keep it down," Slant hissed.

"Is there trouble here?" Two guards appeared behind them.

"None, good sirs," Slant said.

"Then you'll need to come with us," the older of the two said.

Jovan sighed.

"Good news is," Slant whispered, "that takes us right through Red Run and on toward Mamm Kall's."

"Yes. And right to whoever is seeking us out, I would guess."

One guard led the way, while the other took up the rear, a hand on Gelivic's shoulder.

"I'm glad you arrived, guard sirs," Gelivic said.

"Quiet," the guard replied.

"The Patriarch will be glad to see you return me to the temple."

"You're not wearing robes," the guard replied.

"Still. I'll be admitted, and you'll be paid handsomely."

The guards said nothing. Everyone parted for the seven of them as they moved past bawdy houses and rowdy taverns. They came to a point where the street opened up, and none of the houses hung out over the cobblestones.

"Ah," Slant said. "Tinker Alley."

"Why is it called an alley?" Leaf asked. "This is nice!"

"Exactly, my boy," Slant said, winking.

Leaf remained confused. They walked directly toward a large front.

"Why are we going this way?" Gelivic asked.

The windows were dark in the store, but a light sat out on the counter.

"You're on her pay!" Gelivic protested. "I am part of the temple!"

"Quiet, you," the guard holding him said. Then he turned to Slant. "Mamm Kall's in the back. You can take them the rest of the way?"

Slant nodded. "Thanks, boys," he said.

The two guards took Gelivic the other direction toward a side door as Jovan stared after them, a look of surprise on his face.

"He had it coming for a long time," Slant said.

A figure appeared at the door in the dark interior and let them in.

"The look of shock on your face says volumes," Slant said, looking up at Jovan.

"Oh?"

"It tells me you didn't know Mamm Kall was so connected."

CHAPTER 8 — MAMM'S

Kallidova stood at a podium leafing through a large ledger, looking down over the warehouse floor below her like a captain at the helm of a ship. Her ship's sailors—scribes and workers—moved in pairs amongst the stacks of shelves, taking down bags of flour, sacks of grain, odds and ends, and adding them to baskets they had attached to their hips by leather straps.

Jovan stopped at the rails, looking down the twenty feet to the floor, kept cool below the ground level. Kallidova looked up from her books and ledgers, cocked an eyebrow, and returned to her work.

"That's probably all the summons you'll get," Slant said, leaning on a rail.

Zvediz stood against the wall, his arms folded. He was attempting to appear uncaring, but Jovan had the niggling feeling he was uncomfortable.

"Come along, boy," Jovan said.

Leaf kept his eyes on the working floor below as they moved to the side and then down the long walkway that ran along the warehouse wall.

"What are they doing?" Leaf asked.

"Fulfilling orders for customers."

"What kind of goods does she make?"

"She doesn't make anything. She's a merchant. She sells everything to everyone. From my needles to blocks of ice."

"Ice?"

"Yes. Word is she has the steepest price for ice, but she has the cleanest, clearest blocks, that last the longest into the summer."

A man sat on a stool whittling a piece of wood as they came to the corner. He looked up abruptly.

"Business?"

"Kallidova summoned me."

"Your name?" The man glanced over at the woman at the podium, who made a small wave with her hand and then turned back. "Never mind. She says you're good."

Jovan nodded and walked toward the podium. Leaf clung close to Jovan's pant leg.

Kallidova wore an elaborately embroidered dress of reds, yellows, and whites, her heeled boots keeping the hem from touching the stone beneath her feet. Expensive ribbons of silk tied unadorned sleeves of red, marked with black ink stains by her fingers.

"Where have you been?" she asked as they approached. Her tone showed gladness with a tinge of irritation at the frayed edges of her voice. Even with heels she looked up at Jovan; the top of her head, covered in deep blonde hair, ended well below his chin. She was at least a decade older than Jovan, but hid her age with a youthful smile and piercing eyes.

"Traveling north from Geruz. We took the forest paths. Instead of a two or three day trip, we meandered for the past ten. Young children do not travel fast on foot."

"Ah, yes. Of course."

She turned and knelt down in front of Leaf. "Do you see that window over there?" She pointed to the large window in a comfortable sitting area behind her desk.

Leaf nodded.

"It has a view of the mountains. If you look through the looking glass, you may see a drake or even a crag ursa on the slopes."

The boy gasped and ran to the window. He took hold of the swivel-mounted glass and began seeking his quarry on the slopes above.

"I sent two sets of people to find you. How did you stay undetected for so long?"

"We cut through the forest."

"I was starting to think I had mismanaged my investment in you." She glanced over at the boy. "He is well?"

"Yes. Why shouldn't he be?"

"I mean to say, what has he done since I gave him to you?"

"Done? Nothing. He's a boy. He plays all day. Imagines himself a hero of the great battles."

"And his schooling?"

"There has been no schooling. Only the stories he picks up from the old men of the town."

She shook her head. "I had expected you to invest the money I gave you in his education."

"He's only four," Jovan said.

She waved a hand dismissively. "I suppose."

"Why were you searching for me?"

"I had to make sure you were well."

"You mean if the boy was well."

"With your well-being comes his. You had another violent fight. You ought to have been executed for it."

"Lord Valle-Brons and I have an understanding," Jovan said.

"I assumed as much. The man you beat has connections to the throne."

"Then why was he in Geruz and not nipping at the heels of the king and his son?" Jovan asked.

"He was probably looking for something."

Jovan glanced over at the young boy again.

"How is Lord Valle-Brons?"

"Why do you ask?" Jovan turned back to her.

"We were familiar with one another at one point."

"Were you?" Jovan asked, smiling.

"It was a long time ago."

"You warned me this would happen," Jovan said, changing the subject back to the boy.

"I did," she said with a smirk.

"And you're still not going to tell me anything about him?"

"Jovan. I don't know anything. I was hired to find a placement for the boy."

"I can't stay here. It's too close to Geruz."

"Where will you go?"

"I don't know. But I think the best place to head is right to them."

"Take Slant and Zvediz with you."

Jovan sighed and glanced back across the warehouse. Slant smiled and waved. Zvediz had his eyes closed.

"They'll keep you safe."

"I don't need to be watching the boy you gave me as well as your son."

"Son?" she laughed. "Slant isn't my son. He's..."

She glanced toward the sly man by the door, who waved back at her.

"Never mind," she said, rolling her eyes. "Take them with you. If anything, they can provide a distraction if things get tight."

"How much do they know?" Jovan asked.

"About the boy? They know as much as they need."

"Which is?"

"Less than you," she said. "Now go. I have business to attend to."

"I just got in to town and you're already moving me out of here?"

"In the time you've been in town, you've drawn enough attention already. So yes, I am shuffling you along. I have business to conduct in Rightness. I don't need anyone but those I choose messing with the norm."

"Come along, Leaf," Jovan said.

The boy hopped down from his seat and walked over.

"Let me look at you," Kallidova said.

Leaf looked up and smiled kindly.

"Living with Jovan hasn't hardened you?" she asked.

"Papa Jov is good," Leaf said.

"Is he?"

"Yes. Very good. He just gets angry sometimes."

"Is he ever angry at you?"

Leaf let out a little laugh. "Of course not."

"What is so funny?" Kallidova asked.

"I don't think he's ever done a thing to warrant my getting angry," Jovan said.

"Never?"

"Oh sure, he does things that scare me, like walking to the edge of a cliff over water. But he's never done a bad thing."

"Hrm. Interesting," she said.

"You'd prefer I not tell you where I go," Jovan said. It wasn't a question.

Kallidova nodded, but continued to stare at the boy, as though recognizing something in him. Then she shook herself clear.

"Yes, please don't tell me. If I don't know, then I won't be sending people to check on you. I'll trust Slant and Zved to keep their eyes on you. Do you have enough coin?"

Jovan nodded. He touched Leaf's shoulder. Leaf followed him back around the edge of the warehouse.

Slant pushed himself off the wall.

"She wants you to travel with us."

"I know," Slant said.

"We'll need to find a quiet place to sleep so we can leave early tomorrow."

"I know just the place," Slant said.

CHAPTER 9 — UMERNNOSTI

They came out onto the street and followed Slant toward the temple. The crowds were sparse so late into the night. The sound of voices singing in unison came from a house or two.

"Are those hymns?" Leaf asked.

"Very good," Jovan said. "They sing to Saint Neligyne, asking for his guidance."

"You see more people being contrite the closer you get to the temple," Slant said. "It's important to them that it's seen by the priests."

Jovan put a hand on Slant's shoulder. The man stopped and smiled up at Jovan.

"I think that's quite enough of your undermining my teaching of the boy."

"I'm sorry?" Slant asked.

"Kallidova vouched for you and asked I take you with me, to keep an eye out for trouble. But I expect you to keep from causing any trouble yourself. And that means following my leadership, and not getting in the way of how I parent Leaf."

"I meant nothing by it," Slant said.

"You say that," Jovan said. "But you've failed to notice how road worn I am. You have continued to insinuate your own disregard for religion without ever consulting my thoughts on the matter."

Slant said nothing. They stared at each other for a time, and then Slant nodded once and turned to walk away.

"The place I have in mind is just over here," he said over his shoulder.

Jovan followed after Zvediz, who had Leaf's hand in his once more. They came to a single door with two doors either side of it. Upon knocking, someone came to answer from echoing stairs. He wore a brown smock and no shoes. His hair was cropped close.

"Brother Slant," the man said.

"I've brought friends who seek a night out of the cold."

"Very well. This way."

The stairs led down into the earth for several levels, growing chillier, though no air moved. The muffled sound of singing rose from the earth with harmonies not heard from other houses they had passed.

They came to a door. The man in the smock disappeared, leaving them outside for a time.

"They are Umernnosti," Jovan said.

"Yes," Slant replied. "You see, I did not need to ask your beliefs. I read them on you the moment I met you. I apologize for overstepping my boundaries with your boy. I perhaps find myself more humorous than others think I am. I know the Umernnosti. I know their disdain for the other organized religions and their doctrines."

"What gave me away?"

"Your quick acceptance of my saying I was a smoothsayer. You'll allow anyone their beliefs, even if you disagree with them."

"I accepted that because I don't believe you. I haven't seen you do a single thing that anyone would call magic," Jovan said.

"I'm good at keeping it unseen."

"You've done so since we've met?"

"I didn't say that," Slant smiled.

"Will you be able to keep your mouth shut on topics of religion when we leave town?"

"I will try. Where are we going?"

"I have an idea, but I won't discuss it until we leave town. Do you have access to warm clothes?"

"I'll go out tonight and see what I can scrounge up."

The door opened and the man showed them through. Within the sparse and unadorned room, five men and three women sat around a rough wooden table. They held their hands in their laps in silence, watching the men and boy enter.

Slant raised a hand, but Jovan spoke first.

"Simple tenets," he said.

"Simple life," they responded in unison.

"May we bed here?" Jovan asked. "We shall be gone by morning."

"The Four require hospitality. It is the simplest to provide."

"May I ask for truths?"

"So long as it does not disparage another," they intoned.

"May we partake of food, be it only simple?"

"Kindness is only too easily ignored."

"Will you respect the fourth?"

They said nothing but nodded in silence.

Jovan smiled wide and the Umernnosti rose, smiling with him. One of the men left and returned with bread as everyone began to talk in quiet tones. Leaf stayed near Jovan, saying little. Jovan spoke with a man and a woman who called each other "dear friend." He knew them to be companions of one another, though they would not recognize the crown's demand that they be married. They believed that vows were a sin because they could not be kept in life.

Jovan spoke with them about the weather farther north and discovered that the pass to the capital had been uncharacteristically cold for the past month, and it was ill-advised to travel through. Jovan looked over to see the youngest of the women in deep conversation with Zvediz.

"I did not know Zvediz talked as much as I've seen him do here," Jovan said to no one in particular.

"This is where Zved and I met," Slant said, sidling up to Jovan.

"He is Umernnost then?"

"You never asked," Slant said, shrugging in response. "He takes the tenets very seriously. I'm a hypocrite: I suspect the Umernnost beliefs are more religion than they like to let on. I'd probably be considered Umernnost myself if my heritage allowed me to."

"Your heritage?"

Slant pulled back his coat to reveal an orange satin collar. "You're Havat?"

"Is that a problem?" he asked.

"I have no qualms with the Havat. My grandmother was one."

"All of our grandmothers were Havat at some such time. And yet we Havat are still given the boot where others deem fit."

"You'll not find me in that camp," Jovan said.

"I'll take your word for it," Slant said, as though he had heard it a hundred times. "When do you want to leave?"

"Before dawn. Our next road will be long. And we have to beat winter before it comes too far south."

"Then I ought to go find the supplies we need."

"An alternate route out of the city would also be wise," Jovan said. "Leaving by the gate will be too easily noticed."

"I know just the way," Slant said.

Slant disappeared soon after, and the quiet talk went on for another hour before Jovan and Leaf were shown their room, no more than a closet with a large bed.

"May I sleep on the floor this time?" Leaf asked.

Jovan widened his eyes.

"You always give me the comfy bed. Let me give back to you." The boy was smiling broadly.

"You're a kind little boy, you know that?" Jovan said.

Leaf laid a blanket on the floor and lay himself on it.

"Thank you for taking me on such an adventure, Papa Jov," he said quietly after Jovan had taken the bed.

"You're welcome, boy."

Dawn came too soon.

Slant came to their room and knocked. Jovan groggily sat up to see Leaf awake and toying with a little buckle. The leather had deteriorated around it and he was holding it between his fingers.

"Are you two coming?" Slant asked through the door.

"Put the clasp away," Jovan said.

Leaf did as he was told and strapped the belt snug. Jovan could no longer tell that it was deteriorating. They rose and Jovan pulled on his pack.

"How's the weather?" Jovan asked as he opened the door.

"No wind," Slant replied. "But I expect once the sun rises it will pick up."

They came out onto the street. There were no torch flames and the mountains to the east were backlit by predawn light. The temple tried to vie for dominance, but in the dark, all was black. They came to the north gate. Slant led them to an aqueduct in the wall.

"I came out here last night," Slant said. "The water has run dry, but they have a couple of nasty guard dogs in there. Let's see if the treat I gave them still has them dozing."

He slipped away and came back a few moments later.

"Come along. One of them is out cold. The other looks well-enough gone."

Jovan nodded and followed with Leaf's hand in his. Zvediz took the rear.

They walked down the straightaway. Slant had a candle in his hand as the only light. They passed an alcove above the high-water mark. A loud snore came suddenly from within and Jovan nearly threw himself against the other side.

Leaf began to giggle. "It's just a dog, Papa Jov."

Slant shushed them and led on.

They came to another alcove. Slant stopped and let the others pass. He held a finger to his lips. Jovan passed with Leaf in tow and thought he heard a low growl coming from the hole above them.

He looked over his shoulder to see Slant turning to face the hole as Zvediz passed behind him. Slant held a palm out. In the candlelight, it looked as though the smoke from the candle in his hand rose three inches before it wafted at a sharp angle into the hole, and disappeared. The growling subsided.

They came to the other side of the wall and crouched. Slant pushed his way through the others.

"I'll let you know how it looks," he said. He was sucking a finger.

"Did the dog wake and bite you?" Leaf asked.

"No. Just a little burn," Slant said. "I touched the candle flame."

He slipped out and turned to look up, then indicated they follow. They made their way across the field to a grove of trees.

"We'll take the trees for a mile or so," Slant said as they came up next to him.

Jovan nodded and stepped forward to lead the way.

Just as they were about to step out onto the road, now a good mile away from the city, the thunder of hooves forced them back into the dense underbrush.

Five men wearing the colors of the Rightness city guard rushed past.

As their hoofbeats diminished, Slant was suddenly next to Jovan's ear.

"Off on an errand?" Slant asked.

"No way to know. But we keep to the woods."

"Where do we go?" Zvediz asked.

"East. To the Kharavadziy Plateau."

"Will we see the great caravans?" Leaf asked excitedly.

"What are you running from that you would leave the civilized lands behind?" Slant asked. "You seem very keen to leave."

"What do you know of Prince Zelmir Valle?"

"He's carried in a litter wherever he goes."

"Do you know why?"

"Rumor is he's crippled."

"He is."

"You crippled him?" Slant's face lit up with a smile.

"That's not for me to say," Jovan said. "But I was charged with the crime, and I was rumored to have been executed for it."

"And what you did in Geruz was enough to tell those keeping an eye out for you that you're alive."

"I believe so," Jovan said.

"To the Plateau then," Slant said with determination. "I know a faster way than wending along this road to reach the pass. Shall we?"

Jovan nodded and let Slant lead. He would have to take a secret from Slant in trade one day.

CHAPTER 10 — STONEWEKS

The small village of Stoneweks huddled against the quarry. The main street straddled the slag stream that none dared gather water from. Where the quarry had been bitten back becoming flat ground, new buildings had been started.

The open-faced needle forge glowed with the heat from Jovan's fire, though he had quickly turned his industry to that of tempering chisels for the stone carvers. It had been fortunate for Jovan that the smiths in residence had neither formed a guild, nor had any mote of skill. As expected, three of the blacksmiths had come to him to try to convince him to move along on the third night after he had set up shop. But both he and Zvediz had convinced them it wasn't worth their while to bicker or bully. They came to the understanding that he would properly temper their work for them, doubling the price of their chisels. And the masons of the town gladly paid.

The winter had given its worst over a month prior, leaving the place locked in a thin, hard crust of ice, demanding everyone bundle up in thick furs. Leaf had played at gathering up the chalky white snow into piles near the edge of the building, allowing the seeping warmth from the forge to make it just pliable enough to build walls and fortifications for the sticks and stones he had gathered for his soldiers. Slant was rarely at the forge, nor in town, as Jovan charged him with general errand running. Soon after they had come to town he had disappeared for two weeks, returning with a large vat of oil, bought from the the caravan towns of the Kharavadziy out on the plains. It had been the one thing Jovan had needed to improve his tempering, and had arrived before the worst of winter, thus, none of the other blacksmiths could emulate his practice.

Zvediz had proven an apt pupil to Jovan, and served the function of apprentice with no complaint. In three months' time he had said no more than ten handfuls of words. One of which had revealed that he had been apprenticed to a silversmith, before being blamed for the theft of several ingots of silver. None more was said, and he did everything in diligence that Jovan had seen in few men in his time.

There was a fifth person now often seen at Jovan's forge, though he was more a fixture than any help. Tekhom was an odd-looking man. Above his thin legs sat a barrel chest and shoulders, with long, slender arms that ran to his knees. His head sat cocked and foreword, as though he suffered a neck deformity that sent his long, thin-haired beard not down his chest, but over his shoulder. And yet, there were times the man stood upright and looked every bit normal, save the long arms.

Tekhom was never trouble, only a man lonely for company. He spent hours perched on a stool, his fur cloak trailing out behind him like the tail of some exotic bird, watching Jovan work or Leaf play in the snow. One day, the man spent an hour watching Zvediz pump the billows, only to continue staring for three hours after the man had gone. He did help occasionally when there was suddenly a need for another set of hands. He shared the town's gossip, and one time even foretold a need for ten chisels no other blacksmith in town knew of, allowing Jovan to prepare and sell the goods for the full profit.

Once, Jovan had asked about his origins from others at the tavern. Rumor had said that Tekhom was a trapper who got caught in town as winter blocked him from his hunting paths. Another thought him a priest, on the run from his mission. In the end, Jovan knew less than he did before.

"It is interesting," Tekhom said, offering bread and cheese to the others as they took a break from the day's work. The sun had broken through and set the entire town to a sparkle of frost. Zvediz had taken the opportunity to head to the quarry to gather blunt tools to be honed. "A boy's play is as intense as a man's work over a forge. I often wonder if the work of play is more formative to a person than years as apprentice."

"Perhaps they are able to learn more in less time," Slant said. He wolfed down the bread offered to him and took another piece from Tekhom.

"And yet, play comes so naturally."

"Some masters I've known have taken their apprentices quite young for just that reason," Jovan said. "The boys make more mistakes at such a young age, but by the time they make journeyman, they are better than many masters."

"Intriguing," Tekhom said. "I wonder what play we do then that stretches our souls and spirits."

"Ah," Slant said, winking. "And do priests stifle our play of soul too early?"

Jovan shot a look at him that bade him shut his mouth.

"Perhaps the play of a boy or girl does the same for the soul as it does the body," Tekhom replied.

"A philosopher then?" Jovan asked.

"Are not we all?" Tekhom replied.

"I am a nedeller."

"As you so often remind us. And yet you've not made a needle in a month's time."

"When there is need."

"Then you shall needle!" Leaf said, and laughed at his own joke. The others followed with a chuckle.

"Ah, and there is a stretch of the mind," Tekhom said.

Jovan wiped bread crumbs off his apron and turned back to his anvil. "Fetch me the fine file, Leaf."

The boy walked over to the tool bench and took hold of a small bit of metal, but it was pinned under an ingot. Pulling harder, it swung free. Leaf shouted in exclamation and put his finger into his mouth to suck on the bead of red that appeared. The boy walked over and handed Jovan the file with the other hand.

"Put it in cold water," Jovan said.

Leaf nodded and walked over to a pile of snow dribbling down into a water bucket. He pulled his hand out and looked at the finger, and then looked again.

"Boy?" Jovan asked.

"It's gone," Leaf said, holding up his finger for Jovan to see.

Tekhom raised an eyebrow. "Sometimes pain is the first step," Tekhom said.

"What is that supposed to mean?" Jovan asked.

"The stretching of the soul," Tekhom said. "That boy healed himself."

"That's not true," Jovan said.

"Jovan's right," Slant said, sidling up to the older man. "It was me."

"You?" Tekhom said.

"Yes. I'm a smoothsayer."

"Quite an expenditure," Tekhom said. "You ought to be more careful with how you bandy power like that about."

"It was a little thing," Slant said with a shrug.

Tekhom raised an eyebrow and took a long, deep breath. "There was a new group of men come to town today," he said, changing the subject.

"Nothing new there," Jovan said, using the file to make the finishing touches on the chisel he worked on at his bench.

"They came down from the pass."

Jovan turned and looked. "Why are you telling me?"

"They were asking after a man and his boy. No one gave anyone away. But it's a small enough town for anyone to see with their own eyes."

"Where are they?" Jovan asked.

"The Plank."

Jovan looked over at Slant, who nodded. Jovan sighed and carefully wiped his hands free of metal shavings. He pulled on a long, red Kharavadziy woolen cloak and walked out into the hard winter wind.

There were only two taverns, and both were tents set up on the leeward side of one of the larger buildings in town. The Plank was the nicer of the two, with fairly fresh planks laid down for everyone to walk upon. Jovan walked up to the tent. He stood outside the entry flap and waited for the wind to die a moment before he stepped in and closed it behind him.

"Jovan," the man behind the stack of crates that acted as a bar said. "Same?"

Jovan nodded, and the man soon had a large stoneware bottle uncorked and placed in front of him. Jovan took hold of the bottle and pulled it toward him, but the barkeep's grip was firm. Jovan looked up and into his eyes. The man across from him scowled and jutted his jaw in the direction of the back corner. Then he let go of the bottle and placed his hand down on the bar with his thumb hidden. Jovan placed four copper bits on the bar, enough to buy three bottles, and then turned to take it to another seat.

The barmaid, Yara, stood with a large bowl filled with bread rolls on her hip, talking to the three men who sat at the table closest to the hearth. Their belongings and clothes were strewn across several of the nearby tables and on the hearth itself. Furs, cloaks, packs, all sat wet atop the surfaces as they thawed from their descent from the pass above the little town.

"How hard can it be to make a tavern with four walls?" one of them was saying loudly. "I'm still cold." His head was small upon his short and strongly built body, made bulkier still by the filthy badger coat he had refused to remove, even sitting so close to the fire. He looked like the sea turtles that basked on the stones below Geruz, but this sea turtle had a scraggly black beard, and several of his finger joints were missing, including his entire left pinky.

"Ha!" another said. This one was tall and built like a lumber hauler. "You still owe me and Olv the silver you bet us we wouldn't make it. At least the beer is readily available, and the women ample."

He finished off the tankard of beer in his hand and handed it over to Yara, trying to take a swipe at her rear as she turned to go and refill it.

"Don't get your hopes up, Varg," the obvious leader of the three said. He sat tall, and wore browns almost the color of his sun-browned skin and matching hair. "She's the only girl I've seen in town since we entered. And she turned her nose up at your smell."

The short turtle of a man guffawed.

"You're welcome to laugh, Pragg. But Varg's right. You owe us. Perhaps a thumb knuckle?"

"Bah! Only the Bear gets knuckles from me." Pragg looked down into his tankard again. He lifted it up to finish it off. "I'll take the lead on the next."

"That's fair," Varg said.

Yara returned and placed fresh beer in front of each of them, keeping the table between her and the lecherous eyes of Varg.

"You can continue to stare at us as a stranger, or you can join us for a beer as a comrade," Olv said, not looking at Jovan. But Jovan knew the words were for him.

Jovan lifted his bottle to his lips. "I do not drink with strangers."

"A stranger then. I'd know your name, so we can become friends."

"Jovan."

The large man, Varg, clenched both fists, then hid them under the table.

"You've come down from the pass?" Jovan asked. "That is not an easy road, even in the summer."

"We're hunters," Pragg offered.

"Was the season for white pelts no good?" Jovan asked.

"We don't hunt pelts," Varg said.

"Jovan, you say?" Olv asked.

Jovan nodded.

"Perhaps then you'll tell me: has another come this way in the past few months with the same name?"

"If it were so, I should like to know what you would have with him?"

"We were sent on a hunt. To find him."

Yara stood behind the table now, by the hearth, the bread bowl clutched to her chest. She squeaked as Jovan saw the swing of the club coming at him from the side. The fourth man was as big as Zvediz, and the club he held could have knocked out a bull. Jovan stepped back with a lunge. The man took a step to match his stride, and stepped off the planking that lined the floor, into one of the mud holes. His boot sunk deep and then stuck.

Jovan took hold of one of the stools that sat at the table next to him, and then glanced at the bartender, who nodded. Jovan lifted it and stepped forward. The man was trying to pull his boot free. Jovan brought the stool across the man's face, then lifted a boot and kicked down on the man's back. He could feel the audible snap of the man's leg as his weight pulled him over.

As the man howled, now holding his knee, the others were rising to their feet. Their stools fell over as they brandished clubs.

"You're quite the easy quarry," Olv said, "coming straight to us when we started asking around."

"People talk," Jovan said.

"They do. Those who talked without telling us, though? We'll be taking what we offered to pay them from their own hides."

"I doubt they'll take kindly to you saying that."

"You promised to take lead," Varg said to Pragg, "but Sill has already done so."

"Then I'll take what I owe from him," Pragg said, raising his club at Jovan.

They hesitated to take a step forward.

"Who seeks me?" Jovan asked.

"We're not ones to say," Olv said. He stood back, allowing the other two to step forward.

"The prince has heard I'm not dead?"

Olv's face lit up. "Ah, a criminal on the run. Perhaps you'll come with us. Be obliging and perhaps we won't turn you over to whatever bounty you're escaping."

"I doubt that," Jovan muttered.

"You're probably right," Olv replied. "Pragg. He's hesitant to defend himself. Clear your debt and let's bury him. Then we can seek out the boy."

Leaf.

Jovan's ears became suddenly hot, and his vision focused on the men in front of him. The canvas that fluttered at the edge of his vision began to glow red, as though a fire blazed outside the tent.

Pragg stepped forward and Jovan met his stride. As the club came down, Jovan caught it, twisting Pragg's wrist to force him to drop it into the mud below. Jovan took hold of the man's throat and forced him down into the mud, face first. He let go and stepped onto the back of his head, as a stone in the middle of a stream, heading for Varg, who stood dumbfounded.

Jovan pulled out a canvas needle, tucked in his boot, as he stepped back up onto the planking, and sunk it into the man's thigh. Enough blood spurted that he knew he'd hit an artery. He'd bleed out if he didn't care for himself soon.

As Varg howled, Jovan thrust his fingers up under his jaw, snapping his mouth shut. The man staggered and fell onto their table, tankards flying into the air. Jovan lifted the edge of the table, and the man slid off the backside, his head striking the edge of the hearth.

"You ought to have picked better men," Jovan fumed, spinning toward Olv.

"Inconsequential," he said. "I had no need of them in the first place."

He stood on the other side of the hearth and reached a hand out toward the flame. A roar to match the rage that coursed through Jovan's head rose. Suddenly, a rope of flame spun out of the hearth and surged up in front of Olv.

"This will cost you dearly, forcing me to use such a gift," he said.

The serpentine flame twisted and writhed, trying to escape the unseen grip Olv held on it. It suddenly surged forward across the table to Jovan, and then, just as suddenly dissipated. Zvediz stood behind the man, his fist still clenched above the vedmak, who'd crumpled with a wince of pain.

Jovan was on top of him in an instant. He hoisted him up against the side of the hearth, threatening to shove him into the flames.

"Why do you hunt my child?" Jovan shouted.

"We were asked only to bring him to our employer," Olv said, looking up with dazed eyes. "Please don't kill me."

"Why shouldn't I? You meant to kill me."

"Please."

"You're a vedmak. Nothing can contain you but death. Unless you make an Oath."

Olv grimaced. "If you promise not to kill me, I will make an Oath."

"I will promise not to kill you, if you tell me who your employer is."

"The Bear."

"You'll need to tell me more."

"If you begin to ask around for him, he will find you. Make no mistake."

Jovan nodded.

"The Oath," Jovan said.

"What Oath would you have me make?"

"You will swear your forgetfulness of me, and you will go and join a Kharavadziy caravan."

Olv took a deep breath and nodded. Jovan watched the man's eyes roll back in his head. A whiff of light came out of his mouth. Then he passed out.

Jovan slapped him hard across the face, enough to leave a bruise, and to ensure he was not faking his deep sleep. Then he rose.

The barkeep approached Jovan and Zvediz. "They'll be sent to work in a quarry."

"Not this one. Make sure he leaves town going east. You don't want the trouble he'll bring."

"And what about you?"

"Spring is coming in a week or so. I'll travel north and look for a way across once the thaws have begun."

"You'll be missed in town. In so short a time, you've brought respectability to the smithing trade."

"Perhaps I've taught enough to the other boys that they'll continue to do good. Will you buy my shop and see it sold?"

"I'll give you fifty silver for everything."

Jovan held out a hand and they shook on it. "You'll make twice that. And don't sell the anvil to anyone save Marz. He's the only smith worth any salt. He needs a new anvil anyway."

"I'll see to it."

CHAPTER 11 — THE LONG WALL

The wind that blew hard from the east was warm enough to melt the snow from the ground, but cold enough that the cloaks did little good to warm them as they walked. The Long Wall, a tall cliff that rose a thousand feet toward the sky, ran off to the north for miles ahead of them. The mountains that stood above the strata of rock could not be seen from below.

Zvediz led the way, leaning forward as he trudged along. The bushes that sprinkled the plains offered no shelter, and the wind had been blowing since the day before without sign of stopping.

Slant and Jovan walked on each side of the little boy who did not complain, but held his arms close to his chest and pressed on. Jovan and Zvediz had taken turns holding the boy, but Leaf had offered to give them both a stretch.

Zvediz stopped ahead. Jovan approached to look down. A trench in the earth had formed, running from the Long Wall toward the plain to the east; the water coursed several yards below. It would be easy enough to leap over the gap.

Looking to his left, Jovan saw the crack ran straight and true toward the strata.

"Let's see where this stream begins," Jovan shouted over the wind.

They turned and walked along the crack. Jovan picked up Leaf and bundled him into his cloak to share their warmth.

"I'm all right," Leaf said into his ear.

"I'm sure you are. But we must conserve our heat."

They came to the wall. A wide crack rose up ten feet, and the water sat only a few feet below the rim now.

"I'll take a look," Slant said. He reached down and tested the water depth, then dropped down into it, waist deep.

He waded up against the water, and disappeared into the earth. After what felt far too long they heard him shout, the words coming up out of the crack.

"Follow! It's safe!"

Zvediz dropped down and then took Leaf into his arms to keep him dry, and waded up into the cave. Jovan followed soon after.

Inside, the air was still, but did not have the smell of animal, nor the stale smell of an old, moldy cave. Slant had lit a torch and held it aloft. The air was surprisingly warm.

"It's not much of a cave," Slant said, "but it will do. We won't be able to start a fire, unless we go get some bushes to burn."

"If the winds continue until tomorrow we'll hunker up here and fetch burnables," Jovan said. "Otherwise, let's simply rest for now until tomorrow."

The others agreed and began to unpack their bedrolls.

Jovan set his roll next to Leaf and then tucked the boy in tight before putting his own blanket over the two of them. The wind howled outside; the single torch, lodged into a crack in the rock, slowly burned down.

Jovan opened his eyes to a blackness that matched the back of his eyelids. The silence of the now dead wind left him feeling as though he floated in nothingness. Then the warmth of the little boy next to him reminded him where he was. Zvediz's snore reverberated across the cave once, and then fell back to nothingness. Jovan slid again into the void.

A gray light seeped into the space and Jovan cracked his eyes open.

Slant was already up, and using a knife to break up a bush he had uprooted and brought back into the cave.

"How long have you been awake?"

"The wind died down about midnight," Slant said. "I couldn't bear the silence."

He cracked a stick in two, if only to break the quiet. "At least it was a near full moon last night."

"Any game out in the moonlight?"

"Some hare. But they didn't venture far from their burrows."

"I think I still have some dried meat," Jovan said. "We can mix that with some oats."

Slant nodded.

"Do you know how far the Long Wall stretches?" Jovan asked.

"I heard a few men in Stoneweks say it ran for twenty-five miles."

"How far would you say we made it yesterday?"

"Ten."

"That's what I was thinking. If the wind doesn't pick back up, we can make the rest today."

"It's not much farther past the Long Wall to the pass to Vhelrad," Slant offered.

"We're not going to Vhelrad," Jovan countered. "We'll be taking the pass over into Belkhal."

"What's in Belkhal?"

"Enemies, I assume."

"You're not making any sense," Slant said. His flint struck home and showered the tinder. A few quick breaths and he had a blaze glowing.

"Whoever is looking for me, for whatever reason, is looking afar for me. I don't doubt they tore apart the entire Havoy District to find me. Now they look abroad."

"So you go right into their den."

"To seek out the Bear."

"Yes," Slant said. "The bear's den."

Slant took another handful of sticks and reached to put them into his fire, and then froze. He glanced up at Jovan. "That's not what you meant, was it?"

Jovan shook his head.

"You're going to seek out the Bear?"

"You know who I'm looking for?"

"I have heard of the Bear. But I know better than to seek him out. He'll kill you just for thinking about him."

"I will not continue to run. The world is too small to run. So I will seek out the hunter and ask him to stop."

"You fear little," Slant said.

Jovan did not reply.

"I saw what you did to that vedmak," Slant said. "He walked past the forge before you came back. He wouldn't give me the time of day. He was muttering something."

"He was under an Oath," Jovan said without looking up.

"How did you convince him of that?"

"The threat of his life was enough."

"No vedmak makes an Oath lightly. It comes at a great cost, and a great risk."

"You know a lot about magic."

"I do," Slant said.

"Papa Jov?" Leaf said, rolling over. "I'm hungry."

"There will be food soon."

Leaf saw the fire and leapt up, suddenly awake, and began to crawl over the rocks, exploring the insides of the cave. There was no outlet, save where the spring trickled. A crack that ran up the wall disappeared into the darkness. Leaf slipped on the water-worn surfaces several times, but suffered no more bruises than any boy tumbling about a field.

Within a couple hours, they made their way onto the plain once more. Zvediz had dislodged some rocks and tumbled them down into the stream bed below as stepping stones, allowing them all to leave with dry clothes.

The wind had died, leaving the landscape a blank parchment of windblown white snow. The only scribblings of a heavenly scribe were the dead grass that poked up out of the canvas, while the few bushes illuminated the border of the page with a story none could read.

They moved easily north, with no gale to fight them, though their path did not run straight, as drifts rose in their way.

Leaf spent much of the time on the shoulders of the three men, so they made good time.

The sun disappeared behind the mountains, plunging a still cold around them. They approached the end of the Long Wall, which terminated abruptly. Coming around that final corner revealed a dense black forest, quickly growing darker in the failing light.

A thin line of smoke rose up from the forest, indicating someone lived not far within. Jovan pressed toward the beacon. As they entered the darkness of the woods, he could make out the single fire of a lantern hanging from a doorframe.

"I will go up to introduce myself and then the rest of us," Jovan said. "If we all go, we may receive a cold shoulder."

"No," Zvediz said. "You stay. I will go. I know forest tradition."

Jovan stopped and nodded to the big man.

Zvediz trudged off into the woods toward the door, leaving them alone in the hundred yards that stood between them. As Jovan's eyes adjusted, he could see it was more than a hut—a full-sized house, raised above the forest floor on the trunks of four trees at its corners. A few stone pillars were also raised to support sagging eaves, a stone back wall to the forest. The sounds of chickens squawking came from a coop under the house as Zvediz approached the stairs and ascended with creaks of wood.

Zvediz remained just off the porch on a few stairs up to the raised house as he knocked soundly on the wooden post. After a time, the door cracked open. There were words exchanged before the door opened wider. A hunched old woman stepped out onto the porch, cradling an axe in her arms.

CHAPTER 12 — WAYS OF THE WOODS

After what felt like half the night waiting, Zvediz turned and waved his arms for them to join him. Jovan hoisted Leaf up.

"I can walk myself," Leaf said.

"Yes, but I'll not keep our host waiting."

They approached the small clearing. Snow-covered logs sectioned off what might have once been a yard for children or a garden. Up against the woods, a two-doored outhouse sat. One door hung from its frame in disrepair, and a beaten path ran from the remaining door to the house. The old woman had her hair braided, running to the porch behind her, so long it was likely she'd never cut her hair.

Jovan stepped up to meet the woman and took her offered forearm as she dropped the axe behind the doorframe. "Thank you for allowing us to approach," Jovan said.

"Please, I'll have you all in. I have food for you and a place to seek shelter." The tightness of her voice spoke of formal education. She turned to Slant. "And you are?"

"Slavint Yunev."

"You are brethren?"

"Of the Havyun Sept."

The woman nodded and smiled. As she turned and knelt before the boy, Jovan saw the orange ribbon tying her braid and realized what Slant referred to. The old woman was Havat.

"Hello, young boy. What is your name?"

"I am called Leaf."

"Called Leaf? Then that is not your name?"

Leaf screwed up his lips, not knowing what to say.

"I only jest with you. Forgive an old woman." She stood and turned to go inside. "I am called Toniz Shayk. I welcome you to my small home in the forest. I have just finished eating, but I've more than enough food and drink for you."

Leaf ran up and into the house behind the woman. Zvediz came after, while Jovan and Slant collected their things in the corner.

They joined Zvediz and Leaf at a table as the old woman spooned out thick stew into wooden bowls. The place was a mess of cobwebs. In the corner, old furniture sat in a large pile out of the way, while the area by the hearth was the only clean area and well-used. A worn path in the wood led from a single chair to another small room. The old woman indicated they sit down, and then went to sit in the chair that even for her small frame seemed too small for her.

She sat and watched them eat in silence.

"This is bitter," Leaf whispered.

"Mind your manners," Jovan said.

"It's the juniper berries," Toniz said. "I am partial to them, but they do leave that bitter aftertaste."

Leaf scrunched his nose.

"Boy," Jovan said sternly, "this is not like you. Now eat your food."

"He's a young boy. He's allowed a little leeway," the old woman responded.

"He has never turned away food nor been rude to another soul," Jovan said.

Toniz shrugged.

Zvediz put both hands in the air to stretch with a large yawn. A sudden wave of weariness fell over Jovan, too.

"You can sleep in the bedroom," Toniz said. "I imagine you've had a hard day walking along the Long Wall."

Jovan nodded and stood. "I apologize," he said through a yawn, "for not staying up to chat with you. It must be lonely here in the woods."

The old woman stood to show the way.

The side room had a bed. Zvediz found himself a corner, lay down, and immediately began to snore. Slant, who had been uncharacteristically quiet, sat against a wall and folded his arms over his chest. Jovan waved a hand for the boy to take the bed and then he sat down on it, as well. He only managed to remove a single boot before falling over onto the pillow into a deep sleep.

What felt like hours later, he heard the crying of a full-grown man. The man lay on a road with a carriage tipped over on his back, crying out in pain and anger. Jovan had seen him before, the golden hair braided back over one shoulder. As Jovan approached, the man, not much more than a boy, yelled in defiance at him. Another figure shot out from the shadows and on down the road, from torchlight to torchlight.

And then Jovan was the man on the ground, but a golden-haired figure stood over him.

"Why can't I move?" Jovan cried out.

"Your legs are numb?"

Jovan nodded as he woke from the dream.

Leaf had his hands on Jovan's chest. Jovan felt his mind clear as something seeped out of his head and down into his chest. The feeling came back to his feet and legs and hands. Jovan shooed the boy away and sat up. His chest was hot and he couldn't breathe. He touched his chest to feel the leather there singed as though a coal had been put atop it. He threw his legs over the edge of the bed, unable to draw a breath. He began to cough violently. A plug of green dislodged and fell to the ground. A bitter taste was left in his mouth.

"What was that?" he asked. He turned to look at Leaf, who stood there.

"The old woman put something bad in the soup," Leaf whispered.

Someone in the outer room moved, creaking a floorboard.

"Go and lay next to Zvediz," Jovan said. "Pull a blanket over you."

Leaf did as he was told.

Someone approached the door to the room and began to push it open.

"Boy?" It was Toniz. "If you're awake, we must leave. We can't stay here."

The old woman stepped into the dark room. The fire in the main room blazed. Too much. It would catch the place on fire. A fire burned in Jovan's mind. The old woman meant to kill them and take the boy.

Jovan came out from behind the door and took hold of the woman's arms as she yelped in protest.

"Who are you?" Jovan roared. "Why have you done this?"

"Why are you not asleep?" the old woman rasped. "The larger the heart, the faster it acts."

"Answer my question," Jovan asked. A bright flash of flame burst out of the hearth as it caught the pile of kindling set out intentionally on the stones. "Or I leave you to burn inside this place."

The old woman said nothing.

"Tell me!" Jovan roared.

"I'd rather die than admit my failure."

"The Bear?" Jovan asked.

The old woman's eyes lit in glee. "Ha. I don't fear him. If the Bear also seeks you, then you have little time left in this life."

Jovan felt a tug at his belt and looked down at Leaf.

"Please, let her go," Leaf implored. "There is no harm, see?"

Slant and Zvediz were shaking their heads groggily and moved to stand. Slant wiped green from his lips onto his sleeve.

"How?!" the old woman screeched.

Jovan dropped her. Toniz staggered to her feet and rushed out of the room toward the door. Jovan watched her change directions, reaching for the axe not far from the hearth that now blazed. Flames were licking their way up the wall. She turned back to look at the door and the men beyond.

"The boy comes with me," the old woman shouted, "or you'll die."

Jovan felt Zvediz come to stand behind him.

"You won't fare well," Jovan shouted over the roar of the flame.

"I have lived long and never failed!" the old woman shouted.

She took a step forward as flame burst from the fireplace, engulfing her.

Jovan slammed the door closed as the flame belched toward them. It was hotter than Jovan could stand. He fell back into the bedroom.

"We need to go through the wall here!" Slant shouted.

"It's solid stone," Jovan shouted. "We don't have time."

"We can't make a run for it through the flames or we'll all burn."

Jovan caught a movement out of the corner of his eye. Leaf stood in the open doorframe looking at the flames creeping toward him. He did not seem to notice the heat. He lifted a hand.

"Leaf!" Jovan shouted. "No!"

Jovan shut the door to the bedroom again and pressed his back to it. Even through the wood, the heat pulsed.

The boy took a step back with one foot to brace himself and then pressed a hand toward the door and to the wall the other two men fought to bash their way through.

"Nal!" Slant swore in surprise as Zvediz pushed his hands through the stone wall as though he was pushing through a sack of flour.

"This stone is like sawdust!" Zvediz shouted.

Jovan touched the wooden door. Despite the fire on the other side, the wood was cooling and the grains of wood were less defined. The bits of light that snuck through cracks thinned to nothing. Even the beams that crept up and along the ceiling turned to gray stone.

"You can stop now," Jovan shouted as Zvediz continued to dig through the compromised stone wall.

Jovan took hold of Leaf and leapt over the bed, throwing himself through the hole left by Zvediz as he crashed through, Slant coming just after. The four of them landed on the ground not far from the house, and turned to watch as the roof collapsed on the flames. A moment later and the weight of the house fell off the stilted pillars and into a heap of smoldering ruin.

Leaf looked up at Jovan with a smile. "I made the wood into rock."

"At what cost," Jovan muttered to himself.

"Your boy," Zvediz said sternly, "is vedmak."

Jovan nodded solemnly, and knelt down to see if anything was wrong with the child.

"That was a costly spell, converting the stone into wood and the wood into stone," Slant said. "But the boy doesn't seem harmed or drained."

"You don't seem surprised," Jovan said. "Then you knew?"

"I've known for some time. I don't think a day has gone by that he hasn't cast power. But all small casts. Nothing harmful to himself. But that? I've never seen someone use that kind of power. It costs too much."

"I'm fine," the boy said.

"Why?" Slant asked. "A grown man, trained in the ways of the vedmak, would have collapsed under that strain. It might even be the last spell he'd cast if he hadn't already forfeited his soul." Slant knelt beside Leaf. "Where do you draw your power from?"

"I don't know," Leaf shrugged. "But it's there. It always has been."

CHAPTER 13 — HIGH PASS

"He was how old when he came to you?"

"Two years," Jovan replied. "Though, perhaps a little younger than that."

"And he's been toying with this ability since then?" Slant asked.

"Two weeks after he came to me is when I first suspected."

"What did he do?"

"Helped a mouse free of a trap."

"That doesn't seem like too much."

"He set its tail, which had broken clean off."

Slant pursed his lips dubiously. "That's a nearly impossible casting in and of itself, especially for someone untrained. I mean, unless someone was feeding him extra portions of soul while he did it. But that wasn't happening."

They finished piling the dirt over the graves they'd built for the dead family they had found the next day, frozen under a thin layer of snow just behind the tree line. The old poisoner had been ruthless. Jovan tried not to think of their faces in slumber, cut short by the cold winter outside.

"Even if he did do that," Slant continued, "the amount of power spent would be soul-shattering."

"I know little of magic," Jovan said. He turned and looked directly at Slant. "I don't want to know."

"I don't think you have much of a choice if your boy is a vedmak."

Jovan sighed. He looked across the yard. Zvediz leaned against a rock eating an apple, watching Leaf play among the fallen trees.

"I'm only barely trained myself," Slant said. "I escaped before they forced me to learn too much."

"Escaped what?"

"I was sent to the vedmak school when I was a lad. They found out I was a Havat, and tried to beat that out of me." Slant sighed. "Such good memories."

"So you are a vedmak?"

"As I said when we met, I'm a smoothsayer."

"You're no prophet."

"Not a *sooth*sayer, a *smooth*sayer. I can sense magic. I prefer to use magic to bend things to go my way."

"Yet Leaf's ability eluded you at first?"

"I have always had the feeling that he was magic-able, but it took me some time to catch him doing it. When he did, I felt no surge, or something 'more' than I usually do. It's as though he's always using magic."

"That doesn't make sense. Shouldn't that hurt him?" Jovan asked.

"It should. We only have so much magic we can use. Every spell costs something to our soul. Like a bone break."

"A bone break?"

Slant smiled and sat down, crossing his legs under him. He picked up an upturned stone next to the grave.

"We are body and soul," Slant started. "Our body is mastered by our mind." He touched his forehead. "While our soul is mastered by our spirit." He touched his chest. "Ghosts, after all, are souls without spirit, the equivalent of a body without a mind—someone in an asylum."

"I understand this," Jovan replied. "Few disagree with this, least of all the Umernnosti."

"Yes. Of course. Now, we use our bodies everyday. Driving nails into wood, hoeing fields, digging graves." He motioned to the piled up earth next to him. "Sometimes we push too hard. We take a misstep and our bones break. They heal, for the most part, but generally, you are forever damaged. That bum leg will always work against you. Eventually, after enough breaks, we'd be useless, do you follow?"

Jovan nodded.

"Then there is soul. Those trained in its use, the vedmak, can use the soul for things like touching a pair of dice in our minds to turn them to the side we wish. We can encourage a flower bud to open sooner rather than later. Little things, but difficult, nonetheless. These might cause small cuts on our soul, cuts that heal with no scars to show. But then there are spells. Magic that cannot be denied. They go so against the fabric of our physical world that force is exerted back on our souls and breaks them. Thus, every spell brings us closer to useless. If we spend too much and destroy our soul..."

"You'd end up a lost soul, a ghost."

"Close enough."

"So what do I do with Leaf?"

"I couldn't tell you. If you turn him over for testing, you won't see him again. They'll take him away for an apprenticeship. And once there, no one leaves to go visit family."

"And if I don't, he dies."

"That may be," Slant said, looking over at the boy. "But maybe not."

"What do you mean?"

"I can speak with him. Maybe even impart some wisdom to him and see what takes. Prevent him from harming himself."

Jovan sighed and then nodded. "Do what you can," Jovan said. "I won't have him destroying himself."

Jovan walked over to stand next to Zvediz.

"Can I trust you to continue with us?" Jovan asked.

Zvediz looked over at Jovan. "Why do you ask?"

"You are Umernnost. Magic is considered an evil."

"You are Umernnost, too," Zvediz replied. "Do you consider it an evil?"

"I believe it can lead to great evil."

"While Umernnost, do you see me in an Umernnost community?" Zvediz asked.

Jovan shook his head.

"I walk my own path to the heavens. And there are those I care about who have shown they are not evil, despite the sin of magic. Thus, I walk a path of learning, to a better understanding of the world through my own discovery. You might do well to do likewise."

Jovan watched Leaf turn over a rock and laugh gleefully as a mouse shot out across the snow.

"Yes. I will continue on this path beside you, as I have promised," Zvediz said. "Your boy is good. And yet he is ved-mak. What can be learned from this?"

"I don't know," Jovan said. "What?"

"I do not ask you," Zvediz said. "I ask myself."

The following day, they took a path that led off into the woods toward the north. Zvediz often stopped to consider the snow-dusted forest floor, searching for signs of trouble, though nothing gave him full pause.

It took five days to pass through the stretch of woods, which let out again onto the plains. The slow rise up to their position gave them a clear view of the entire Kharavadziy Plateau. In the swirling snow, many miles off, Jovan could make out a stretch of a caravan community.

"I think we're not far from the Kardag Pass," Slant said. "If my education serves me correctly, we won't know until we see it."

"I know the way," Zvediz said. "We have miles to go to its foothills."

Jovan nodded, and let Zvediz once more take the lead.

As night fell, sparse trees rose around them and the ground grew gradually steeper. The hills were black against the backdrop of the cloudy sky, and close enough to block the view to the mountains beyond them.

Zvediz called for camp and they gathered up branches to prepare a quick shelter in a small copse of trees.

Slant continued to speak with Leaf, showing him small tricks, and even produced a spark of flame on his fingertips. Leaf looked on with interest, but Jovan had seen the boy do many of those things in the privacy of their home. He was taught nothing new. Jovan hoped that the least Slant could do was teach him to better understand what it was he did when he used that power within him.

"Now," Slant said. "One of the easiest minor casts to use, though also the easiest to abuse, is the twist of luck. It can be something as simple as recovering from a trip. And when you panic, even a little, that can be your undoing. If you are surprised as you fall after catching your foot on a stone, you can easily right yourself at too much a cost of your soul."

"What do you do?" Leaf asked.

"I let myself fall. More often than not. And when I do recover, I do it in a way that simply moderates the pain."

"Can you show me?"

Slant nodded and rose, smiling. He walked toward the other side of the fire next to Jovan, and then caught his foot on the log as he stepped over it. He yelped and fell forward. Jovan felt the second it took for him to pitch forward last thrice as long as it should have, as Slant rolled his shoulder forward faster than the rest of himself to take the ground with the curve of his back.

He rose and hopped to his feet, his arms out, and took a bow.

"You didn't do anything!" Leaf said.

Slant winked. "But I did," Slant said. He glanced over at Jovan. "At least I've still got enough in me to mislead someone who should have caught it."

"I caught what you did," Jovan said. "But I was right next to you."

Slant raised an eyebrow.

As the fire died down, they huddled together and watched the clouds above clear away, revealing the stars.

"Can a vedmak do anything?" Jovan asked.

Leaf was already snoring against him.

"Can you smith a sword?" Slant asked.

"I might be able to. But it's not my specialty."

"There you go. You can embroider, being the needle-maker that you are?"

"I have, but I've never been as good as others. I more understand the how of doing it well than anything else."

"Vedmaks can develop a specialty. Most don't, because they generalize too much."

"What do you feel Leaf will do with his talent?"

"That is for him to decide. What will you do with your seeing eye?"

"My eye?"

"Your eye for magic. Not many can feel and understand what happens around them the way you felt my twisting of luck."

"I don't know what you mean."

"You are gifted yourself. Or else you would not have understood what I had done as I tripped over that log."

"I am a needle-maker. I'm no vedmak."

"Suit yourself," Slant said.

No more words were spoken.

As the sun rose, it revealed the road they had camped next to.

"Another fifty yards and we would have seen this," Slant said, laughing.

"It is the road we must follow," Zvediz said. "This will take us to the pass."

The road cut back and forth as it paralleled the natural slope of the mountains. A few times they had to find ways over washouts running with sluggishly cold water. At the end of the first day, they came to what Zvediz described as the first pasture. Snow covered the large space to the north. There were snow-covered divots in the earth that marked long-abandoned fire circles. They stayed near the edge by the trees, and built up a shelter in a cutout that once may have held the walls of a cabin, now long since used for kindling by travelers.

Jovan was up before the others, Slant having stayed up late teaching Leaf how to melt the snow with their magic.

With an axe, he began chopping at a fallen tree.

He chopped in a rhythm of three swings, followed by a pause of the same length. After making it through the log once, he heard something in the woods that repeated the rhythm with thumps on a tree.

He paused and listened. He didn't hear nor see anything.

He swung at the log again, and again the woods replied with an echoing three thumps.

He repeated the action, and in the middle of his pause, he swung a fourth time as the replying thumps began, and then faltered at his breaking of the rhythm.

He looked back toward where the others slept under a shelter of canvas, and saw three figures coming out of the woods nearby. A male stone elk led the way tentatively out into the pasture. Not far behind, a female and her full-grown calf joined. While the cow and calf were unadorned, the magnificent bull was a sight Jovan could never forget.

He was muscled like a southern studding bull, but his neck rose a full two feet above his shoulders. Along the spine of his neck, horny growths began and then grew in size until they came to the two large, spiraled horns that rose far above the top of his skull. Reversed thorns jutted backward down the horns.

The animal froze in mid-step and quickly turned to gaze at the man. The great beast twitched its ear. His snorts formed clouds of steam that were thick and refused to dissipate. He bellowed out a call that reverberated through the quivering bone plates of his neck and horns.

The other two stone elks took off bounding toward the wood edge and disappeared into the trees. The elk began to paw at the ground as if working itself up into a frenzy.

Jovan did not move, though his grip tightened on his axe.

"Calm down, boy," Jovan muttered to himself. He glanced to the left. A tree stood not far away. He could get behind it and at least keep it between them.

He darted toward it as the bull began to barrel forward. He reached the tree and caught it with his arm to avoid hurtling past. He caught a glimpse of the bull, who had changed directions to come straight at his cover. Jovan pushed on it to check that it was firm. The impact was jarring. Jovan pushed away as the bull swung its head around and tried to hook his antlers past the wood and over Jovan's head. The horns caught just enough, and the bull had to adjust himself free. Jovan ran toward the next closest trunk, though it was a dried out, standing-dead tree.

The bull charged again, with horns low, and thrust them up as they came to meet the wood. The rotten trunk exploded, and Jovan launched himself over a small berm and down into the sandy dirt below. The bull turned, now enraged, and leapt over Jovan and into the field. It threw itself upward and came down, rushing toward Jovan, thrusting once more. Just then, the horns lodged in the exposed roots that grew out of the sandy embankment. The bull began to flail and foam at the mouth. It would break free sooner or later.

"I'm sorry to destroy such a magnificent animal," Jovan said in a low voice. The beast huffed and stopped struggling for an instant. "But I cannot have you charging us down while we pack up and leave your field. I can't trust you."

Zvediz stood twenty feet away with a spool of rope in his arms, still yawning and wiping his eyes free of sleep. Jovan sighed in relief.

Together, they further entangled the animal.

"I hate for you to lose your rope," Jovan said.

"It has gone to save a magnificent beast," Zvediz said. "As we cannot use the whole animal, we will not allow it to go to waste."

"How long do you think it will hold?"

"An hour or two," Zvediz said.

"Then let's get moving. Remind me to buy you a new rope later."

Zvediz nodded.

Within a short time, they had packed up their things and moved down the road. It took until midday to reach the high road that looked back down over the meadow. Jovan looked to where the stone elk had been tied. But instead of an elk, the sight, though far off, was horrific. A stain of blood covered the area, and the elk was nowhere to be seen.

He looked over at Zvediz, who nodded ominously.

"It's gone," Jovan said.

"Yes. And I heard the telltale knocking this morning," Zvediz replied.

"Then we're hunted."

Zvediz nodded again, and began walking away.

"Shall we keep an eye behind us?" Jovan asked, running up to walk alongside him.

"No. Nothing will happen until night. So long as we keep moving."

CHAPTER 14 — VODYANOV

Jovan woke to a rough hand on his shoulder. He reached for the axe next to him, but it was missing.

He began to panic as the low voice whispered, "Jovan, it's Zvediz."

Jovan sighed and nodded. Five days they had been climbing the pass. The days were warm, but the nights were cold. The men had taken turns keeping watch behind them. The signs of their being followed by something never ceased. The mornings were filled with the less distant sounds of knocking on wood, while their evenings remained eerily devoid of the calls of birds.

"It will be morning soon. I must sleep," Zvediz said, handing him his axe.

Jovan rose and worked himself awake.

"Shall I start a fire?" Jovan asked.

Zvediz shook his head. "Wait until the eastern sky brightens. I fear you would draw a night attack."

"Did you see what it was this time?" Jovan asked.

"No. But I smelled it."

"What do you think it is?"

"Have you ever been to the town of Kelnoz?"

Jovan had not.

"They make beer for the surrounding area. Their runoff from the brewery and town waste dumps in a marsh ten miles away. When the wind shifts, it can carry the fetid smell of that swamp. That is what I smelled."

"Vodyanov," Jovan muttered.

Zvediz only nodded and rolled over to catch the last hours of sleep.

Jovan took a seat on a stone and sat looking back down the path. The wind was still, but the faintest whiff of the vodyanov wafted up the hill. He fought down the urge to gag.

After an hour, the sun began to color the horizon. Jovan had already gathered up enough wood to make a fire. He built it up against a stone to block some of its light downhill. He pulled out his flint and steel and began to cast sparks into the kindling. Soon the blaze grew, consuming the firewood. The air seemed to clear with the burning heat.

The knocking began. It came from directly over the meadow they had crossed to make camp.

Suddenly, Slant crouched next to him.

"It's hard to sleep with that rancid smell, isn't it?" he said.

"Yes. We cannot continue with a vodyanov pursuing us."

"You think it's a vody then?" Slant asked.

"I want you and Leaf to go ahead."

"You think you and Zved can take care of this yourself?"

"Are you volunteering to help?"

"Good point. No."

"Do you know anything about them?"

"They don't like fire—I think it's the heat or some-thing—but that doesn't stop them. I remember a story about a Medved, a bear-man, making a trade with one. He promised the vody a pot of honey. Inside the pot was burning embers. The vodyanov picked up the pot and it burned him. He spilled it out on himself and the sparks flew into the sky and became stars. Something like that."

"We don't have a pot. So I don't think we'll be making any trades today," Jovan said.

"I'll get some food made and we can go. Maybe leave some out to stall it."

They dropped travelers biscuit and dried meat into a pan of boiling water, and ate. Leaf was quick to finish and pack up his bag.

"Go with Slant," Jovan told him. "Zvediz and I are going to stay behind and cover the fire."

"Very well, Papa Jov."

Within a short time, Leaf and Slant were out of view.

"Thank you for staying here," Jovan said to Zvediz.

Zvediz only nodded.

Jovan turned out the rest of the pot onto the glowing em-bers. Soon a smoke of burnt food rose into the air.

"We should go to the edge of the woods," Jovan said. "See if that doesn't draw it out."

Zvediz pulled out a fireplace poker, one he had taken from the cabin, and laid it half into the fire.

"What is this?" Jovan asked.

"A surprise for our friend."

They walked alongside one another, moving up into the short, sparse trees, and waited. Jovan tugged at his ear and fought the urge to clear his throat as the anticipation settled onto his shoulders oppressively.

It wasn't long before the creature came lumbering out of the woods to examine the field.

It stood no taller than Jovan, but its huge toad-like head did not rise above its shoulders. It easily outweighed both of the men combined and almost walked on all fours. Its arms, bigger round than Slant's torso, were as long as its body, and felt along the ground as the two short legs waddled behind it. It held a rock in one hand and lifted it and struck a tree next to it three times and then stopped to listen for a responding knock. Nothing came.

"Well, at least that confirms who was knocking," Jovan muttered under his breath.

"And what killed the stone elk," Zvediz responded.

Tendrils fell from its massive chin, sweeping the ground, seemingly by intention. It stopped and bloated up its cheeks, then let the air out with a silent puff. The smell from its breath fell over Jovan and Zvediz, who blanched and took a step back, almost fainting in the awful stench. The vodyanov's eyes were glazed over with cataracts. It approached the stone that harbored the dying fire. It placed a hand covered in stony scales on the warm surface, and recoiled from the heat. Then it hung its face over the fire and opened its mouth to breathe. The tendrils that hung from its face recoiled and quivered.

Then, it reached down and took hold of the poker and lifted it up to regard it, but suddenly tried to drop it. The flesh on its hand clung in melted strings to the hot poker. The creature began to shudder and quiver. Jovan saw Zvediz put both of his hands over his ears. Jovan quickly followed suit, almost too late.

The vodyanov's bulging throat belched out a sound like a sealed barrel popping, followed by a screech that reminded Jovan of a copper parlor kettle steaming. The thought did not do justice to the shrill roar of pain and anger.

The vodyanov turned frantically this way and that, perhaps looking for something to put its hand into, such as a pot of water. The cataracts, a second eyelid, folded back from its eyes. The large black wells of its pupils closed slowly, as it turned to look at the trees Jovan and Zvediz hid behind. It forgot the pain on its hand and huffed, filling its throat sack again, and then bellowed as it loped awkwardly toward them on all fours.

Jovan tightened his grip on his axe and then stepped out from behind the tree. But Zvediz was faster. The big man had nothing in his hands, save his fists. As the monster ran up at him, Zvediz moved faster than Jovan could follow, meeting the creature with equal force from the opposite direction. His fist came down on the side of its face.

The vodyanov's head moved in one direction, but both arms moved up to grab at the big man. The arm closer to Zvediz swung wildly, but the second took hold of Zvediz's leg and pulled.

Zvediz lurched to one knee and thrashed out with the other leg and hit the creature's. It bellowed in anger and dropped down onto the man, threatening to crush him. Jovan stepped forward with the axe and brought it down on its back, only to slide off. A layer of thick mucous-like slime now covered the creature, secreted from its flesh. A rank odor burned Jovan's nostrils. The thing continued to press down on Zvediz, who roared with the pain of eight hundred pounds upon him. The vodyanov looked up at Jovan, who held the axe in his hands. The slime that clung to it was thick and already drying in a crust.

Jovan drew his large knife from his belt. The vodyanov swung out with a hand to keep him at bay, and then reached under itself to take hold of Zvediz. He heard a yelp of pain. The evil in the creature's eyes told Jovan it knew what pain it was causing, and willfully so.

Jovan gritted his teeth and threw himself at the creature. It reared up, letting up the now slime-encrusted Zvediz, and took Jovan in both its arms to squeeze the life out of him instead. His right hand was still free, so he brought the knife down into the creature's eye. The second lid was as tough as saddle leather. He drove the knife down a second time, and then a third. A small bead of liquid formed. The creature threw Jovan away and took hold of its eye.

Jovan gasped for breath. Out of the corner of his vision he caught sight of Zvediz rushing forward, holding Jovan's axe in his hands. He brought it down on the creature's hindquarters. It looked up with terror in its face, turned, and fled back down the mountain.

Zvediz stood a moment, and then collapsed. Jovan rushed to his side, the slime that covered his arms was drying up, and threatening to cement him in place. Zvediz's mouth and nose were caked.

Jovan took hold of the hard, crusty stuff and tried to pry it from Zvediz's face. It encrusted his own hand, making it hard for him to do anything with his fingers.

He rushed over to the sack leaning against a tree, and pulled out a flask and began to douse Zvediz's face. But nothing seemed to work to free his mouth from the hard coating.

Zvediz groped for his knife and held it out to Jovan. Jovan nodded and looked down into the man's eyes.

"I'm sorry if this hurts," he said.

Zvediz nodded.

He pressed the knife point to the crease of the man's lips, and then with a practiced hit on the butt with his palm, the knife jabbed, stopping suddenly, hitting the closed teeth behind. The big man sucked life-giving air through that tiny hole, his chest heaving to breathe. Jovan took the knife and worked his way across the lips. He only drew a little blood once, but Zvediz waved him away from fretting over his handiwork. Soon a slit across his lips had opened up enough for him to breathe, and after a time, he sat still and took easy, calm breaths.

Jovan had a hard time moving himself, the rock-hard crust clinging to his clothing. He helped the big man to his feet, and they walked over to put their packs on. They moved slowly up the path, often taking stops for air.

As the midday sun slowed overhead, they came upon Slant and Leaf sitting next to a stream that fell down into a deep pool. Fish lay butchered on a rock and Slant's pole plied the eddies below for more.

Both men dropped their packs, and without a word walked down into the frigid pool of water. They walked until their chests were covered by the numbing liquid, and just stood there.

Zvediz put his face in the water and scrubbed and scrubbed without pause for air. Jovan soon followed suit. The hardness eventually washed away, but the stench lingered.

"What is that smell?" Slant shouted down at them.

They did not respond. They just continued to scrub. At one point, Jovan looked over to realize that Zvediz had taken off his outer shirt, and then his tunic. Within moments, he no longer wore anything as he waded toward the waterfall, where he lay his clothes out over a rock under the drop.

He stepped out of the water and began to gather wood for a fire, not worrying about the cold nor the wet. The blaze he soon had going towered, and he stood before it far too close, perhaps hoping to burn away what was left of the vodyanov stench from his body. Eventually he retrieved his clothes, and let them dry near the fire while he wore only a simple white tunic over his massive frame.

"I am sorry we did not kill it," were the first words he said. "But I also would not have cared to take a trophy with me in order to prove I had done it."

"What was it like?" Leaf asked.

"They say the vodyanov was once a woman," Slant said. "A baker by trade. She was strong of arm and well-built. But she was not attractive. That is why all bakers ply their wares at night, you know." Slant winked.

Jovan recalled the baker woman of Geruz. She might have baked all night, but she was most certainly someone to look at when she made her way to the tavern.

"Vodyanov sought to make bread fit for Vun, the squirrel god who climbs the tree of the spirit, who is the oak, from whence the breath of spirit comes. And so she set off. She met on her road a bear who told her that only one thing could satisfy Vun: bread made from the honey of Pchal, his sister. And so Vodyanov sought out the Queen of Bees, the goddess of the mind. And in the buzzing throne room, the baker stood before the queen, who saw her for what she was: a baker who sought to rise above her station. Pchal denied her the honey, and told her she must leave the next day. Vodyanov went to her room, and in great anger struck the wall, only to find within a flow of the golden fluid. And she devised a plan. She took all her clothes and her pack, and covered them in the golden liquid until she shone. She put layer upon layer on herself, and slowly walked out of the queen's kingdom to travel home to make the bread she so desired. But the honey was sticky and heavy, and she walked slowly home. It took years and lifetimes for her to reach the place of her birth, now built over by a town. She was forgotten and cast out, covered now in the sticky substance that only immortals can stomach, her face wasted away by years and trials."

Slant finished his story and sat in the firelight in silence for a time.

"But what did the vodyanov look like?" Leaf pleaded, heedless of the story Slant told.

The men laughed at him and told him what he wanted to know.

"You don't think it will come again?"

"Evil creature as it was," Jovan said, "it learned fear today. It will think twice before coming for us."

CHAPTER 15 — THE BLUE TOWER

Theirs was a mile-long approach to the base of the tower. It rose far above atop a mountain of yellow stone, getting its name from the single run of blue stones that was visible across the circumference under the highest set of windows. They approached the door set in the rocks, but Zvediz turned to the left and continued on. Jovan came closer to the door to see it was merely a carving in the face—a false door meant to bring hope where there was none. Zvediz proceeded toward a switchback that would take them a mile away, and then back again.

"That's nothing but irritating," Slant said.

Once they had completed the second switchback and turned toward the tower, Jovan saw that they had only had a view of its highest parapet. The short, squat citadel seemed built to support the singular tower. The crenelations were variegated with yellow stone, cut from the surrounding mountains and the azure blue of lapis lazuli.

"How many men are stationed here?" Jovan asked.

"Not as many as in the past," Slant said. "Mind you, I've never been here. But I've heard men call it 'the station at the end of the world.'"

"Why?"

"Because if you're stationed here, you won't be leaving unless the end of the world has come."

"Criminals then."

"No," Slant said. "Thieves, drunks, liars."

"Criminals," Jovan repeated.

"You ever met a soldier that wasn't one of those?"

Jovan chuckled.

"The criminals are kept in the king's prison. These are the soldiers that still have enough worth to keep an eye on the east, but not enough sense to remain uncaught in their little habits."

The road became level and wide enough for two carts, but fell steeply on both sides. To their right, it fell off down the switchbacks. To the left, a boulder field without a trace of life went out to meet the Belkhali lands below. Jovan looked out over the land covered in small rivers running through a carpet of farms, and could only just make out the blue stain of the sea on the western horizon.

A single figure stood atop the gatehouse to the Blue Tower. It was five times larger than the bailey in Geruz, and that great room and barracks housed fifty men at times. Jovan wondered how many more could be stationed here in a time of war.

"Business?" the figure called.

Jovan could see the figure had a bow leaning against the wall and held a half-eaten loaf of bread in his hand.

"We're seeking shelter before continuing down into Belkhal," Jovan shouted.

The man nodded and disappeared without further question.

The guard unbarred the door and pulled it open for them, and then pulled the loaf out of his mouth to speak.

"You can go into the guesthouse over there and wash up. We're having dinner soon. I wouldn't be late. The boys tend to strip the platters clean right away."

He was a young soldier, who didn't seem old enough to have seen more than the first month of soldiering.

Jovan nodded and followed his directions. The guesthouse was a ramshackle stable with old mattresses laid down in the animal stalls and doors to close them off from one another. He turned his nose up.

"A free bed is a free bed," Slant said.

Jovan nodded grudgingly.

The pump soon had water pulled up from some ancient and musty spring. They left their things, though Jovan watched Slant pull out and hide some of the more expensive belongings in a crook in the rafter. Jovan followed suit and kept some of his tools on him. Leaf had to be coaxed down from the loft he had climbed into to explore before they walked across the narrow courtyard to the main building.

The fireplace roared and laughter filled the main room. Jovan came around the corner to see a single table with ten men around it. They each had tankards of ale in their hands and jested with one another. They wore yellow and blue coats that were wind-faded, but not filthy. One of them looked up and nudged the young solider at the gate.

He stood and approached.

"Come on over," he said. "Find yourself a seat and we'll get each of you a tankard."

Jovan followed the lad and took a seat, with Leaf between him and Zvediz, while Slant sat across from them next to a soldier who nervously rattled two dice in his hands.

"You come from the Kharavadziy Plains?" one of them asked.

Slant nodded. "Though not so much the plains as the edges. We just came from Stoneweks."

"Quarry workers then?" another asked.

"Smith," Jovan said.

"And what've those old caravaners been doing?" another said.

Jovan was about to correct him, that they had not been on the plain, when he saw the grizzled voice came from a very old man.

"The same as usual," Jovan said three times before the man finally understood him.

"You were quick to let us in," Slant said. "You didn't think we might be robbers come to hide in the pleasant lands of Belkhal?"

"Ha!" one said. "A pleasant land. You know what Belkhal is? Just another place for boyars to tax and pillage and then put the blame on us who do the soldiering."

"I told them to let you in," a voice said over Jovan's shoulder. A man wearing the markings of captain held a serving tray of food. He reached over Jovan and placed it down in front of the four of them. Then he proceeded to bring trays out of the kitchen and serve them to his men.

"I let you in because you're the first to come up the pass from Kharavadziy. Now we can hear tell of how the pass is, and if we need to watch for anything."

"Whom am I addressing?" Jovan asked.

"Captain Samov Zin," he said as he took the seat across from him. He had a narrow face and a thin, dark mustache that stood out in contrast to his well-kept blonde hair. "I should ask the same of you."

"Jovan Nedeller," he replied. None of the guards seemed to recognize the name. Jovan nodded to himself and relaxed visibly. "This is Slavint Yunev and his friend Zvediz. The boy is mine: Leaf."

"You're the Boyer of the Ring!" one soldier exclaimed as he pointed at Zvediz.

Zvediz nodded.

"Very well," Zin said, ignoring the interruption. "And to where do you travel now?"

"I'll be setting up a shop where I find the need."

"The need for needles," Captain Zin said, laughing.

Jovan forced a smile. It wasn't the first time he had heard it. Leaf, however, laughed to hear his own joke said by someone else.

"The pass down into the Belkhal foothills is still icy," Captain Zin said. "It took our last wagon of supplies an extra five days to reach here. At least it was in time to share a feast with you as guests."

"I'd warn those heading down into Kharavadziy to be cautious," Jovan replied.

"Oh?"

"We encountered a rather mean-spirited vodyanov just yesterday."

"And survived?"

"We may have blinded one eye and maimed a hind leg."

One of the soldiers banged his tankard on the table. "Tell us more!" he shouted.

Jovan then described, with no elaboration, what had happened.

The room was silent as they listened. They could tell from the way he spoke that his words were truth. As he finished, someone leapt up to feed the fire, and quickly refilled their tankards.

"Tell them how you ended up here," one of them said to the young soldier that had admitted them to the tower. The boy blushed.

"Keep the stories coming," Captain Zin said. "More stories, more feasting."

The boy proceeded to work out a story of a cobbler and a cow, involving some ill-aged radishes and a lordling to the south. The story was forced and it reeked of falsehoods.

After another three soldiers told their stories, it was obvious they were elaborating their own tales, if not making up new ones entirely. They were all borderline ribald, and Jovan was glad to see much of it went over Leaf's head.

An old guard finished his story and turned to the captain. "I think it's your turn, sir."

The captain nodded. He waved the old soldier to fill tankards once more, and then took his back, brimming with a foamy head.

"You know," he said, "there is plenty I did before I was sent here. But the best stories come from my being boon companion to Prince Zelmir Valle."

Jovan blanched at hearing this and lifted his tankard, drinking deeply to cover his look of astonishment.

"There are things you do in your youth that you regret. I regret nothing. Except having introduced my secret love to him, or perhaps he would not have taken her from me."

"We all know that," a soldier said. "Tell us more about what you did after that."

"I'll only tell you what they don't know I did. What I got away with," he said.

The assembly began to bang their tankards on the table to urge him on.

"The prince, to this day, does not know what I did to his favorite golden arm band. But he complained of the stench that seemed to hang around him for two weeks."

Everyone laughed.

"The prince never suspected it was I who moved his favorite book to the highest corner of his library. I doubt he's found it yet."

The laugh was less substantial. But there, nonetheless.

"But let me tell you about when I replaced the prince's ointment with a substance that set his rear to burning."

Everyone roared their desire to hear it, and he began a long and almost unbelievably elaborate tale. As he fell silent, Jovan spoke up.

"And these tales, that is what brought you all to be stationed here?"

"For some," Captain Zin said. "For others," and he touched his chest with an air of sophistication, "I only reveal that which has not yet been discovered."

The men beamed at their captain.

"Tell us your story, Slant," Captain Zin said.

Slant cocked an eyebrow. "What kind of story would you have me tell?"

"Enough truth to make it real, and enough falsehood to make it good."

Slant nodded and rose slowly. "Belkhal was once covered in forest. The Medved, the bear-people, lived amongst the men." Slant walked over to the fire.

"The Medved worshipped Medi as their father and Pchal as their mother, while men were pulled to and fro by Vun and Rovol. The squirrel, Vun, gave his secret wisdom to those who sought him out. But Rovol, the wolf, who lived then upon the mountains, scorched the souls of those who sought him, and these were the first vedmak.

"One of the vedmak, a man named Tiho, had the fleetness of Vun, and moved this way and that, his soul parched by Rovol. With his swiftness he sought out Medi, who held court amongst his people. And it was as they feasted that Pchal arrived with her own hive court. It is said that Tiho was the first to witness a meeting between the two.

"The queen shared her mead with her husband and with the gathered. Tiho took a sip and saw the marriage of body and mind. And thus he felt he knew what he must do. As Tiho rose to leave, Medi graced him with a gift of his choosing.

"He was offered an arm band that would make him stronger than any man.

"He was offered a pelt of fur that could not be pierced.

"But Tiho pointed to a basin of half-drunk mead that sat before the bear-god.

"'If you would allow me, I would take that basin. For I would use it to quench the burns upon my soul, and to understand the limit of the gift with which I am already burdened.'

"The queen of mead took up the basin, and in her hands she formed it into a gourd. From an attendant, she took a wax stopper and plugged it. She gave it to him, and he took it in his hand and left.

"Forth he strode, and he sought out Vun. The spirit squirrel listened as Tiho promised him a taste of his sister's mead. For it was what Vun relished most. But Tiho made him promise to arrive at the sacred circle found within the forest. And the god agreed.

"Then he sought out Rovol, the slavering wolf. And by the howls and grinding of the earth, he was not difficult to find, for the burns on Tiho's soul grew hotter as he came to him. And so he found and ran alongside the god that had once marked him with fire.

"'What? Do you seek another burn upon you? Shall I devour another portion of your soul?' Rovol asked.

"'No. I plead you to share a gift I have received from your sister and brother. For within this gourd sits her mead.'

"And Rovol ceased his running.

"'This is a gift you would freely give?'

"'If only you would receive it at the sacred circle.'

"Then Rovol agreed, walking alongside Tiho to the circle.

"They both entered that circumference of stones. Vun came and stood alongside them at the table from which man's first meal was taken.

"'It seems odd to sup here as we once did all those years ago, with man and beast, and not have our brother and sister here, as well,' Vun said.

"'They have sent their blessing,' Tiho lied. He held up the gourd. 'Together, let us drink.'

"'You must first provide your stipulation,' the wolf said.

"'What is this?' Tiho asked, feigning astonishment.

"'We promised to those we supped with in this circle that we would provide a boon.'

"Tiho knew this. But none had ever come this far. And so he spoke. 'I would receive a length of spiderweb from Vun's oak.'

"Vun produced the thread and Tiho took one end.

"'I would ask that you take hold of this thread, by which we shall swear an oath,' Tiho said to Rovol.

"'I have no hands with which to do this,' Rovol said. 'Place it over my neck.'

"And so Tiho did. Then Tiho took out the stopper and drank deeply from the gourd. But he did not tell the gods before him that he had bit his own tongue, and blood from his mouth seeped into the gourd. And thus he offered it to the two. Rovol drank deeply, and then all that remained was given to the greedy Vun. The silvery cord that ran from Squirrel to Wolf began to turn color to that of blood. They did not notice as they savored that which sat in their mouths. But Tiho knew. And the burn upon his soul diminished. He took hold of the thread and used Spirit and Soul to bind himself to the thread.

"'What is this?' Rovol said, pulling back. But the thread tightened, for Tiho had tied it tightly around his throat.

"Vun took his own steps back, but the thread was his own, and he could not let it go. 'What have you done?'

"'I have bound you both together and to me, that no man may be burned again. That the vedmak know the allotment of magic that they have.'

"'I have done nothing,' Vun said. 'And yet you bind me.'

"'I have given you a gift,' Tiho said. 'You now hold the noose that harnesses the soul. The wolf that scorches shall no longer do so but by your will.'

"'You assume I wish to rule anyone, that I wish to master others. Leave that to Pchal and Medi. I will not take this gift.'

"'You have already offered me a gift and I have taken it. So you are bound.'

"'A quarter you have drunk,' Rovol stated. 'And so I curse you with only a quarter portion of the magic you once held so dear. Yet I submit to this leash you have put upon me. It shall forever bind me to the administrations of Vun.'

"Tiho stood alone in the circle. The burn on his soul was gone. Yet he feared for the rest of his life to cast even the smallest of spells, lest he expend the pool of magic that he had within his soul. Many students he taught. And all knew they now risked much where once they had no fear."

"Quite the story. But what of it was true?" the captain asked.

Slant shrugged. "Who can know? It could all be true. It could all be false. Still, you wanted a story. Seemed like a good one to tell as we bid you all good night."

Slant moved calmly to leave and Jovan followed with Leaf and Zvediz.

One of the guards walked them to the guesthouse. The door closed and Slant stood beside it to listen. Once the guard had gone, he turned back.

"We have to find a way to leave before the night is over," he said sternly. "I never told them my name was Slant."

CHAPTER 16 — MESSENGERS

"How is it they know you?" Jovan asked.

"I'm not sure," Slant said. "Could be an old crime catching up to me. Could be they recognized me from boyhood."

"By association, they'll suspect us, as well."

Jovan walked to the door to peek out. Captain Zin was marching through the stables with four guards behind him.

Jovan swore.

"What?" Slant asked.

Jovan explained. Slant sat down on the bed.

"Let's hear him out," Jovan said. "We won't go down without a fight, regardless."

Immediately, a rap came to the door. Jovan reached out, taking a deep breath, and opened it.

Captain Zin stood there, the four guards across the stable at attention with spears in their hands.

"May I come in?" he asked.

Jovan nodded.

Captain Zin stepped into the stall and closed the door behind him.

"I see you haven't unpacked yet," he observed.

No one said anything.

"I suppose I can't blame you for wishing to leave so soon. I ought not to have revealed that I knew who you were. It was a slip of the tongue and a mistake."

"Is there going to be trouble?" Jovan asked.

"You tell me," the captain said. He took a seat on a chair and leaned back with his hands behind his head. "I'm just the messenger."

"Messenger?" Jovan asked.

"From Kallidova. She sent word to me to keep an eye out for you."

Slant visibly relaxed. Jovan did not.

"You know too much of us," Jovan said. "I think you owe us an explanation."

Zin held up a finger. "I owe you nothing. Remember that. I received word from this woman, Kallidova, over a month ago. She gave me a description of you and paid her reward upfront. This was a much better offer than the bounty I've seen out for you."

Jovan clenched his fists.

"No need to get yourself in a twist. I'm not going to turn you in. I don't feel like going to the capital for a reward. I think the prince might kill me if he saw my face anyway. In fact, now that I've seen your boy here, I think he might kill me regardless."

Jovan glanced over at Leaf, who had fallen asleep. "What is that supposed to mean?"

"I knew the child's mother. And I suspect that knowledge might be more dangerous than the sin I committed against the prince when we last saw each other."

"You knew his mother?" Jovan asked.

"Knew. Yes."

"I think you and I have a conversation due, then."

"I'm afraid that's all I can say. Mamm Kallidova asked that if I saw you I convey a message to you. I was going to wait until tomorrow, but one of my guards has disappeared since dinner. So I suspect that he was keeping an eye out for you, too. You'll need to leave as soon as you can."

"What was the message?" Slant asked.

"Her warehouse was burned down not long after you met. She wants you to look for her in the place she first met Slant."

Jovan tightened his arms across his chest. "She won't be happy, if the warehouse was burned on our account."

"What do you think, Zved?" Slant turned to his friend.

"Perhaps we'll catch up with the guard."

"Give him my regards," the captain said.

"Which guard was it?" Jovan asked.

"The young one, Athasin, who let you in the gate."

"He's newly stationed here?"

"Yes. It seemed odd to get one so young. They usually try to beat out the problems when they first join up. Most here are serial offenders."

"We'll see what we can do to catch him," Jovan said.

"It looks like we won't see much sleep then," Slant said.

"No," Zin said. "But we can make it easier for you to travel if you'd like. Can you drive a cart? Ours is due back down the mountains."

"We'd be obliged if we could take that," Jovan said. "It'll mean less questions from those on the road."

"I'll give you the paperwork and you can turn the wagon in at any barracks you like."

"I'd like to get a look at the maps down the pass," Jovan said.

Zin left with Jovan in tow, while Slant and Zvediz carried the sleeping Leaf to the cart and moved their belongings into its bed.

Jovan followed after the captain to his study and closed the door behind him. Zin turned and looked at him with widening eyes as he quietly lowered the bar in place. Jovan held a finger to his lips.

"Do you recognize me as well?" Jovan asked. "Nod if you do. But do not say a word."

Zin nodded slowly.

"Then I think we have an understanding. If I find out you've said anything about our being here, then I'll share your secret. I doubt you'd like the prince to know the truth."

Zin continued to nod. Jovan let out a long breath and walked over to the table to look at the maps.

"Now. Tell me about the roads from here to the coast."

Zin kept himself at arm's length from Jovan, and proceeded to tell him what to expect.

"I owe you my life for what you did that day. I heard rumors that you had been executed for what happened."

"I'm alive, but it took more lies to make that happen. Or more so, I should say, my not ever denying or acknowledging what really happened. The rumors themselves became the truth."

"Then we have an agreement. I'll keep the men from speaking of you, and you won't tell anyone what you saw that day."

"Correct."

They shook hands. Jovan turned and unbarred the door and left.

The two dray horses that pulled the cart were not happy about being forced out into the cold, dead of night. They moved laboriously, and the empty barrels and crates packed in the back rattled constantly.

"At least we're not going down the east side of the pass," Slant said. "The vodyanov would have little trouble finding us."

"Yes," Jovan replied. "But if the soldier we're pursuing has found a hole to hide in for the night, he'll hear us coming and either stay where he is and pick a new course, or pick up speed and we'll never catch him."

"I think word of us is going to end up going ahead of us regardless. Since it seems everyone is looking for us."

"Did you catch the boy's name?"

"Athasin," Slant said.

"And where is it we're to find Mamm Kallidova? Where did you first meet her?"

"Where we were going anyway. The capital, Khorapesh."

"How far to the capital?"

"At the rate this wagon is likely to travel, I'd put us at five days," Slant said.

"Eight," Zvediz said. He sat in the back, with his cloak pulled tight around him.

"You think I'm that far off?"

"Eight."

Slant looked at Jovan and pursed his lips. "If Zvediz says eight, it'll be eight."

"We should ditch the wagon at the first barracks we find or this will be slow going."

"I was taking that into account, actually."

"Why is it she used that as her code? Saying we'd find her where you first met? How did you meet her?"

"I met her at a sept meeting. We're not kin, but she is Havat. She sought refuge for a time, after she had a falling out with her lover and Verth wouldn't take her back."

"Verth?" Jovan asked. "Verth Valle-Brons?"

"Aren't you from Geruz? You're old enough to know that she was once the lady of your town."

"I did not know. I returned there after my apprenticeship elsewhere. Then, Sephaly?"

"Verth and Kallidova never had children, as I understand it. Sephaly came into Verth Valle-Brons's care long after he left his wife and returned to his town to rule by himself."

As the sun rose behind them, they came in view of the town of Rivall, built in a western facing crescent around the lake that formed below the Boryuv River's only waterfall. The blue roofs of the town glinted with frost from the spray that fell over the place. A few people walked cautiously along the streets, trying not to slip while they attended to their morning errands.

The road turned to cobbles several hundred yards outside of town.

Jovan let the animals move at their own pace. They pulled toward a trough outside the local barracks, knowing the streets well. Slant broke the layer of ice on top so the horses could drink, as Jovan walked up to the door and knocked.

After a time, the bar lifted, the door opened on smooth hinges, and a burly man looked at Jovan, sizing him up.

"You bring the cart from the Blue Tower?"

Jovan nodded.

"Have the paperwork?"

Jovan nodded again.

"We don't usually take it from here. Can't spare a man to take it downriver."

"Meaning?" Jovan replied.

"I don't want to pay you for it."

As Zin had explained it, whoever took it into the capital would get the biggest pay. But barracks were required to pay a small fee if it was brought in farther from the capital.

"You are required to, though, are you not?"

"I'd offer you two silver."

"That's half the price we were told we'd get by Captain Zin."

"Zin's a fool. There is paperwork we'll have to fill out, including the name of you and your companions."

Jovan kept his gaze steady.

"If you simply relinquish the cart and walk away, I won't require you to fill out any paperwork."

Jovan nodded. "I will leave the drays there at the trough."

The man nodded and closed the door. The bar did not drop back into place.

Jovan stepped away and sighed.

"Let's get moving," he said quietly to the men, picking up the still sleeping Leaf.

"What's the trouble?" Slant said.

"I gave the cart over too easily, to avoid paperwork. It might give them the excuse they need to come after us. I'd guess that Athasin told them about us."

Zvediz nodded and picked up his pack and Jovan's. They quickly moved toward the edge of town, though the slick cobbles made it difficult.

As they rounded a corner, they heard a door slam far behind them. Jovan looked over his shoulder to see twenty guards marching down the street. Jovan turned back and began to walk faster.

"I don't like this," Slant said.

"Nor do I. Twenty soldiers is a bit much for us to handle."

Leaf roused in Jovan's arms.

"Papa Jov? What's the matter? Where's the cart?"

"We have to go. Soldiers are following us."

"Why?"

"I don't know."

Leaf looked over Jovan's shoulder at the soldiers. Jovan felt a chill run down his spine and a few seconds later heard a yelping crash as soldiers slipped on ice. They couldn't seem to stand up where they fell.

"Nice work, boy," Slant said. "That will only hold them for so long, though. If they bring out horses, we'll never get away."

"Then I suspect we'll never be free of them," Jovan said.

"Unless we split up," Slant said.

"I'd rather not," Jovan said.

"We must split up," Zvediz said with finality.

The big man stopped at the entry to the city. He put down his pack and pulled out another cloak. This one had bits of green tassels hanging from it. He handed it to Jovan.

"Wear this and find somewhere to hide. Wait until mid-day, then continue down the road. Ask for an Umernnost named Jeg in the next town. They will see you to the capital safely."

Jovan took the cloak and Zvediz's arm in his. "Thank you."

Slant didn't say anything but gave a wink to Jovan. Then he turned and crouched next to Leaf. "Be wise," he said. "Mark how much you feel leaves you when you do things. Got that?"

The boy nodded.

Jovan picked him up and walked into the underbrush. They moved off the road until they could only just make out the gate. Then he pulled the large cloak over the two of them and they watched. Six riders soon came rushing out of the small town and thundered down the road.

The sun rose high, warming the bushes around them. At one point, a rider came back into town at a canter. Not long after that, ten more men left the town on foot, though they did not look keen to leave the comfort of their barracks. They chatted as they marched and soon their talking faded into silence.

"Why do they look for us?" Leaf asked.

"I don't know, boy," Jovan said. "But I mean to find out once we're in Khorapesh."

"What's there?"

"Those that are looking for us."

CHAPTER 17 — KHORAPESH

The city of Khorapesh spread out before Jovan and Leaf, who sat upon his shoulders, down the amphitheater-shaped bowl to the sea. Jeg had been more than helpful in getting them to this point. Now they waited with all the others seeking access to the city, the gatekeepers taking their time working through the line. Since the eastern gate entered into the richest estates, the guards were not going to let vagabonds and workers enter from that side. It took some explaining for Jovan to convince the guards that he was a maker of needles, not trouble.

From the top of the street they looked down over the walls of the houses of rich merchants that lined the lane. Finely kept shops opened to travelers and merchants silently smiled, not boisterously hawking their wares as they might closer to the pier.

The gold and green of the city decorated every corner. People did not bustle, but moved with self-importance. The tops of houses were steeply peaked, with carved curves at the bottom, for casting away rain or snow. Each household they passed sat a tier lower than the one above. The sound of trickling brooks told Jovan that water flowed from house to house, and with it, he had no doubt, the constant bickering of ensuring the higher, richer neighbor above did not put things in the water that would run downstream.

Leaf wordlessly exclaimed at the sights. They came to the bottom of the steep street to the first square. It was not wide, but the inns and the shops that rose four stories around it had people shouting platitudes to one another. An innkeeper of a small establishment sat on a stool, watching passersby.

"You look road-weary," he said, as Jovan walked by.

Jovan nodded.

"What trade are you in, good man?"

"My Papa Jov is a needle-maker," Leaf said proudly.

"A respectable trade," the man said, smiling to himself. "If you look for a clean establishment to eat, wash, and bed in, I'd be obliged to have you. I have one room left available, and I pride myself in honest, valuable service."

"Convince me I should spend my silver with you and not elsewhere."

The man pursed his lips. "Perhaps I won't be able to keep you more than a single night," he admitted. "I would ask four silvers for an evening and all that entails."

Jovan scoffed. "I would not pay one silver on any place, no matter now nice the meal, bed, and company."

Jovan turned to leave.

"My family makes a fine meal. I've an aged wine that is older than you, the bed is down, and the bath and razor are hot and sharp."

Jovan paused but did not turn around.

"I also know this city better than most. I can find who or what you're looking for. A vacant shop that might meet your needs? A person of interest you seek to do trade with? I can find them for you."

Jovan turned back around and walked up to the man, who now beamed. "While a needle-maker, I work the finest needle points and the strongest awls. I would know what work you might need as well."

"I'm sure we can come to an arrangement."

Jovan reached into his purse and pulled out three silvers. "I can give you these for the meal, the bath, and the information you offer. I think you'll find my work I offer in trade will more than pay for the rest, if not for a second night's stay."

The man nodded. "We shall see. We shall see. Come. Let my family pour you both a hot bath while we prepare food for you. What food do you fancy?"

"Fancy?"

"Why sure as sure, my wife will make you whatever you like," the old man said. "For the price you pay, it's the least that I can do."

Jovan looked down at the boy. "Well? What do you say, boy?"

Leaf's eyes got big. "Raisin cakes?" he asked.

"The finest." The old man winked. "How about a nice bit of dried ham and cheese to start. And maybe some fine beef?"

Jovan nodded.

They entered the home, for it looked more a home than an inn.

A woman not much older than Jovan entered.

"This is my daughter, Ilge. She'll show you to your room."

She curtsied in a dress of expensive embroidered brocade of white and blue. Her mouse-brown hair framed her face. While not overly attractive, her cheeks blushed as she rose and their eyes met.

The girl turned and guided them down the hall past the wash closet.

"This is the evening wash closet. Once you leave your travel sacks and boots in the room, I'll show you the bath. We should have the hot water ready for you in no time."

They did as she said and entered the wash closet. Steam poured out of an old cistern that rose up from under the building.

"My great-grandfather built this home over an old spring," Ilge said. "An advantage that caused this part of town to spring up around us."

She led them into a tiled room obscured by steam. There was a lower bath deep enough to sit in comfortably. Nearby, two basins stood. She brought the arm of a pipe over and turned on the faucet. Then she took out jars full of herbs and salts.

"Before you go down into the water, we would ask you to bathe well in the basins. This will keep the water clean in case others arrive."

Jovan nodded. She bustled out and closed the door behind her.

Jovan tested the water. The basin was filling fast and the water was overly hot. He winced and then saw buckets of cold water resting beside. He turned off the faucet and cooled the water down until it was acceptable. The second basin was already filled with cooling water.

"Climb in, boy. Get yourself clean."

"How?" Leaf asked.

Jovan looked over. "Have I never bathed you?"

Leaf shook his head.

"I wiped you down until you were old enough to."

"But not a bath."

"Strip down and get in."

The boy nodded and was suddenly stark naked. Jovan slowly took his own clothes off, grunting at the tight muscles that longed for the hot water. Leaf squealed as he slipped in. Before Jovan took off his last garment, he approached the stand next to Leaf's basin and picked up a bar of soap.

"See this?" he said.

Leaf nodded.

"Rub this all over you. Then use the water to wash it off. Do it until there is no more dirt."

The boy took the soap and sniffed.

"It smells like a girl," he said, wrinkling his nose.

"It won't kill you."

He turned and moved to climb into his own basin. The water hurt enough. He took his own bar of soap and a brush and began to scrub everything as well as he could. He opened his eyes and saw their host bustling about. He already had Leaf's clothes in his arms. He took Jovan's and walked toward the door.

"I'll see your clothes are well cleaned. For now, please accept the robes hanging over there." He indicated the other end of the bath.

Jovan nodded and watched him leave the room before he rose and stepped out onto the tile. Naked, he walked over to the steaming pool and slipped down in the water that was even hotter than his bath. Just as he closed his eyes, Leaf leapt out into the water with a splash that drenched Jovan's head.

Jovan spluttered, and then laughed as Leaf looked up, standing chest-deep in the pool.

"It's so deep!" Leaf said.

"It is. Move your arms around if you fear slipping."

Leaf began to violently move his arms. It gave Jovan another laugh. One of the first laughs he had had since before Stoneweks.

After a few long minutes, Leaf had the hang of it and began to move incessantly about the pool.

After a long while, a little bell rang near the door.

"I think that means we are wanted at dinner," Jovan said.

Leaf waded through the water toward him.

"What am I to wear?"

"Looks like these robes are it," he said. "Hopefully the common room isn't drafty."

After pulling on his own robe, he helped cinch Leaf's loose robe meant for an older boy.

They walked through the door by the bell and down the hall. The heat grew as they approached and they came out into the fire-warmed common room. The old man stood behind the chair at the head of the table. He indicated they take a seat. Leaf climbed up into a plush chair and Jovan took the seat next to him. No sooner had he done this than a side door opened and Ilge came out with an older lady behind her. They both carried food, placing down a slab of red meat in front of them next to a wall of tubers, as well as raisin cakes stacked on a plate between Jovan and Leaf.

Leaf reached to take hold of the cakes and saw Jovan give him a glare of warning.

The two ladies soon returned with more plates and took their own seats. Another was set for someone who had not yet arrived.

"I expect," the old man said, "that our other guest will be delayed. I shall say a prayer. We try to show the respect for the gods that they deserve."

He touched his forehead and belly, then his chest and each hand. "Guidance and blessing, respect and mercy."

Jovan grunted, then nodded to Leaf, who finished reaching for the cake and stuffed it into his mouth.

"How long have you been on the road?" the old man asked.

"Too long," Jovan said. "I should like to hope we've come to the end."

"As do I," he said, winking.

"Do you know I was rather rude," Jovan said. "I never caught your name."

"Aramz," the old man said.

Jovan coughed through the cake in his mouth.

"Aramz Bather?" Jovan said.

"One and the same. You've heard of me?"

"Who hasn't? I've heard songs."

"Not many of them good, I'm sure."

"I wouldn't say that," Jovan said.

"'Miser Miser, None So Wiser' is my favorite."

Jovan smiled. He knew the song.

"Word used to be that it cost a gold to stay here," Jovan said.

"When I was younger, there were more that sought my company. I still get that pay some days. Like today."

"A gold? I paid you only a few silver."

"Ah. I haggled over the price with you out of whimsy," he said.

"What do you mean?"

"Your stay here has been paid for."

"Oh?"

The door opened and a woman entered.

"Jovan," Mamm Kallidova said as a means of greeting. Her face was framed by the white furs piled up on her shoulders and cascading down her back. Atop her head she wore a black sable headpiece that matched her own hair. Her cheeks and nose were red from the cold night fast falling outside. She turned to their host. "Aramz. I apologize. I was delayed." Then she turned to the ladies. "Good evening Mamm Vansa, Mamm Ilge."

The old lady rose two inches as a curtsy and sat back down. Kallidova opened her coat to reveal a deep purple brocade, embroidered with a lighter hue. She let the furs fall off the back of her frame and into the arms of Ilge, and then took the hat off her head to place on top of the pile. She sat across from Jovan as Ilge disappeared with the furs.

"It pays to bribe the guard," she said. "They kept you in line at the gate long enough for me to rush over here and make arrangements for your stay."

"Why are you here?"

"You knew I was going to be in town. Where are Slavint and Zvediz?"

"We had to split up once we came down from the Blue Tower." He turned and eyed the family sitting at the table with them. "Should we be discussing this in front of them?"

"So you were out on the Kharavadziy Plains? Good. I sent most of the prince's people looking for you down in Godariy. Looking for a bearded man with all the Dzeda traders there will keep them busy enough. And it is no trouble to discuss before the Bathers. My gold has bought their loyalty to me."

Aramz Bather smiled with a nod.

"Am I owed a bit of an explanation then?" Jovan asked.

"Owed? No. You said you were going into the nest of the vipers. I knew you'd be here eventually. And then when they came and destroyed my own little empire, I decided to do the same."

Jovan pursed his lips.

"Regardless, I've paid for your stay here. Perhaps you'll find somewhere else to go later, but for now I've rented out the entire inn to conduct business and begin afresh."

Jovan looked at Aramz. "I'd like my money back, if the room has been paid."

Aramz shrugged. "Seems we had a deal. If you invest a bit in your stay, you'll be more likely to respect the location."

"You are a miser," Jovan growled.

"You knew this to be true," Aramz chuckled.

Jovan muttered to himself, but calmed as Leaf put his small hand on his.

"How did you fancy your life on the road, little Leaf?" Kallidova asked.

"Well, Mamm," he said.

"So polite," she smiled. "He reminds me of my daughter at that age."

"You had a daughter?" Jovan asked.

"Yes. Have. It has been a few years since we've seen one another, though."

Everyone ate their food in silence. The hosts cleared their plates and then did not reappear.

"So, what is your plan?" Kallidova asked.

"I don't owe you an explanation, if you will not give one yourself."

She shrugged.

"I will seek out information about who it is who hunts me. And then I will ask them to stop."

Kallidova laughed. "You think the people who hunt you, if they are willing to burn my warehouse to the ground for being involved with you, will let you live?"

"That is what I will do."

"I have already made a few connections in town myself," she said. "Or perhaps I should say, I've reconnected with people I knew years ago. I'll see if they know of any good locations to set up a shop."

"You not only came looking for me here in Khorapesh, you also returned to an old life."

She took a sip of tea. "While it was many years ago, I had quite a life here. A very different life from what I lead now."

"Is that what prevented you from caring for Leaf yourself?"

"What gave you that impression?" She looked up from her tea in shock.

"You're a well-connected and wealthy woman. I am at a loss as to why you chose to place him with a laborer in a small town rather than raise him yourself."

"To be perfectly honest, you were at first chosen for your vicinity to the town of Geruz. It was important to my client that the boy be placed there, rather than in a large city."

"But in Geruz you would not have been able to conduct your own business."

"I could not stay in Geruz for personal reasons. But I've remained nearby. Rightness is not the largest of market cities. But large enough."

"And this client of yours. They are respectable?"

"They have Leaf's best interest at heart."

"You do, too," Leaf said.

"Anyone who meets you does." Kallidova smiled.

She poured another cup of tea for Jovan and herself.

"Where do you go first?"

"After the only name I have of one who seeks me: the Bear."

Kallidova spat tea across the table and coughed.

"The Bea—" She let the word fall short. "You can't be serious."

Jovan nodded. "Everyone is so afraid of him. I imagine this Bear survives by the myth of his name. I will go into his den and discover what it is he wants. If he kills me, I die. If he lets me live, then I find out who it is who really hunts me."

"You do not know?"

"Given your reaction, I can only assume you believe that it is someone else who destroyed your warehouse."

"I do not know who it was. But I know it wasn't...him. I would not be alive if it was."

They stared at each other in silence.

"Papa Jov?" Leaf said. "Who is the Bear?"

Kallidova hissed. "Stop saying his name. Ears hear. It is best to be in the practice of not saying it."

Leaf furrowed his brow.

"I do not know who this Bear is," Jovan said. Kallidova shrank back further. "But I believe he is not a good man, and I intend to speak to him about it."

"I'm regretting staying here now," Kallidova said to herself. "But I've already paid for it. And I know Aramz would never return the gold I gave him."

CHAPTER 18 — CRIME

Cold seeped into the bedroom as morning dawned. A knock came at the door and Jovan rose, groaning as he did so, to answer it. Aramz walked in with a platter of herbs and cups sitting atop a stack of their folded and dried clothes. His daughter carried a heavy water bucket.

Going to the wardrobe, Aramz pulled out a small but heavy iron cauldron and set it down in the center of the room. Ilge poured the water and then left. Leaf was rubbing his eyes free of sleep as Ilge reappeared holding a red hot bar of iron with tongs. She approached the cauldron and dropped it in. The warm steam that rose cleared the air of some of the cold. Herbs dropped into the water gave off scents that encouraged wakefulness.

Ilge returned with two more iron bars, warming the room with steam.

Aramz ladled out tea from the cauldron into cups and offered them both to Jovan and Leaf.

"We will have breakfast for you soon, when you are ready to come through."

"Thank you, Aramz," Jovan said.

The man nodded and left.

"What will we do today, Papa Jov?"

Jovan looked down at the boy and sipped the tea.

"I wish I had someone to leave you with," Jovan said. "But I expect trouble would catch us unaware. I think today we'll simply go and see the city. That will take time enough."

"So we can find a new shop?"

"Yes. And so we can discover why everyone seems intent on harming us."

"I wish we could find a home," Leaf said. "I think I'm done traveling."

"I am too, boy."

Breakfast was a simply toasted bread. The jars of preserves for the toast more than made up for the simplicity. Jovan had to stop Leaf from putting a sixth type on the first piece of bread he took. The womenfolk thought it adorable.

Kallidova did not come down to join them and they did not wait for her. Jovan went through his pack to make sure there was nothing he might fear losing if someone searched his room. He tucked silver into his boot and into the small satchel he carried on his hip with a roll of tools. The trip had not hurt his savings nor what he had earned in Stoneweks.

Leaf had taken out his "Sword of Danger" stick. He had gone through six since they had parted ways with Slant and Zvediz.

"You cannot swing that around as we walk," Jovan said.

"I know, Papa Jov. Today it'll just be a walking stick."

Jovan nodded. Together they walked to the front door.

Aramz came out from another room to see them off. "Where will you go today?"

"I'd rather keep my business to myself," Jovan said. "But we go to see the city, and to see if we can't find a place to set up a shop."

"Very well. Tonight, over dinner, I'll make sure you know of each district and what it contains."

Jovan walked out of the Bather Inn, Leaf's hand in his. A layer of frost clung to the buildings, the cobblestone slick where the icy touch of night had melted under the footsteps of early workers. Only a few paths led to and from the main street, and spoke of early deliveries of bread and milk to the surrounding homes.

The sun would be a long time coming up over the city, though its light was already fully spread across the sea, where shoals of fish swarmed and leapt as boats launched out to try to bring in a quick and early haul.

Servants walked bundled up against the spring frost, with baskets in their arms as they ran errands for their employers not yet up from their late night revelries. A pair of bakers stopped their carts alongside one another to talk about the latest news, including the happenings of the castle that loomed to the north of the rich estates. The king was away on some business with another boyar looking to cause trouble. The prince was wasting little time in spending the people's taxes on his own predilections.

Down the long street, Jovan could make out the bazaar beginning to fill up with vendors. The shouts of merchants taunting one another as they raised their stalls could be heard even at this distance.

Jovan chose to avoid it to start. If it was the first thing Leaf saw, they'd quickly become distracted and lost, if not separated. Instead, they took a zigzagging path through the rich upper tiers of the city. Their appearance was frowned upon, since Jovan had not yet found clothing suitable for either of them. But from several overlooks they were able to get a better measure of the city, and one talkative old man pointed out the guildhall that Jovan would need to seek out as a needle-maker.

Each evening they returned, took a hot bath, and ate with Mamm Kallidova, who had her own errands. Each day after, Jovan and Leaf continued to explore. And each day, Jovan felt more confident in his surroundings and less fearful that anyone kept an eye on them.

On the fourth day, they finally went to the bazaar. As Jovan had expected, Leaf was taken in by the sights.

Every merchant's tent was more garishly colored than the one before. Some were brightly dyed, showing fresh crafts made on long winter nights by crafters in cottages near the capital, while others bore the fading color of having been set up with oft-sought-after goods all winter long. Leaf darted from stall to stall. He did not ask for the things he obviously desired. But with wonder, he commented on the importance of this item or cooed over the beauty of another.

He dawdled longest at a woodcarver. The man sat with a long and very thick plank of wood that he chopped at with a large knife. Jovan saw a tent next to the man selling papers for hearth and forge char. Jovan kept an eye on Leaf as he stepped aside to hear the man's prices.

Leaf watched the woodcarver work the long plank into a smooth staff with intricate carvings following the natural grain.

As the man finished, he took an axe and cut off the rough top. He held the rough portion out to Leaf.

"Care to try your hand, boy?" he asked.

Jovan finished his conversation with the collier and came over.

"May I, Papa Jov?"

Jovan nodded. Leaf stepped behind the booth table and took the piece of wood and the man's big knife. The carver showed him how to hold the piece braced against the chair, bringing the sharp knife down.

"If you don't respect the knife and the wood, you will cut yourself or gain the nastiest splinters."

"Have you ever gotten one?" Leaf asked, looking down at his work intently.

"Of course," the man said. "We've all gotten careless."

"Then I will never be careless," Leaf said, seeming to decide for himself.

After a few more minutes, Jovan suggested they needed to move along. When the man offered the little piece of wood to Leaf, Jovan had the impression that he had just purchased him the entire bazaar.

Leaf held the rough piece reverently as they walked, bearing only a few nicks from his work upon it. "I need to get a knife so I can finish my work!"

Jovan chuckled and promised that he'd consider getting him one.

As they returned to the Bather Inn well after sundown, Jovan lay the already slumbering Leaf down on the bed and pulled the covers up over his little frame. The boy breathed deeply and then burrowed himself into the mattress.

Jovan turned toward the bed and thought to crawl in himself, but then decided otherwise. He opened the door and stepped out into the hall. A single candle burned, lighting the way toward the baths. He took a taper from an alcove, lit it, and then proceeded into the darkness of the steaming bathing room. It was long past when everyone else slept, so he moved quietly as he lit two more candles and prepared a bath to wash in. He did not wait for the water to be warmed, but simply dipped himself down into the cold water and soaped himself off. Then he crawled out and slipped with a wincing hiss into the hot pool. He lay there and closed his eyes and let the warmth and blackness seep in.

He opened his eyes, to the same blackness, and cursed for the candle having gone out. A faintest hint of moonlight came in from the clerestory window. He moved to rise, to find a way to light it again.

"Perhaps you should not," a voice said. Jovan froze. The voice had a heavy accent he did not recognize. It was deep and throaty.

Jovan sank back into the depths. An immense figure stood across from him above the pool as a pair of attendants removed his robe. He lumbered down into the water with a grunt, then a moan of enjoyment as the heat sank in.

The hulk of a man settled into the water. Even then, it didn't seem to come up to his chest.

"I ought to make arrangements to come here more often," the figure noted to himself. "This is much nicer than waiting for servants to heat up enough water for me in a copper tub."

The man said nothing for some time. Jovan said even less.

"Jovan Nedeller, I understand?"

Jovan nodded and grunted.

"I thought about having my men bring you to meet me somewhere else. But I heard of your reputation and I decided I didn't want to waste a few good men on the chance to cause a little fear and trepidation in you. I see now that it would not have caused any fear in you. So I'll have to settle for trepidation."

"You know my name," Jovan said. "But I don't know yours."

"You do, in fact, know who I am. I've already lost at least four of my men to you. Including a rather expensive vedmak."

"Why have you been hunting me, Bear?"

The figure roared out in laughter.

"You see?" he said to no one in particular. "I cannot cause fear in you. What I wouldn't give to have a man like you working for me."

"Perhaps you will allow a candle to be lit, and then we can talk as civilized men," Jovan said. "Eye to eye."

"No. You already do not fear my name. I would not have you see me for who I am."

"Very well," Jovan replied. "Then I ask again: why are you hunting me?"

"Not hunting. Merely interested. Why does the prince seek you and your boy? He doesn't even know your name. And from what I have been able to gather, he wants you alive. So you're no enemy of his. He asks for enemies dead. Or at least, as close to death as possible. He's gone to great lengths to ensure that you and the boy are unharmed."

"The men you sent looking for me in Stoneweks didn't seem to mind trying to harm me."

"They found you in Stoneweks?" He lifted his hand. "Send a courier there. Get those men to return my money."

"Don't bother looking for your vedmak," Jovan said. "He's not there."

"Isn't he? Then perhaps you'll tell me where he is?"

"You still have answers to give me."

"Very well," the Bear said. "As I said, the prince wants you alive. Why?"

"I am thought to have hurt him several years ago."

"What harm to the prince could you have possibly gotten away with?"

Jovan did not reply.

"Ah. You're the man who made his legs useless."

Again, Jovan said nothing.

"An interesting happenstance. I do not think that is why he seeks you. And do you know why I think this? Because he does not know who did it. He spent the first year of his time bedridden tearing apart the kingdom looking for that man. Word is, the king found out who it was and had him executed."

"Why do you hunt me?"

"I think perhaps I am done hunting you," the Bear replied.

"Why?"

"Two reasons. For one, I have now shared this bath with you. Among my people, those that do so are friends. Secondly, you are the enemy of the prince. I do not care for him myself. And so, because we share a common enemy, we are now doubly friends."

"And yet you know my face, and I do not know yours."

"Interestingly enough, I do not know your face," the Bear said. "I have kept that bit of honor between us. When we meet again, and know each others' faces, we shall either be enemies or we shall be thrice friends. If that is the case, then we shall be brothers."

"Your vedmak was seeking my boy as well as me."

"This is true."

"What do you want of him?"

"I was asked to seek him out as a favor to a friend."

"If you call me friend, then you shall leave him alone."

"I can agree to this. The knowledge of your location is enough for me to speak with the friend for whom I am doing the favor."

"If anything should happen to my boy, I will burn your kingdom down around you."

"Such threats," the Bear said, clicking his tongue.

"Promises."

"The promise of a protective father. I would expect nothing less. In fact, I'm honored that you would think to do anything to me should harm befall your boy. But I accept your promise. Let me give one to you, as a friend: I shall see to it that no harm befalls you nor your boy. And if I catch a hint of danger coming your way, I shall endeavor to warn you."

"Why?"

"Perhaps because I like you. But the truth? I'll be as clear as a glass window: I have a vested interest in your boy's future."

"I don't like that you know more than I do about my own child."

"Let's not lie to one another. He is not your child. He might be in your care, but I understand that he bears as much resemblance to you as I do."

The Bear groaned as he stood. Water dripped off his frame for some time as he lumbered up out of the water.

"Take care to watch better over your shoulder," the Bear said as he began to move round the corner. Then he stopped. "It was far too easy for my men to follow you the last few days."

CHAPTER 19 — DEBT OWED

Jovan woke and touched his face. He could feel the sagging bags that had formed. He rolled over and got to his feet. The groan that came from his chest reminded him of the Bear's own growl. Leaf sat up on the edge of his bed, looked over, and yawned.

"Where will we go today, Papa Jov?"

"Eat first. Decide later."

Leaf quickly dressed himself and ran off to the dining room.

The table had another splendid spread of preserved meats and sweet cheeses. Only the girl Ilge served them. Once the food was put out, she took the seat next to her father's empty place.

"My father and mother have left on business for the next few days. And I was asked to give you a message."

Jovan looked up, but continued to chew.

"Mamm Kallidova has asked you seek out the area around the Gilded Wing Inn. She will meet you there after sunset. She has things she wishes to discuss with you."

Jovan nodded. "Where will I find this inn?"

"It is located under the wall by the Wash. Below the castle cliff."

Jovan rose and took a large loaf of bread and tore open the end, stuffing some of the sausage and cheese into it, and then plugged it up with the bread he had taken from it.

"For the road," Jovan said, and gave a bowing nod to Ilge.

Leaf grabbed several small biscuits filled with dried fruit and followed Jovan back to their room.

"From here on, we leave our room with all the things we can't live without," he said to the boy.

"Are we not returning?"

"I do not know. But I have a feeling that one day we'll come and find this place too dangerous to return."

"I have everything I need," Leaf said.

"Good. I want you to keep my roll of tools in your sack."

Leaf nodded and took them from Jovan's outstretched hand.

"What will you do if you lose me?" Jovan asked.

"Find Mamm Kallidova?"

"Good boy. She may be your only friend in this town. But even then, only trust your own wisdom."

"Yes, Papa Jov," Leaf said somberly.

The day was washed with a warm sun and matched by a warm sea breeze. It wasn't long before Jovan held Leaf's cloak so he could run and gape at every sight and sound. They made their way down to the bazaar first and then off to the north toward the Wash. Jovan had avoided the neighborhood for as long as he could. It was spoken of in hushed tones amongst those of the upper tiers, and on the piers it was seen as the place money was made, if sometimes barely legally.

The tide had come in, and as they approached the Wash, they saw a landscape flooded with water, with homes and businesses hovering over the surf on stilts. Far off to the east, the sand was visible where the tide was beginning to retreat. Far above, atop the cliffs, sat the royal estate. Tulip-topped towers peeked out over the walls onto the city it ruled. They were visible here more than anywhere else in the city, as though the castle complex watched for anything out of the ordinary. Jovan took a seat on a stack of empty crates and told Leaf to stay close as he looked out over the Wash to read the landscape.

It did not take him long to decide the Wash was not the place for him to set up shop. It looked as though the winters would be harsh and it would be harder still to keep warm. A swathe of homes had been newly built and the homes near those had the look of fire damage. The people that lived out on the tidal plain gave Jovan weary and suspicious glances from their homes and shops built on thick stilts. Jovan stood and beckoned Leaf to follow him as they walked north along the edge of the Wash toward the cliffs where the Gilded Wing Inn could be found.

There was a stink of revealed grime coming off the sand where the Wash met the cliffs. Jovan did not doubt that the city used the area as a runoff pit for sewage and garbage. No sooner had he thought that, than he watched a wagon full of refuse back up to the pier and dump its load out onto the sand below. Some boys who were scampering about on the sand stopped their playing and looked to be deciding if they would scavenge through the mess. Leaf began to move toward the edge to watch, when Jovan put his hand on the boy's shoulder.

"You'll get yourself sick if you do what those boys are considering. And they aren't the sort of boys you want to associate with," Jovan said.

"What do you mean?" Leaf asked.

"You can't just run up to boys from the Wash and ask to play. They'll be as suspicious as their parents. Maybe one day. But today we're about business."

Leaf nodded and followed, though Jovan kept catching him looking toward the boys as potential playmates.

As they walked several blocks away from the wharf's edge, each street was cleaner than the last.

The Gilded Wing was not hard to find. Hanging unabashedly on the front of the large tavern inn was a wooden wing painted yellow. The windows were dark and the street around it quiet.

An old man sat on a chair outside his own shop, a broom held in his arm like a halberd. Above his place hung a spool of old rope.

"You looking for something?" the old man asked.

Jovan shrugged. "An empty shop, to tell you the truth."

"Not many this time of year," the old man said. "Everyone has come to town to make their fortune."

"Still, I'm looking. I've a mind to be particular."

"Not many that can afford that," the old man replied. "What's your trade?"

"Needle-maker."

"You didn't think to try the upper tiers? Sell your goods to the ladies and maids up there?"

"Not much money in that. Gathering pennies every day, with only the hope of taking business away from another? No. I'm looking to find a place to set up shop so I can meet the needs of all.

For woolers and tailors.

For fishers and sailors."

"Ah. Then a man who truly knows his trade," the old man winked. "You've been to the guild hall then?"

"Not just yet. I'd rather find a place to set up shop first, and then ask permission."

"You'll be riling up the local Havats. The clan here has their fists tight around the tailor trade. The other needle-makers owe them allegiance. They won't work with the Guild Hall either."

"Then there are no needle-makers in the guild?"

"Can't say there are. Might not let you in either, for fear of causing war with the Havies."

"Where might I find the Havats and come to an understanding with them?"

"Hard to say. They don't have a shop. They move through the town by wagon, like the tinkers."

"I'll watch out for them. How's the neighborhood?"

"Around here? Stinks at low tide. But then, so does the whole city if you've got a nose between your eyes. But otherwise, not a finer place to ply a trade."

"You're a rope-maker?"

"Rope merchant. I buy the goods off those that make them. Wives, sailors, boys with fingers to tie and untie a knot."

"I appreciate the knowledge," Jovan said. "We ought to keep moving, to look for that empty shop."

"Take that street there," the old man said. "Talk to the old lady with the nasty cat. Milva is her name. Tell her Zurl sent you."

Jovan nodded his thanks and gave Leaf a penny to give to the old man. Zurl took Leaf's hand in his and gave a silent blessing before they continued on.

The old lady saw them coming before they saw her. She picked up the lethargic cat she was untying from a hitching post. The cat lay in her arms with vacant eyes. The woman had the same look in hers, along with a small spark of suspicion.

"Mamm Milva?" Jovan asked.

The old woman pursed her lips. "Why do you want to know?"

"A friend sent me along to speak with you."

"What friend?" she snapped.

"Zurl."

"What does that old coot want?"

"I'm the one looking for something, actually. He thought you might know of a vacant shop. I'm looking to set up in one."

She scowled and turned up the street. She turned back. "You coming?" she snapped again.

They walked behind her. The cat lolled its head over the woman's shoulder to watch them with disinterest.

She shuffled three doors down and came to an empty store front. The next door down had a quiet flower shop with only dried goods hanging in the window, while across the street stood a glover.

"What do you do?" Milva asked.

"I'm a needle-maker."

"You mend?"

"I'm not a tailor. I make and repair needles." He repeated his little motto to the woman.

"Hrm...," she said. She opened the door and pushed through. She held it open for the two of them.

The doorway opened into a very small front room. A tall desk stood right inside with little room for anyone to stand within. Behind that was the workshop and a set of steep steps into the loft. Jovan moved around the desk and looked out the back door.

"Who last lived here?"

"Turned out to be a smuggler."

"There's a forge outside, I see. But it needs work."

"I'm not fixing the place up for you," she said.

"How much are you asking?" Jovan asked.

"Straight to it, huh?" She walked toward the door. "Place has already been rented out."

"Why did you let us look inside then?" Jovan asked, then clenched his fists in realization. "Let me guess: Mamm Kallidova?"

"I think that was her name, yes. And I had nothing better to do."

Jovan took Leaf's hand and marched out onto the street.

The old lady was cackling to herself as they left.

There were no other places available as they walked up and down the area, waiting for nightfall when Mamm Kallidova would see them at the Gilded Wing.

Leaf began to comment on his hunger, so they made their way to the inn, which had only a few patrons within.

It was a large inn, housing a stage wider and deeper than most he had seen. According to one of the locals there was a troupe of performers promised to entertain that evening once others filtered in.

A whole leg of cow was on a spit in the hearth. The fire had been stoked and soon after Jovan and Leaf took a seat at a table, a boy snuck up to the hearth hoping to avoid, unsuccessfully, being boxed around the ears for being late. He stood and turned the spit slowly, knowing he'd be long at it before he'd be allowed to pull up a chair, if there were any to spare.

A bread merchant pulled up to the door and began unloading a delivery of baskets. Jovan could see guttersnipes sneaking up and pilfering a few loose loaves from the back of the wagon outside while the baker was within.

After the baskets were all on the bar, he haggled a price with the barkeeper. He wore a broad grin of one who had gotten the better deal as he walked away.

A bell sounded from somewhere in the city. Barmaids suddenly rushed out from some back room and took their places, waiting for something. The moment dragged on long, with only the rustling of barmaid dresses breaking the silence.

Leaf shifted restlessly.

Suddenly, a commotion came from the street, and then fifty men all wearing matching blue hats shoved in, fighting for spots at tables, all the while talking.

One of them boasted of having completed more harnesses than the others. It was then Jovan finally caught the distinct whiff of leather and brass.

"Those hats they wear?" Jovan said to Leaf.

Leaf looked around and nodded in excitement.

"It marks them as journeymen. I don't doubt they're all journeyman leatherworkers who work at the local leatherworks. I've heard tell of factories in the city here. They churn out apprenticeships and journeymen, and then underpay them. They don't have the skill to go out on their own."

"Like the smiths in Stoneweks?" Leaf asked.

Jovan nodded. "I don't doubt that explains the Stoneweks smiths' poor quality." Then Jovan took a deep breath in and leaned forward. "Don't repeat those words, Leaf. It's not kind to speak ill of people's quality of work. Even if it is poor."

"Isn't it the truth?"

"Their own poor work will pay itself in kind. The best you can do is note and then learn from such quality."

"Do you think you can sell awls to them?" Leaf asked.

Jovan laughed. "You know my work better than me sometimes. Perhaps I should find that out."

"Perhaps you should," said a voice.

As Kallidova approached, Jovan thought he caught a scent of smoke following her, perhaps from the men who stood outside burning herbs in pipes. She took a seat next to Jovan and lifted a hand. She was clearly known and thus immediately received a loaf of bread, asking for a second one to be brought. She doled out pieces to Jovan to Leaf.

"How long have you waited?"

"All day," Jovan said.

Kallidova looked astonished.

"We've been in the area all day," he chuckled as she sighed relief. "We've been here none too long."

"And how has the search for a shop gone?"

"Unsuccessful."

Kallidova laughed. "Then I have news for you. I've found one. It's rented out by an old, shrewd lady."

"Mamm Milva?"

Kallidova laughed again. "Then you have met her?"

"She showed me the shop and then decided to inform me it wasn't available."

"She'll get a good surprise when she finds I rented it for you."

"We shall need to discuss reimbursement."

"Later. For now, use your money to rebuild your shop. I consider it an investment, upon which I hope to make a return."

"Why have we met here?" Jovan changed the subject.

"You said you wanted to come to the heart of the enemy. Tonight, I'll be giving you another gift. Let us say three gifts in total. First, the shop. Second, the entertainment you'll see here tonight. And third...you'll have to wait and see."

Over time, half the men finished eating their bread and drinking their ale. They disappeared into the falling night to seek entertainment elsewhere or to return to their homes.

A man appeared at the bannister of the second level, dressed in more furs than Jovan had ever seen on a single person. His paunch, along with the furs, made him appear like a ball. He had a red face, framed by more fur. He held a staff in his hand, which he began to pound on the floor. The place quickly grew silent.

"The Dervok Troupe!"

Suddenly, two lithe men leapt up and out from the balcony. They wore motley greens, reds, and blues. They landed on the floor below at the same time and stood with a flourishing bow. Down the stairs several musicians brought their instruments, strumming wildly. The collected crowd began to clap. Their cheers became a roar as six figures, all wearing loose clothes and masks glided down the stairs together and went to stand against the wall alongside the stage, suddenly freezing like statues.

The large man commanded his troupe from above. Three minstrels took the stage. One held a simple drum and beat out a tune, beginning to sing. He drew his voice up into a nasally tone, denoting he'd be singing a romantic ballad, while two pretty minstrel girls accompanied on their lutes behind him.

As the song finished, the six masked figures appeared on the stage almost suddenly. They began to pantomime the creation of the land. There was a mask of a wolf, a squirrel, a bee's hive, and a bear. The other two figures wore blank masks. They seemed to represent the sun and the moons, or possibly the brothers: Luck and Death.

Leaf was entranced. Jovan smiled broadly with amusement, and even Mamm Kallidova seemed to enjoy herself.

After some time, the entertainers took a break and sat at several tables. The roast leg on the spit was removed and soon meat was taken to paying customers.

As the two minstrel girls took the stage again, the outer door opened, letting in a burst of cold air from outside. The bartender walked toward the door and prepared to bark at whoever left it open, when two burly guards entered.

They said little, but pushed into the middle of the room. People quickly held their beers as the jostling threatened to splash them, and with the guards' goading, they pushed their chairs and tables out of the way. Four more guards suddenly shoved into the inn, bearing a litter between them. The forward guard had cleared away those sitting at the table nearest the stage. Jovan saw the barkeeper slinking back. The man knew what was happening and knew better than to get in the way.

One of the barmaids was able to sneak to the door and pull it closed as the litter was placed down onto the table. With practiced moves, the guards disassembled the top, revealing a young man sitting within. He had hair as golden as the sun and pale skin with striking features. It was there his good looks stopped, for the scowl he wore creased his face heavily.

"Prince Zelmir Valle," Kallidova whispered. "But you knew that already."

"And you knew he was coming. What have you done, woman?" Jovan asked.

"I have done nothing. Only given you the gift of seeing your handiwork."

"I do not wish to see this."

"But you will not rise," Kallidova said. "Or else you will give us away."

Jovan crossed his arms. He had lost his appetite for the evening.

The prince was less entertained by the actors. And even they seemed to have lost their joy in their work. A juggler dropped one of his balls and it rolled off the stage. He finished his act and jumped down to retrieve it. As he rose, he had a look of shock on his face, having accidentally turned his back to the prince when he stooped. When he turned, the prince beckoned he approach. The juggler overacted a look of shame and reproach, hoping to dissolve the situation with humor. The prince's arm flashed out from his box, a rod in his hand, slashing it across the man's painted face. Blood streaked across his cheek as the welt ruptured.

"You will perform again," the prince said. His voice was shrill and filled with hatred.

The juggler nodded and took the stage. Sweat and blood cut through his paint as he tried with great concentration to perform a second time.

The prince clapped his mirth, though he did not smile. As the juggler finished, the prince asked his name.

"Vlahz," he said.

"Note that down," the prince said to a guard. "I do not think Vlahz here is good enough to perform at the palace. Ever. His name is struck."

The juggler let out a sob.

"Now, those two pretty ones. Have them perform again. At my table."

The master tapped his staff again and the two girls with lutes appeared. One of them moved hesitantly. The other came to the tableside and leaned up against it, bending over suggestively.

"What song would you hear, my prince?"

The prince scoffed. "Something...rousing."

She smirked and began to play a staccato of a beat.

A man near the door rose and began to leave. The prince shot a look around.

"Where are you going?" he said.

The man glanced toward the door. "Out for a breath."

"Not without my permission you do not."

The man slunk back to his seat. No one made a sound.

The girls began to play again. The prince thought it humorous to ignore the girl practically throwing herself at him, giving his attention to the younger, shy one.

"This is becoming unbearable," Jovan muttered. "Did he learn nothing from his injury besides bitterness?"

"Learn?" Mamm Kallidova said with a soft whisper. "Yes. He did learn something. Do you understand the Will of Cause?"

"Yes. What we do has an effect. Good begets good. Evil begets evil."

"You see, Prince Zelmir here thinks that the great evil that was visited on him paid a good deal of coin against what he would do in the future. He is allowed to do these petty evils because he feels the bill has already been paid."

"Unless the pain wrought on him was in payment for sin he had already committed."

"Who can say? But that is what he is."

"Why did you seek to show me this?" Jovan asked.

"To assuage your guilt."

"You assume guilt upon me."

"No? No guilt?"

Jovan caught a glimpse of someone moving to go out the back door. He far too obviously tried to bring his hood up over his head. But not before Jovan saw who it was: Captain Samov Zin.

Jovan rose, taking Leaf's hand in his. The guards shuffled as the prince turned to watch him go. He heard the ruffle of Kallidova's skirts following him. The prince raised his voice to stop him, but Jovan did not. The prince made some ribald joke and everyone laughed. The guards did not pursue him. Jovan smiled to himself. It turned to a scowl as he ran with the boy in tow to circle the inn. Captain Zin was nowhere to be seen. He turned back and sighed.

Mamm Kallidova approached slowly. "Let's find our way back to the Bather Inn. We've all had enough entertainment for the evening."

CHAPTER 20 — CASTLE

Mamm Kallidova came in to dinner after Bather had blessed the food and took her seat across from Jovan. Leaf was quietly eating.

"I did not expect you to be here," Kallidova said to Jovan. "I thought perhaps you'd be in your new shop."

"You have found a place?" Ilge Bather asked.

Jovan nodded. "Our benefactor here seems to have provided many things for us—including a shop for us in a part of town that is not too unseemly."

"I'm sure my father will be glad to hear it when he returns."

"I have been waiting, in fact," Jovan said to Kallidova, "for your return tonight."

"And why is that?" she asked.

"I need to ask you a favor."

She laughed lightly. "You owe me enough already, I believe. What could I possibly do for you?"

"As you are the only person I trust, I would ask you to stay here tonight. I have business I must conduct, and I need someone to stay here with the boy."

"I am here," Ilge said.

"Yes. But Mamm Kallidova has a vested interest in the boy."

"I will keep an eye on him," Kallidova said.

"Leaf, I must go out tonight."

"Where?" Leaf asked.

"I have something I must attend to. Tomorrow we'll go down to the new shop and move our things in."

Leaf smiled. "I will go right to sleep then. I want morning to come quickly."

Jovan excused himself and went back to their room. Leaf was not far behind.

"Behave yourself while I'm gone," Jovan said.

Leaf giggled. "What trouble can I get into while I'm asleep?"

Jovan nodded and took up his roll of tools, tucking them into his side satchel. He pulled a cloak over his shoulders and went out into the night.

The wind was cold and wet, and promised to get worse by the middle of the night. Jovan bundled himself tighter and made his way through the streets. He was glad to find he was not the only person. The guards that came at regular intervals made no note of him. The castle loomed far above and grew larger as he approached.

Oddly, the gate was not barred, and people moved freely in and out of the place. The cold stone of the edifice was wet and black in the torchlight. The windows above seemed to hang in the night.

Jovan paused at the gate. A guard stood nearby.

"When last I came here," Jovan lied, "I had to check in with the gate."

"The gates are always open when the king is not here," the guard said. "Makes it easier for the prince's companions and whores to visit him."

"Hrm," Jovan grunted.

"Should we be checking your credentials?" the guard said when Jovan didn't move.

"I'm here to deliver a roll of needles to the seamstress," he said as he pulled his own tools out to wave at the man. "I was asked to deliver them tomorrow, but I have them ready a day early."

"Go on in. If Mamm Cillis asked for them tomorrow, she'll probably still be irritable that you didn't deliver them yesterday."

Jovan nodded his thanks and entered.

He circled around the main building, came to the servant's kitchen entrance, and stepped through the door. There was a back hearth in the kitchen, which glowed warm as cooks prepared for morning, rolling out the dough to rise. A little girl watched him walk by with intense eyes. Under her flour-covered hair, Jovan thought he glimpsed the same color as Leaf's. He smiled at her, then turned back to the large woman he'd approached.

"What are you waiting for?" she asked. She wiped flour from her face with large arms, and then moved it onto the apron across her middle.

"I was told to meet one of the maids about a new set of needles."

"Probably Cillis. Go up those stairs. The butler up there is in his books, and likely the bottles," she said, nudging the lady next to her.

Jovan took the stairs up a long tower. It opened up to a well-lit corridor. A door stood open and a man within sat at a desk, with hundreds of bottles stacked on shelves near him.

"Who are you?" the man asked with a slight slur in his voice.

"I'm to seek Mamm Cillis. I have new needles for her ladies."

"On down the hall. Don't go too far or you'll come out in the royal quarters."

Jovan nodded his thanks.

"Far too easy," he muttered to himself. "Why would the capital of the kingdom be so easy to enter. Does the prince fear nothing?"

He walked confidently past door after door. One held a circle of ladies embroidering a tapestry. Jovan assumed that Cillis was the matronly woman who commanded the attention of the others. Jovan did not pause but continued down the hall. His heart pounded in his chest. The door in the next hall, even more lavishly adorned, was also empty. Rich green tapestries hung over yellow exotic wood panels. He walked across the thick wool carpet to the top of the stairs, and stopped. He could hear carousing far down below.

There were voices of people coming up the stairs. One voice stood out above the others—the nasally voice of the prince himself. Jovan turned and began to hurry back down the hall. He came to the door into the servant hall and passed it by, continuing deeper. The doors he touched were locked, barring his escape. He came to the double door at the end and found it locked, as well.

He knelt by the lock and considered it. It was an old style with a maker's mark from several generations prior, and generally out of favor. He reached into his satchel and took out a heavy steel darning needle, shoved it into the keyhole, and gave it a quick twist. The latch opened. He slipped into the room, picked up the key he'd pushed out with the needle, and returned it to the lock.

The room within had a roaring fireplace. Jovan recalled the old crippled man he knew as a child, who kept the fire blazing in his home, in hopes the warmth would bring feeling back to his legs. If he didn't know better, he'd have thought an entire tree was burnt every day in the room, given the heat that warmed and lit the fur-adorned space. Jovan could hear the voice of the prince drawing closer and closer as his compatriots forced themselves to laugh at his every jest.

Jovan looked over to a bundle of furs that sat piled atop a chair next to the door. The key in the latch turned and he heard the prince barking orders from the other side. Jovan crouched down next to the chair and pulled the large bear pelt over himself.

No sooner had he situated the furs over him, than the door was pushed open and the prince came in, carried on his litter by the six guards who had escorted him to the Gilded Wing the night before. Behind him came a gaggle of drunken friends.

Jovan cursed to himself.

The prince dismissed his carousing friends to return to the women who awaited them below. Once the door closed, he ordered the guards to turn him onto his bed.

They moved gingerly now, and worked him out of the litter onto the furs. One of them took a rod to the back of his neck for no other reason than that the prince felt like it.

"Now go. I would be alone."

The guards said nothing, but set the litter down near the door and left.

The prince lay outstretched on the bed and groaned to himself, both in frustration and boredom.

Jovan drew the needle he had picked the lock with once more and held it in his fist.

He took a deep breath and stood up.

The prince yelped at seeing the bearskin rise and reached for his rod.

Jovan moved quickly, shoving the needle into the keyhole alongside the key, jamming it in place before leaping onto the bed, whacking the rod from the prince's hand so it flew across the room, and covered the younger man's mouth.

"Do not say a word and you shall live through this night," Jovan said.

The prince nodded. Jovan removed his hand.

"Who in the Four are you?" the prince asked disdainfully. "And how dare you come to my room like this."

"I come for a friend," Jovan said. "To understand who you are."

"You won't outlive the night," the prince said.

"I'm surprised you've lived this long."

"And why is that, you creature," Prince Zelmir said.

"You ought to stop insulting someone who holds your life in his hands."

"Answer."

"I walked into the castle and there were few who even noted me. Strange to think a man of my description should be allowed anywhere near you, nevertheless the upper floors of the castle itself."

"Your description? Show me another tradesman with a long beard and a bald head. Ah. Of course. Half of them meet that description."

"You do not know me?" Jovan asked.

"Should I?"

"You've sent enough men looking for me. I felt perhaps we should come to an understanding. Eye to eye."

"Who would I have out looking for you?" the prince asked.

Jovan did not say anything.

"I do feel I should recognize you," the prince admitted.

"You ought to," Jovan said. "I lifted a wagon off your back."

The prince's eyes popped. "You! YOU!" he roared.

Jovan held up a hand. "No need for bellowing," Jovan said. "We need to come to an understanding."

The prince fumed in anger. "We need to do nothing. You broke my legs."

"I did not."

"You left me in that ditch."

"I hid you until I could send help so that the person who had harmed you in the first place could not come back and finish the job."

"You were supposed to be found and executed, and you live?!"

"I live."

"I shall have your head. And I'll drink your blood."

"You didn't know?" Jovan asked.

"I was assured you had died."

"Then who has been searching for me? For my son?"

"You were in the inn last night," Zelmir said. "You left with that boy with the golden hair and that..." The prince suddenly clamped his mouth shut. "Guards!" he shouted.

Jovan moved toward the door, which suddenly flew open. Six guards stepped in and froze, seeing Jovan standing there.

"You may wound him, even break him," Prince Zelmir said. "But bring him to me alive. I want this intruder to suffer."

Jovan turned to Zelmir. "I did not harm your legs."

"I don't care. You'll pay for them, all the same."

The prince looked at the guards, who had their hands on their sheathed swords. "Well?"

"We cannot draw our swords without your express permission," one said.

Jovan did not wait. He charged through the six of them and barreled down the hall.

"Draw them!" the prince shouted.

Jovan was halfway down the hall to the servant's door when he heard the sound of the swords being drawn. One of the guards bellowed for another to sound the alarm. Jovan turned and careened down the servant's hall. The butler stood with his hands full of several bottles of wine. Jovan took hold of him and threw the man behind him. The bottles crashed and the man screamed in terror, falling to the ground amidst the lost vintages now soaking the carpet. The guards followed soon after and found themselves tripping over the man as they swore at him.

Jovan took off down the stairs, holding the central stone pillar and letting himself slide.

"This was a bad idea. Bad," he told himself.

He careened through the kitchen and kicked over pots and pans as ladies began to scream.

He ran without pause. He rushed toward the gate just as the order came for them to be closed. He slipped through the crack, no guard standing there to stop him, as the ones atop the wall closed the gate from above, dumbstruck.

One tried to bring a bow to bear, but it was too late, as Jovan took a corner and raced off into the night.

He did not dare return to the Bather Inn. Instead, he ran through the city toward the Wash. The smell of low tide was starting to dissipate as the tide came in. Jovan hoped he could find a place to hide that would not be flooded.

The stilted houses stood up over the water that came in wave after wave. Far above, bells pealed the alarm as the guards across the city were awoken.

Jovan rushed out over the sand as the sea came in. Debris floated casually in the water, and Jovan slowed his pace as he waded in, moving with a larger float of garbage headed out

to sea. The tide drew him up under one of the more promi-
nent buildings and he climbed up under its scaffolding. The
darkness was cold, but there was a space underneath that
remained above water. He listened as guards searched the
shore. A few took to boats and halfheartedly looked under
the buildings with torches.

Long before dawn, after the tide had once more turned,
Jovan climbed down from the building, shivering. The guards
had been mostly recalled, while others loudly disrupted the
peace as they sought anyone out on the streets at that hour
and up to no good. It made it easy for Jovan to slink from
shadow to shadow as he made his way up to the Bather Inn,
arriving just before dawn. He slipped in the back door and
first went to the wash closet, where he dropped himself into
the pool for a few minutes to warm before donning a robe
and returning to his room.

It was silent. Leaf made no sounds. Jovan sat down on the
bed.

"We'll likely have to move along again," he said.

Leaf usually slept lightly. But he said nothing to this. Jovan reached down and touched the blankets. There was no
little form there. Jovan stood and turned and felt around, his
heart beating fast. The boy wasn't there.

He tore open the door and raced through the dining room.

Ilge came out of a door, rubbing her eyes.

"You've returned. All is well then?"

"What do you mean?" Jovan said. His voice was rising. He
choked down the need to bellow. "Where is Leaf," he whispered hoarsely.

"When the town bells began to ring, Mamm Kallidova said she'd take Leaf somewhere safe."

"She left? With Leaf?"

Ilge nodded as she yawned.

"Where did she take him?" he asked. He turned and walked down the hall and began opening doors. "Which is her room?" he asked firmly, placing his hand on the last door.

Ilge nodded, now wide awake and pulling her shawl tighter around her shoulders.

He pushed the door open, revealing a room devoid of any belongings.

"She took him," Jovan said. "And now I'm a dead man."

CHAPTER 21 — THE BEAR

Jovan took hold of the knife and held it to his own throat, considering the man in the mirror. The eyes that stared back quivered in the quiet anger he reserved only for himself. He took a deep breath and breathed out, "Leaf" as he took hold of the end of his beard and then swiftly cut the long whiskers free. The movements were short and quick, taking off the years of growth that had been a silent pride. A few short minutes later, his chin was visible, cold, and breathing for the first time in many years.

He had forgotten how sharp the tip of his chin was.

He took the warm towel and wiped himself clean. It had been some time since he had shaved, but he was relatively proud that he had avoided nicking himself, other than the one little gash behind his right ear which would likely sting. At minimum, the clean face didn't look as though he had quickly cleared it away to avoid a passing resemblance of the man the castle now hunted.

He double-checked his pack, pulling it onto his shoulders, then he turned and walked toward the kitchen.

"I'll be leaving now," Jovan said to Ilge, who startled as he entered. "If Mamm Kallidova comes and asks for me, tell her she will know where to find me. But if she comes without Leaf, things will not go well."

Ilge nodded as she pushed herself against the wall. Jovan took a basket from a shelf and began to pile it with food.

"You think she just took the boy?" Ilge asked.

"Two of the most powerful people in the kingdom have both informed me they have no actual interest in the boy. And yet at every turn, Kallidova is there. She and her 'client,' are somehow involved."

"She seemed to have the boy's best interest at heart," Ilge said.

"At the cost of my life. Whoever is after Leaf, Kallidova and her client or someone else, needs me dead or taking the fall for this. That tells me that they do not have his innocence in their best interest. I'll not have him turned into a tool for their plans."

Jovan walked to the kitchen door and then turned back.

"I thank you and your family for your hospitality. I have to go and find my son now."

He headed first to the shop, but when he found no one there, he knew his worst thoughts were right. He left his pack in the forge yard and walked out into the street. The sky to the east was bright, but the sun had not shown itself to the city.

He knew what he had to do now.

He headed to the bazaar. A few people huddled against bare walls, keeping each other warm. Jovan walked up to the largest group of them. One of them stood jesting with the others. He wore brown leathers meant to look worn, but Jovan could tell the quality. He had a tight black mustache. One of the men crouching against the wall, a blanket pulled around him, indicated Jovan's approach and the man turned, smiling wickedly.

"What do you want?" the man asked.

"You look to be willing to make a little coin," Jovan said.

The man shrugged and spat to one side.

"I seek the Bear," Jovan said.

The eyes of the collected group started.

"Who are you? And what makes you think I know what your message means?"

Jovan pointed a finger into the man's chest. "Pass the word back that he promised no harm would come to mine. I have business to attend to this morning. I will be returning to the bazaar shortly before the sun sets. That is enough of a message."

Jovan turned to leave. The men didn't move. He repeated the message to other groups around the empty plaza and noticed that a few of them quickly disappeared after he turned his back.

Then he brazenly walked the town, turning down random side alleys and down the middle of open streets. His shaven face brought no attention to the guards that passed him, and after several hours his heart raced less with each passing guard. Finally, he began to make his way back to the bazaar.

The sun was beginning to set and most of the merchants had already sold their wares to leave or were still breaking down their tents. The beggars and outlaws were beginning to congregate again in shadowy, empty corners of the space. A few were approaching merchants and half-heartedly asking for spare change. A pair of guards marched nearby, though the beggars didn't seem to fear them. Most of the beggars shied away from Jovan as he approached, so he knew the message had been received and passed around.

He came to the merchant selling knob-topped walking staves.

He took hold of one of the larger staves from the merchant's table of wares and swung it around, narrowly missing a man who quickly approached from across the aisle.

The other man threw up his hands in protest. "No need for that!" he hissed.

The merchant was moving toward Jovan, opening his mouth to protest.

"The Bear sends word," the man said.

The merchant suddenly clamped his mouth shut and shied away.

Jovan lowered the club and placed it back onto the table. "Take me to him."

The man nodded and turned to go, Jovan following.

They weaved through the bazaar to the southern edge. As they walked, Jovan became aware that others were following parallel to the two of them. They wore varying arrays of scowls, frowns, and knives.

As they came to the edge of the bazaar, ten men now escorted him. They didn't hold weapons or sticks in their hands, but the knives strapped across their persons were just within reach.

One of them held out a sack, obviously intended for Jovan's head. Jovan held up a hand. "No."

"The Bear insists you not know where we take you. If you know where his den is, he will have to kill you."

"Then let him kill me. I won't have that sack put over my head."

"Sack or unconscious."

"If the Bear has agreed to see me, then he doesn't want me dead," Jovan said, turning to the small man. "If anyone lays a hand on me, I'll harm you first. Stop wasting my time and take me to him."

The man cowered and glanced toward someone in the group behind Jovan's back. "Very well."

They began to weave their way through the city.

"A group of men like this, moving through side streets, is sure to draw attention," Jovan said. "If I was looking for a hideout of a man like the Bear, I'd be looking to follow a group like this."

"Group?" the man next to him asked. Jovan glanced behind them to find the thugs that had been following them had disappeared.

"They went quietly," Jovan observed.

They came to a deep alley. Two men stood leaning against the two walls framing it. They stood up straight, gave a nod, and let the two of them pass.

There was only a single door with no latch at the end.

The man next to him kicked over a bottle left sitting on the stoop. As it clattered away, the door swung open silently.

"Go on in," he said, though he did not follow.

Jovan stepped into the dark entryway. A small, seedy man held the door. He pointed to a flight of stairs that led down into deeper blackness.

The hot, sticky heat that rose up out of the stairwell was overwhelming. Jovan took slow, deep breaths. Firelight shone around the corner as he came to the landing and he stepped into the light.

It was a large, vaulted cellar. A heavy wooden table sat in the middle. The tables were empty save the four men playing bone sticks. Coins moved around the table as they placed their bets. A pair of women, disinterested in their surroundings, lounged near the hearth with bowls of foolhead smoke in their hands. A turbaned man approached and silently offered to take Jovan's cloak. Jovan shed the cloak and found himself no cooler. The man indicated he walk toward a pair of curtains.

As he pressed through, he found a hall with layer after layer of curtains. Each he passed cut the heat off further, but the humidity remained. He could hear the trickle of running water somewhere.

A movement of air fluttered the last curtain and he came out into what felt and sounded like a cave, though the room had no light by which to tell. He was aware of the heavy breathing of one sitting on the opposing side of the room.

"Lég nugo," the Bear said.

Jovan did not know how to respond. He did not recognize the language.

The Bear rumbled out a chuckle. "Greetings, Jovan."

"Do you know why I am here?" Jovan asked.

"You seem to have lost something."

"I told you I would find you if something happened to my son."

"You did. And admittedly, I did not know something had happened. I understand you took a little trip to the castle, though. You left your son alone at the Bathers'."

"I do not like how much you know," Jovan said.

"I do not like how unobservant you are. The work it has taken for my men to bury your identity with the guards at the castle has cost me much. If we were not friends, I would say that you owe me a great deal."

"Friends?" Jovan said. "Your men wished me bagged before I came."

"Old habits of theirs."

"Friends look each other in the eye."

"Yes," the Bear said. "This I agree."

The large man hefted himself up out of his seat and shuffled around the room. A tinder was struck and a candle lit at a large table. Then, his back still to Jovan, the Bear filled two tankards with drink.

"Come and join me," the Bear said.

As Jovan approached, he saw the Bear wore furs across his shoulders, muscled arms, and a round paunch of a belly. Jovan circled the table and stifled the gasp that welled up within him. The Bear was no man. The furs upon his frame were not donned, but grew from him, and his face bore a massive muzzle of sharp teeth, two ears atop his head, and a black nose below black beady eyes. He was a Medved—that ancient race of bear-people from the north.

The Bear laughed at the look on Jovan's face.

"I expected you already knew," the Bear said. "I always enjoy the look on the face of someone who comes to the discovery. Please, have a seat Jovan Nedeller. Drink with me that we may become truer friends."

Jovan hesitantly took a seat across from him, grasping the tankard of yellow mead in his hands. "I was expecting to come here, make some demands, perhaps take some frustration out on your men when you let them off their leash. But now, I'll admit, I'm more afraid of not making it out of this room."

"Your first Medved?"

Jovan nodded solemnly. He took a long draw from the tankard of mead. It was sweet and strong.

The Bear sat silently as he drank heavily from his own tankard. Jovan followed suit and worked his way down to the bottom. He placed the tankard down.

"How does this go down now?" Jovan asked.

"Go down?"

"Yes. Now that I've demanded to see you and you've brought me here, what do I have to do to leave here alive?"

The Bear slammed his own empty tankard down and began to laugh.

"Walk out of here alive anytime you'd like!" he roared. "I have never taken a tankard of my own mead with a man. We are now friends. No harm can come to you."

"No harm?" Jovan asked. "Why?"

"Jovan. I have never known someone who simply asked to see me. To demand to come without a blindfold. If it were even possible, I'd have thought you were part Medved yourself. You blundered yourself into the very heart of a friendship with a Medved. If I was to hurt you in any way, I'd be sacrificing my soul to my god. You are as close to a brother as you can be."

"I...thank you," Jovan said.

"Guthfru," the Bear said.

"Guthfru?" Jovan asked.

"My name. Few know it. I entrust it to you."

"Why?"

"You're very suspicious, aren't you?"

"Yes."

"I want you to know that I am trustworthy. If you do, then you will trust me to help you find your boy."

"I don't know where to begin," Jovan said in defeat.

"I have an idea. But you'll need to trust me to begin to look. I must know some things first."

"What must you know?"

"Describe the boy to me, so I may find him." Guthfru came around the table and poured Jovan's tankard full again.

"He is the size of most boys his age."

"Which is how old?"

"Four. And his hair is easily described as polished gold."

"Gold, you say?"

"Yes. Not blonde. But a gold I've only seen on a few people."

"He has pale skin?"

"Yes."

"Then I know where to look. I shall invite you to stay here for several days. I wish to see that the guards have finished searching the town for you."

Jovan nodded drowsily.

"Come, I will show you to your room."

Jovan stumbled on drunken legs as he followed the large Medved lumbering ahead of him, through curtain after curtain, into an adjacent hall.

"How did a Medved come to be a crime lord?"

"It is a long story. Perhaps I'll tell it to you someday. Let's just say I found my mind sharper than those of my own blood. And I was not in a position to take leadership."

"You were cast out?"

"I chose my own exile. Perhaps one day I'll return."

"So you're small for a Medved?"

"What makes you say that?" the Bear growled.

"You could not challenge your chieftain, even if you were smarter. So you left."

"This is true."

"But you're still bigger than me. So that really doesn't mean anything here."

"This is also true."

CHAPTER 22 — LUCK

The sticky heat of the den brought Jovan in and out of consciousness. He thought morning had come and gone, but it was hard to tell in the dark of the room the Bear had provided for him. The sound of people conversing in some other room came to him, and later fell to silence again. Several times he prepared to get up and then decided against it.

He awoke as a man brought a tray of food and placed it next to the mat he slept on. He rolled over after the man left and took the soft spiced biscuits and ate them, finding himself hungrier than he thought he was. He drank down the tea from the mug and then sat up. His sweat had soaked through his shirt and he sniffed at himself in disgust. He reached to grab for a towel and then remembered he wasn't at the Bather Inn. There was no bath here.

He stifled a groan as he stood and walked toward the curtain and pushed through. With each heavy drop cloth he passed, voices got louder. He came to the common room which was now full of people, all of various levels of obvious criminality. Most ignored Jovan as he moved through the room. Several who looked up guffawed.

"You look like well-rested death," one man said. "You just hibernate?"

Jovan ignored him and walked toward Guthfru's room. A man quickly rose from a chair and stepped in front of him.

"Where you going?" the man asked. He was powerfully built, but lean. If Jovan wasn't still trying to clear his head, he could have pushed past.

"To see the Bear," Jovan said groggily.

"He's not here. No one goes into his room while he's not here."

Jovan turned and looked at the room behind him. Two tables were playing bone sticks. Another had a card game going. Jovan stepped away from the curtain. The man visibly relaxed.

He took a seat at one of the tables. A dealer held up a bundle of rib bones, sheared down flat and engraved with symbols painted red, black, and blue.

Men placed bets on the top-most sticks, or hidden colors. The bones fell out of the dealer's hand and cascaded onto the table. Two of them hit the table and bounced away and off. Jovan reached down and picked one up and put it back onto the edge.

The next several hours were a blur as hands of bones were played. Eventually, the groggy feeling faded, and he found he had been drinking tankards of ale and mead mixed with one another. A half-finished chunk of ham sat on the table next to him. One man fiddled around with the bones across from him, letting them fall, and examining the results. He had a long mustache that fell from his lip. His fur-lined hat sat on the table, though he still kept his elaborately embroidered coat tightly closed on his very thin frame.

"You ever have someone read your fortune in these?" the man asked.

"No. I do not believe in such," Jovan said. "It is a heresy, some would say."

"Do you believe in the Four?" the man asked.

Jovan nodded.

"Then you must believe in the other two, as well."

"That doesn't mean I draw their attention to me," Jovan replied.

"What harm can luck do?"

"You think them separate," Jovan said. "Good luck and bad luck. But they are partners. Luck and Death run the con together."

The man chuckled. "The game calls me too strongly."

"Then I don't care to stay sitting here."

"No need for rudeness," the man said. "I simply offered to read your fate. They were once one, you know. Fate became Luck and Death."

"Thank you for your offer, but no."

"You're an Umernnost," the man said.

Jovan sighed. "What makes you say that?"

"One of the few religions that refer to Vhezin and Tov-Ol as Good Luck and Bad Luck."

"It is so," Jovan conceded.

"Then you're required to accept the hospitality offered by a devotee of a god."

"So now you're a priest?"

The man stood and opened his coat and took it off, turning it inside out, revealing the blue coat with white embroidery of a devotee of Vhezin, the Luck god.

"My friend Vhezin thought I might find one seeking a bit of his blessing here," the man said.

Jovan folded his arms. "Say what you've come to say, then. But do not expect a reply from me."

The man flashed a smile.

"A few people know me as Listener," the man began. "I run a game of cups on the street."

He took out three stones and placed them on the table.

"Funny thing is, I use no cups nor stones."

He began to move the stones around with his hands. After a few short moves, one of the stones turned red. Then another turned blue, and the third turned black. A few moments later and the stones seemed to stretch into bones. He laid the three bone sticks out face down so none of the runes were seen.

"What do you seek?" the man asked.

"That is none of your business," Jovan said.

"No need to be difficult. I can still work with this."

The man began to move the bones around. They spun and danced, though none revealed the runes beneath.

"Place your finger down," the man said.

Jovan shot out a single finger. A moving bone hit his finger and flew away into the other man's hand. He took the other two in his left hand and revealed the rib in his right. It bore no rune on the back.

"Ah," the man said with a dramatic flare. "Something pale."

Then the man slammed the bone down on the the table and took a deep inhalation. He covered the end with one hand. He sighed long and hard. When he pulled his hand away, there was a rune that Jovan had never seen on a bone before. It was gilded within the carving.

"Something white and gold," the man said. "Something mystic. But you will run after the wrong one."

Jovan took hold of the bone and pulled it out of the man's hand, only to reveal a second identical bone in his palm.

"What are you saying, seer?" Jovan asked.

The man shrugged. "I said nothing. Vhezin the Sable spoke. I am only a vessel."

"What is your name?" Jovan asked.

"Vigi," the man replied. "Or Listener. Call me what you wish. The Bear likes to keep a token disciple of Vhezin around. Says it keeps him safe. But like a lucky sable tail, we're only lucky to him. Most of us don't last more than a year."

"How long have you stayed here?"

"I think I'm at two years. I don't have much longer to live. But my family is safe."

"He has kept you here on threat of the safety of your family?"

"No!" the man burst out, laughing. "No. I was in real trouble. Tov-Ol was hunting me down. The Bear gave me safety, and safety for my family. In turn, I gave my soul over to Vhezin until he feeds me to his brother, the Black Fox."

Jovan shivered. Few spoke so familiarly of the twins of Fate.

"When shall the Bear return?"

"It's been three days since he left, so not long."

"Three days?!" Jovan nearly shouted. "I thought I was restlessly sleeping just one night."

"Ah. First time hibernating here then?"

"First time here, ever," Jovan said.

"Who are you a devotee of?" Vigi asked. "Ah yes. An Umernnost. Right. Perhaps he's preparing you to be his sacrifice to his father, Medi."

"Sacrifice?" Jovan asked.

"He keeps someone from each of the six. I've even heard this isn't his only den, nor that we're his only pets."

"Pets?" Jovan said.

The door opened and the wide figure of Guthfru shoved through. He wore a cloak and hood over his massive frame. He pulled it off. In the common room, Jovan could see him more clearly now. His body was covered in thick, but short brown hair. The fuller fur that lined his jaw was darker, like a beard across this fuzzy face. His beady eyes glinted in the firelight.

"Night has fallen," he said with a low growl. "Be about your business or stay and revel. But tomorrow, this hibernalia ends, and the time to store up and prepare begins."

The men and women assembled roared a cheer.

Guthfru put his hands on his hips and let out a belly laugh, scanning the room. His eyes fell on Jovan. He motioned for him to follow and then lumbered off into his den.

Jovan moved cautiously after the giant bear-man.

The Medved was puttering about, sniffing at pots and turning to place them on his table. "A few of these will go bad soon. So they better get eaten."

Jovan took a seat at the table.

A man puttered in. He wore a wrap around his head that marked him a devotee of Pchal, the Bee Queen of Mind. He had a loaf of bread on a tray. He placed it down in the center and then began to cut away slabs of airy, soft bread, whiter than Jovan had ever seen. Guthfru had come to the table and broken off the wax top of a jar, which he now held over his own piece of bread. Ever slowly, a thick and viscous honey poured out. Then, taking a knife, he clipped off the honey. As it continued to fall, he moved it over Jovan's own. When the honey had quit its dripping, the Bear lifted his own piece of toast.

"To Heart and Mind," Guthfru said.

"The Bear and his Queen," Jovan intoned back.

They each took a full bite. The sticky honey was hard for Jovan to chew through, but he worked at it.

Guthfru had no such trouble. He chewed and spoke as he ate.

"I have been uncovering many a hill of grubs," Guthfru said. "I'm rather proud of myself, to be honest."

Jovan could say nothing through the honey in his mouth. He continued to chew.

"It all led to one rather significant bit of information. A small boy with golden hair was seen entering and exiting the castle."

Jovan began to cough.

The Bear clapped a heavy paw-like hand across Jovan's back as he reached for a tankard of ale. He cleared his mouth and swallowed. The honey was dry in his throat. He drank more ale and looked over at the Bear.

"That easy?" he asked.

"Easy?" the Bear growled. "I've been at it these three days. Rumor has it you have been sleeping the whole time."

"What of Mamm Kallidova?"

"I do not know where she has gone off to. But I do know the boy has been seen coming and going, escorted each time."

"I must go and see for myself."

"You will not be leaving," the Bear said firmly.

"I will not be staying," Jovan said. "I appreciate your hospitality—I do—but I will not be kept here against my will. And I won't be made a token of yours."

"Token?" Guthfru asked.

"Vigi said you keep people here as tokens, pets, sacrifices to the gods."

The Bear began to roar with laughter. "I do not keep anyone here against their will. Certainly not those I call friend. And Vigi is welcome to leave, but the Black Fox will find him if he does. His face is too well known, and he killed enough men in his time. I don't doubt his enemies will ever forget him."

"Then why do you say I must stay?"

"Because word has gone out again, seeking you. I thought that by now they would have grown bored of seeking you out. No. I will see that the boy is found and brought here. Then we can decide what to do next."

"I do not understand why you treat me as a friend."

The Bear put both paws on the table and looked at Jovan seriously.

"I have told you before. But I will say it again because I want to make myself clear: I have lived among men for over twenty years. Never have I had someone treat me as an equal. You do not fear me. You do not think little nor great of me. For that, I trust you."

"I do fear you," Jovan said.

"You fear these claws. You do not fear my power."

"Because power is perceived. I believe in hospitality. I believe in the tenets of the Umernnost faith: hospitality, truth, kindness, and discernment. Above all, temperance. We agreed at the bath that I would seek you out should anything happen. And so I have."

"So often those are simply threats. Instead, you came here and pleaded with me as one person to another. For that, I want you to understand my appreciation for you."

"Then let me go and seek my son."

Guthfru took a deep breath and closed his eyes. When he opened them, a decision had been made. "We shall go together. In two evenings' time."

"Very well. If that is what it will take."

"That is what it will take."

CHAPTER 23 — SECRETS

The night and day passed. Jovan found himself pacing the den, discovering over the course of the evening that it was a rather extensive group of rooms. He did not like the company found in several of them, and avoided those that gave off the acrid smoke of foolhead or the fake moans of paid comfort.

The day brought a quiet to the place, and by noon many of those that had seemed to be taking up a permanent residence for the winter had gathered up their things and gone out to seek their means of support. Vigi tried again to get Jovan's attention, but Jovan soon noticed he did this to everyone.

The Bear appeared a few times, checking that Jovan hadn't left yet, before quickly going back to his own den once the two of them made eye contact.

As night came down upon the world above, some people returned, reporting on their work, and all paying a stipend to the Bear's turban-topped assistant.

As more filtered in, some with food to share with the throng, the assistant finished up his accounting and disappeared into the Bear's room. He soon reappeared and approached Jovan.

"The master will see you now," he said.

Jovan turned, touching the scruff of his face negligently. He already missed the long whiskers he'd been so quick to shear.

He entered Guthfru's lair. Guthfru had a whole ham before him and was cutting off thick steaks onto plates. He motioned for Jovan to join him.

"When would you like to go and see for yourself?"

"As soon as I can."

"Very well. Then first we must change your attire." The Bear made a motion and the assistant appeared with a package tied up with a thin woolen string.

"You'll put these on. I am told they'll fit. We can't have you looking like the smith you are."

Jovan nodded consent. "And you?"

"I have little to worry about. However, I'd also like you to carry this." He pulled out a short package and put it on the table.

Jovan stuck a large piece of ham in his mouth and wiped his hands on his trousers before lifting the package. Unrolling it, a heavy baton of wroughtwood fell out into his hand. It was a simple design, with a heavy pommel of iron. There was a latch above the handle. He pushed it and pulled the end of the baton off the handle, revealing a long and very fine-pointed stiletto.

"A needle for a needler," Guthfru said.

Jovan nodded. "And a heavy enough pommel to serve me in a brawl."

"The scabbard is wroughtwood. It will suffice."

Jovan rose. "We'll leave after I dress."

Guthfru nodded.

Jovan returned to his own room and opened up the second package. It was a simple handwoven coat that ran far past his knees. The material was stiff, but he was able to move in it easily. The sleeves were wide, but did not get in the way of his hands. He found the pocket on his right side ran deep enough to hold the baton, so he slipped it in. It was a coat fine enough to wear with prospective customers, as well as out on the road.

He marched back to the common room to find Guthfru speaking with several of his men. He looked up and smiled.

"Jovan," he said, and indicated toward the men. "If they do their job well, you won't see them, but I want you to know who looks out for my well-being on the street."

The men all pulled their hoods back and nodded to him as he looked them in the eyes before they once again donned their hoods.

Jovan walked up to Guthfru and touched his coat.

"This is a fine gift," Jovan said.

Guthfru beamed.

"Thank you."

Jovan walked toward the stairs and ascended. He could feel the air behind him stop as the Bear came up behind him, filling the space. Jovan came to the top and put his hand on the door and pushed. It swung silently out into the alley, which bore no men. He blinked against the bright light out-side after so much time in the Bear's caves. The Bear came up beside him, his heavy hood over his shoulders, enshrouding his eyes.

"You seem to know much of me," Jovan said over his shoulder as they walked. "But I know so little of you."

"Not many do," Guthfru said. "But then, not many are brave enough to ask."

"You're not as violent as you make yourself out to be, are you?" Jovan asked.

"What makes you say that?"

"I've known many fighters in my time. I can tell when I am speaking to a violent man."

"But I am no man."

"I understand that. However, the humor you've shown in response to words I've said tells me that perhaps you rely more on people's perception that you are violent than that you truly are."

"And you are more perceptive than you seem," Guthfru said.

"How many men have you killed?" Jovan asked.

"How many men have I had killed?"

"No. How many men have you killed with your own hands?"

"Three."

They walked in silence as they wended their way toward the top of the city. They came out onto the bazaar, which was now deserted.

"When I left my tribe, I was young and foolish," Guthfru began. "I blundered around in my new-found freedom. It was my own fault, I admit, that I stepped into a nasty iron leg trap. It nearly severed my foot off. I howled in pain for days, unable to open it. The trappers who eventually found me blessed their stars for having caught not a bear, but a Medved. They spoke in a language I did not yet know. But I understood well-enough my predicament. I soon realized they did not know how to approach me. So I laid myself down, and feigned weakness and sleepiness.

"They approached me. One of them unlatched the chain from its deep spike, and I rose up and killed each one in turn. Three fell easily. The fourth pleaded for his life. I let him remove the trap from my leg. He escorted me back to his cabin and nursed my leg back to health. It seemed the fear I had caused had shaken loose the humanity he had hidden away. He taught me your language. Together we contrived a plan and came to the city."

"You mean your turbaned assistant?"

"Yes. Gergor is the hunter. He knows I could have killed him."

"And now you're the most feared man in the kingdom. Perhaps more feared than the prince himself. And yet the only people you've killed are the three hunters who sought your life?"

"You do not believe me?"

"No. I don't," Jovan said. "If you are willing to have men killed at your behest, what difference is there?"

"You are a violent man, who continues to do violence yourself, believing that since you've never killed a man you are different," Guthfru said.

"You assume I have not killed," Jovan replied.

They came to the square outside the entrance to the castle complex.

"Let us find somewhere warm," the Bear offered.

As they walked, Jovan kept near the walls, while the Medved walked beside him nearer the street, his hood obscuring his face. They regularly passed guards, though none seemed to pay them any attention.

They soon approached a single, sizable inn with large windows facing the castle. Guthfru motioned for Jovan to enter ahead of him. A stage was set beneath the window. Anyone watching the stage could see the backdrop of the castle behind it.

"I suppose that speaks to the loyalty of the innkeeper," Jovan said.

"The appearance of loyalty," Guthfru offered.

They took a seat at a booth screened by heavy wood, looking toward the stage and the castle. A pretty girl wearing layers of heavily embroidered clothes came and set down two hefty flagons of ale.

"I'll bring you some bread and meat," she said demurely.

"Thank you, Bilya," Guthfru said.

The girl curtsied and turned to glide quickly to the kitchen.

"Attractive girl?" Guthfru asked, watching Jovan's eyes follow her.

"What do you mean?" Jovan responded.

"I'm asking if you find her attractive," the Bear said. "One can learn much about a man by who or what he sees beauty in."

Jovan laughed. "I thought perhaps you asked because you yourself did not know. You're not a man, after all."

"This is true, but you are wrong. Do you not see a fine horse and see beauty in it? Do you admire a finely carved lute even if you can't play one?"

"I concede that to you."

"Well?" Guthfru asked, motioning toward the girl across the room. "Your thoughts?"

"She is rather pretty," Jovan replied. "Her headdress hides her hair, though, and with how much blackening she has in her eyebrows I could not guess at the color. So that tells me she's either even younger than I suspect, because she hasn't learned how to apply her color well, or she's of a lower class than her clothes seem to say. So regardless, she doesn't interest me."

"You'd prefer someone older?"

"More than anything," Jovan began, "someone who wears her class. If a girl comes from a humble home, she should dress accordingly, even if she's trying to attract someone of better means."

"Don't we all dress for the part we wish to play?"

"I do not," Jovan said. "If someone seeks for me to save them from their poorer life, where does it end?"

Guthfru shrugged.

Jovan turned his head as someone walked through the bar, jovially slapping people on the back as he moved.

Guthfru turned to see who he stared at. "Should I know who this is?"

"Captain Samov Zin," Jovan replied. "He was at the Blue Tower and has somehow ended up back in the city, despite his having been sentenced there."

"Samov Zin, son of Daru Zin, the Boyar of Belkhal?"

"I wouldn't know," Jovan scowled.

"There is no way the son of a boyar would be sent to the Blue Tower, regardless of what he did."

"If half the things he told me were true, then I would think he would be sent to the end of the empire to rot there."

"Who did he offend?"

"The prince, from what I understand."

"The boyars hold more power than the king's own son, and the king has little love for that man's father."

"Then why is he here?" Jovan asked. "Why did he help me come to the city? Why is he so near the castle if he is now enemy of both the prince and king himself?"

"Shall we ask him?" Guthfru asked.

Jovan nodded.

The Bear made a motion and the innkeeper approached.

"That man?" Guthfru growled lowly, motioning toward Zin, who flirted with the girl, Bilya.

"Zin?" the innkeeper asked. "What of him?"

"Have Bilya take him to a room where my men can prepare him for a private conversation."

CHAPTER 24 — BOYAR

"I merely want answers," Jovan said. "No harm."

"I will leave that to you," Guthfru said.

They watched Zin, a silly grin on his face, follow Bilya into a back room. Soon after, there was the soft sound of a scuffle. Bilya came out and tucked a stray lock of her hair behind her headpiece, giving a wink to the Bear.

Guthfru rose and led the way out one door, down a hall, and to a room, outside of which stood the innkeeper. Guthfru handed him gold. "Keep the ale flowing for the men, and see if you can make a little noise."

The innkeeper nodded and returned down the hall.

"What do you want?" Jovan could hear Zin ask before he entered.

Guthfru held the door for Jovan, who followed. Four men held Zin down while one bound him to the chair he sat in. Then, the men filtered out.

Jovan said nothing, while Zin's eyes darted back and forth between Jovan and the cloaked figure before him.

"Who is this?" Zin thrust his head toward Guthfru.

Jovan did not respond.

A din of laughter and clinking tankards rose in the distant common room.

"Why have you done this?" Zin asked. "Do you know who I am?" He tried to shift in the chair, and huffed in frustration. "You can't do this to me. My father is a boyar. You have no right."

"It matters little to me who your father is," Guthfru growled from beneath his hood.

"Best not to question the Bear," Jovan said calmly.

Zin's eyes widened and his mouth clammed shut.

After a long silence, Zin sighed. "How much does he know?"

"What do you mean?"

"If you think you have to bring the Bear into this," Zin said, "then I assume you've told him our secret."

"He has told me nothing," Guthfru said. "Only that you were at the Blue Tower and now here. I proposed that the son of a boyar would never be sentenced to such a place."

Zin nodded. "It took some doing to be sent there."

"I think it's time you shared what brought us both here," Jovan said.

"Depends on what your friend here thinks of the prince. I won't be sharing if he's loyal to that prat."

"I dislike the prince as much as the next person," Guthfru said. "Though he and his men have kept many of the brothels in my control in business."

Zin laughed. "I'm sure I've kept one or two of them open from my own pocket."

Neither Jovan nor Guthfru smiled.

"Very well. You, Jovan, are here because you unwittingly saved my skin those few years ago."

"It would seem so," Jovan offered.

"What is this?" Guthfru asked.

"It is believed," Jovan said, "that I overturned a cart onto the prince's back, destroying his legs. But I found him like that. I ran for help, despite the prince gaining consciousness and begging me to stay. Before I went for help, though, I saw a figure fleeing. That figure made the mistake of looking back. It was Zin."

"And yet, I cannot take the blame for what happened," Zin said.

"Explain," Jovan said.

Zin took a deep breath. "There was a girl—Vlada." He blushed. "A daughter of one of the southern boyars. I had met her while I travelled south with my father as a boy. Even as a young naive lad, I had the intention of wooing her. I made the mistake of inviting her here to Khorapesh. I don't doubt she would have come here eventually. But when she came, I introduced her to Zelmir. He took a liking to her. She had his golden hair, which spoke of a 'cleaner' blood. He had every intention of seducing her to be his. Maybe he was jealous of my own way with women, since he was often forced to pay for any pleasures he sought. I suspect he took advantage of her. In the end, she was impregnated. The prince barely seemed to care. He disappeared into his study, taking only the counsel of his cousin Sephaly, who had been summoned to the capital from her town of Geruz."

Jovan frowned. "The simpleton daughter of Lord Valle-Brons?"

"She was not always that way," Zin offered. "In fact, she came to me and begged my help. The time was drawing near for the birth of the child and Vlada had become ill, the last portion of her pregnancy not treating her well. Even Sephaly seemed to have become more weary than I had ever seen her. But the girls both insisted that I help them escape, to take Vlada south to give birth in Geruz. I don't know why I gave in. She carried the prince's child, and my own hatred of that betrayal had festered in me. But I relented.

"The prince pursued. As we drew near to Geruz, I held back to keep the prince at bay as they fled ahead."

"How then did the prince fall beneath the wagon, if not by your hand?" Jovan asked.

"He was riding toward me down a long hill that ran to the road. He was fifty yards ahead of me and I doubt he could tell in the twilight who I was. His horse suddenly threw a shoe and Zelmir went flying into a ditch alongside the road. There was an old abandoned cart there, and as he struggled to rise, it collapsed and brought down half the berm over onto him. I stood and stared at his limp body for some time, debating what I should do."

"So it was just an accident? Pure and simple?" Jovan asked in disbelief.

"Pure and simple. That was when I heard you coming and I knew how it would look, so I fled."

Jovan nodded. "I had been sent back down the road by two hooded women as they came rushing through Geruz," he said. "When I saw the prince, pinned under the wagon, I ran back for help. But I was soon put under arrest for the crime. The prince didn't seem to think it'd been an accident. Thankfully, Lord Valle-Brons gave me a second chance and called for my release. A little more than a year later, the boy was given to me."

"Who is the boy?" Guthfru asked.

"I have never known. He was brought to me by Mamm Kallidova."

Zin twitched.

"You know where she is?"

Zin shook his head. "No, but her fingers have been in this since the beginning."

"What happened after you fled?"

"I ran away. Joined the army."

"How did you end up at the Blue Tower?" Jovan asked.

"Kallidova asked me to go there and watch for you. Once you passed through, I came back here."

"Why?" Guthfru interrupted.

"I'm sorry?" Zin asked.

"Why did you return here?" the Bear asked.

"To find Kallidova. And get my money."

"Then you don't fear the prince?" Jovan asked.

"Why should I? He's a fool. He thought you did it. I understand you paid him a visit. He won't stop yowling about it."

"Then why are you here, near the castle, near the man you say you hate most?"

"I heard the boy was seen nearby. I saw you and him with Kallidova the other day at the inn where the prince was holding his court of fools."

"It would seem we're here for the same reason," Jovan said. "To find Kallidova."

"Take these bindings off me and perhaps we'll find her together?"

"I don't think so," Jovan said. "I intend to find out why Kallidova took the boy from me, and then I will be on my way."

"Perhaps she took him back to return him to his mother—" Zin bit his lip like he'd said too much.

"And who would that be?" Jovan asked.

"Who do you suspect?"

"That he's the prince's," Jovan said.

Zin smiled broadly. "No. The prince sired no son."

"You said that the girl was pregnant."

"Yes. But I found out later Vlada had a girl. The boy is not the prince's."

"Then what do you know?"

"I suspect he belongs to Sephaly."

"Lord Valle-Brons's daughter?" Jovan asked.

"Surprising, I know. Bookish and quiet. Of course, that raises the question of who the father is. I imagine the father is the man who took an interest in Sephaly years ago."

"And who would that be?" Jovan asked.

A knock came at the door.

Guthfru answered it and turned back. "The boy has been spotted leaving the castle."

Jovan turned to leave.

"What about me?" Zin asked.

"You stay where you are," Jovan said. "I don't trust you. You'll get in my way."

"In the way of what?"

"Answers."

CHAPTER 25 — BREAK

Jovan stormed through the common room, the giant bear-man trying, almost futilely, to keep up with him. The man who had brought the message to them stood leaning by the door.

"A little golden-haired boy was seen leaving the castle. He can't have gone far."

"Show me," Jovan said.

Jovan was practically pushing the man ahead of him as they moved toward a side street. Ahead, another man of Guthfru's, one Jovan had seen in the den plenty of times, stepped out of a doorway and pointed, making a series of small gestures to their guide.

The guide suddenly took a right down an alley and flew ahead to the other end before pausing and peeking to his left down the street. Jovan came up to his shoulder.

"I see the back of his head," the man said.

Jovan started forward to look when Guthfru's paw fell on his shoulder.

"I hope you understand that I abhor inflicting violence." Guthfru's eyes pierced Jovan with sincerity from beneath his hood.

"I understand," Jovan replied, then he turned to look out of the alley.

It was easy to pick out the golden hair of Leaf. He walked with two men at his shoulders, though they did not seem to be forcing him along. He held the hand of the larger of the two men, who wore the faded yellow and green of a militia man, though he looked to be bulkier than Jovan. The other was a slighter, thinner man in a long black leather tunic.

Jovan growled to himself. "Slant and Zvediz."

"What did you say?" Guthfru asked. "You know Zvediz and Slavint?"

"Yes," Jovan said. "How do you know them?"

"Anyone who has ever bet on a fight in Khorapesh knows Zvediz, the Boyar of the Ring."

"And Slant?" Jovan asked.

"Not as many know who he is. He's done work for me from time to time."

"When did he last work for you?"

"Do not question my loyalty to you, my friend."

"Very well," Jovan said.

"So easily?"

"Some say it is a fault. Slant saw it in me when we first met. Said I had the ability to see through the sheep pat."

"I agree with him," Guthfru said.

"It seems I must end my friendship with them now," Jovan said. He sighed and then marched out into the street.

They were moving at a pace that would not draw attention, though Jovan knew that Zvediz preferred the slower pace, regardless.

Once he was half a block behind them, he called out. "Zvediz! Slant!"

Slant took only a small glance behind him before he grabbed Leaf's hand and began to flee. Zvediz stopped in his tracks as the boy's hand slipped from his, and then slowly turned around, his fists balled up.

"This makes it more even for you, at least," Guthfru said.

"See your men continue to follow Slant."

"Jovan," Zvediz said.

"Zvediz," Jovan replied. "I will provide you one chance to turn my boy back over to me."

Zvediz shook his head. "You do not understand."

"Then use your words." Jovan had stopped thirty feet from the man.

"We have always had the boy's safety in mind."

"Since when?"

"The beginning. We were asked to find and bring the boy. That Kallidova trusted you gave us reason to trust you."

"But now that I'm not his protector?"

"Our loyalty is to his safety."

"You will take me to him."

Zvediz shook his head. "I am bound by the fourth."

"Then I invoke the fifth and the sixth."

Zvediz sighed and raised his fists. "I am sorry, Jovan. I truly am."

Jovan felt adrenaline coarse through him with an impending sense of dread. Zvediz lumbered toward him. He swung with a testing fist which Jovan easily side-stepped as he put a punch into Zvediz's ribcage. It was far too easy. Zvediz's head spun to look at Jovan. He was leading by toying with Jovan. Jovan did not try to take another swing. He let the man come at him, and soon realized he was being shepherded. He turned the table on the bigger man and began to juke in random directions.

Zvediz knew his business and picked up the pace of his swings. He left his side open, but Jovan refused to take the bait. More force went into the larger man's swings. Jovan decided to take another attempt as Zvediz turned his back to him, and hit Zvediz hard on his back. The bigger man's elbow suddenly flew back and took Jovan in the side of his head, making his ears ring. Jovan stumbled back and lost his footing, falling into a pile of used crates, wood flying everywhere.

His head hit the wall. The sudden and coppery taste of blood in his mouth sent a surge of strength through him. Zvediz smiled.

Jovan flew forward at the man, his hands curled as claws, the anger rushing in his ears. The big man almost laughed at him as he let Jovan's hands try to cover his fists, before he shoved Jovan back into the pile of debris. Jovan rose again and came up at his opponent, who now stood over him. Five times he rose and fell as Zvediz thrust him back into the mess of wood. He roared in frustration, making him stronger.

Then, something fell from his coat, and he scrabbled to grab it. It was the wroughtwood blade, fallen free from the sheath in his deep pocket. His foot caught the wall behind him and he lurched forward, lower than he intended, the sharp blade piercing Zvediz's leg.

The big man roared. It was a muted sound through the rush of rage that flowed through Jovan's blood. He rose and the top of his head hit Zvediz's jaw as it came down, his bulky frame buckling over to clutch the piece of wood sticking out of his leg.

"Not fair fighting!" Zvediz roared.

Jovan did not care. He shoved at the man, who's foot caught and he fell back, as Jovan's hand fell to rest and grip the wood jutting out. He did not intend it, but the piece came free, and Zvediz screamed.

Jovan turned to look back at the pile of wood and pulled out a longer plank. He came and stood over Zvediz.

"Jovan!" Guthfru roared. He could tell by the tone in the Bear's voice that he had called him multiple times. "Do not kill him."

"He must!" Zvediz yelled. "He invoked the sixth: death."

Jovan lifted the plank, but felt the anger draining out of him. The plank became lead and he let it fall. He saw the blood pouring from Zvediz's leg.

"No," Jovan said. "You will live."

"Why?" Zvediz asked.

"I invoked the gods of Good and Bad Luck. I'll not give Tov-Ol what belongs to his brother."

Zvediz nodded. "Thank you."

"The cost of my breaking that invocation requires you to break one."

"Name it."

"Break the fourth. Break your silence."

"You would have done better to ask for the second, for a truth."

"Tell me where Slant went."

"The shop. We found your bag there."

Jovan nodded. He touched Zvediz's wound.

"You will not die," Jovan said.

"You are a good man."

"Not good enough that I won't find you and kill you if you lied."

Zvediz looked Jovan in the eye and nodded.

Guthfru walked up slowly. "You bested the Boyar of the Ring," he growled. "After this, I ought to put money on you."

"After this," Jovan replied, "I'm leaving."

"I suspected as much."

"Will you see to his wounds?" Jovan asked the Bear. "See no harm comes to him. We respect each other enough for me to promise his safety to him. I must go the rest of this road alone."

"Yes," Guthfru said. "I have enjoyed our time together. If ever you are in need, send word to me, and I shall see what I can do to help."

"Thank you, Guthfru," Jovan said, taking hold of the Bear's arm.

The Medved took hold of Jovan's arm in return with his massive paw-like hand. They looked into each other's faces and nodded. Then Guthfru crouched next to Zvediz, picked him up easily, and lumbered off toward his den.

Jovan turned in the direction he had seen Slant go with Leaf, and took off at a run. He came out of the alley before he realized where he was. The Gilded Wing stood across the small square. Jovan could just make out the bar. The man leaning there glanced over his shoulder and saw Jovan. Slant darted out of view.

Jovan charged across the street and past the front door to reach the side door he had seen Zin leave from the other evening. As the door began to open, Jovan stopped it hard with his foot and felt it hit Slant across the top of his head. Taking hold of the handle, he pulled it outward; Slant's hand still held the other side as he fell toward the ground in a heap. Jovan caught him by the front of his tunic and heaved him up until their noses met.

"Slavint," Jovan said through clenched teeth.

"Hello again, Jovan," Slant said, wincing as his hand reached up to touch the cut across his brow.

"Where is the boy? Zvediz told me he was at the shop, but it looks like you're here instead. Where is he?"

"Jovan, I'm not in a position to negotiate with you, obviously. But I also can't tell you. Since you seem to know where you're heading, I won't stand in your way."

"Stop talking circles."

"I'm not," Slant said. "I'm simply not denying that you were headed in the right direction."

Jovan shook him once. "Stop it, Slant! Tell me where my son is!"

"I can't."

"Why not."

"Because I don't know."

"What do you mean? You just fled with him."

"I did not," Slant said. "That wasn't Leaf."

"Wasn't Leaf?"

"No. It was Periphina."

"Who is Periphina?" Jovan asked. "Stop confusing me." He pulled Slant out onto the street. "We're going to the shop." He began dragging Slant down the street.

"You're not going to like what you find," Slant said.

"You're not going to like what I do to you if you don't start talking sense. You owe me a secret, anyway."

"I do?" Slant asked.

"I told you when we left Rightness that I was the one suspected of maiming the prince."

"True," Slant said. He put a foot down to slow Jovan. "You're strangling me."

"I don't care. I no longer trust you."

"I don't blame you for that. But I promise I'm not going to run. Let's walk together as civilized men."

"No trickery," Jovan said, loosening his grip.

"I'm not the one you need to worry about regarding trickery."

They turned a corner and came to the old man selling rope. He looked up at the two of them, showing recognition of both.

"Not far now," Slant said inanely.

"Tell me who this Periphina is."

"Leaf's double, it would seem. Zvediz and I have been charged with keeping near her since we came to town."

"His double? A distraction for me? So Kallidova could keep Leaf from me?"

"That's an interesting point of view," Slant said. "You call him yours, but Kallidova, as I understand, placed him in your care. And these last two weeks little Periphina has been blabbering on about how Leaf is hers."

"Why are you mixed up in all this?" Jovan asked. "You're Kallidova's lover?"

"Lover? Hardly. No. I owe her much, though. Or I should say, I owe Sephaly much."

"Sephaly?"

"Yes. She's Kallidova's daughter."

"You failed to mention that," Jovan said, "when you told me that Kallidova was Valle-Brons's former wife. In fact, as I recall, you said quite the opposite: that Kallidova and Verth never had children."

"Yes. But that secret is not the half of it. You want a secret? I'll tell you one that will more than pay you back for the one you paid me. I told you Kallidova had a falling out with her lover, and Verth didn't take her back. What I didn't tell you was that she also had a pair of twins by that lover: Sephaly and Prince Zelmir."

Jovan stopped.

"Surprising, huh?"

"Zin thought that Leaf might be Sephaly's child," Jovan muttered. "And that a girl named Vlada had a daughter off the prince. If the prince and Vlada had a girl, who I assume is this Periphina, and Sephaly had Leaf, then Kallidova is their grandmother."

"Sephaly had no children. I would know."

"What does that mean?"

"She and I..." He shrugged. "Shall we go into the shop? And meet the little girl? I asked her to run on ahead. Though there is no telling if she followed what I said. She does what she wants."

Slant led the way up and into the shop. A golden-haired child sat with a book in front of her on the floor. She looked up and gave a broad smile, though her eyes were dead and uncaring.

"Jovan," she said. Then she looked at Slant with disdain. "Brought him right here, did you?"

"He brought me here," Slant said. "By all rights he might have killed me right after he took down Zvediz."

"That's impressive," she said, looking back at Jovan. "You don't look the worse for wear, though."

"I can take a lot," Jovan said. "Where is Leaf?"

"I appreciate your being straight to the point. Illifan and Kallidova have already left town."

"Who is Illifan?"

"You call him Leaf. Illifan is his name."

"Going where?" Jovan asked.

"That is not something I intend to tell you."

"You will."

"I will not," the little girl said.

"You're older than you look," Jovan said. "Why are you speaking like an adult?"

"Why is Illifan wise beyond his age?"

Jovan did not answer.

"We were imbued by our mother, given portions of her mind and her spirit and her soul. Or perhaps I should say: I was given a part of her mind and Illifan a part of her spirit. That is why he is so wise, and better at tapping into the shared reserve of soul that escapes me."

"I don't understand," Jovan said.

"Perhaps that's something better explained by Slant."

Jovan turned toward Slant, who held his hand up toward Jovan, words wandering across his lips. A white smoke shot out from his mouth, like a frosty breath, and hit Jovan between the eyes. The strength in his legs gave way and he fell to the ground.

The girl came and stood over him. "The question you ought to have asked is why I've stuck around this city for as long as I have?" she said quietly. "The answer is: I needed the prince to find you here, so he can remain distracted by his desire to have you tortured before you're killed."

CHAPTER 26 — ESCAPE

Jovan lay in a pool of blackness, feeling nothing save the nagging call to wake. A dull pressure pushed down on his chest. Slowly, it subsided before he felt a stronger shove against his rib cage. The pressure repeated itself several times until he found it irritating. Blurry vision suddenly returned to him as the pressing shove became pain.

"Wake up. Wake up!" someone shouted.

A gasp of air shot into his lungs, reducing the pain. Samov Zin was crouched next to him, pushing against him.

"Stop kicking me!" Jovan growled.

Zin fell back into a seated position. "I wasn't!" he shouted.

"Why does my side hurt?" Jovan said, trying to roll himself over. The pain had just become a burn inside his chest. "How long have you been here?"

"Not long. You've taken a short panting breath every few minutes. I imagine that's why your chest hurts."

"Sit me up," Jovan said.

"You don't have time to take a breath. As I made my way here I saw the guards forming up at the castle gates. I would guess they're coming for you."

"I suspect you're right," Jovan said. "The little monster said as much."

"Monster?"

"Yes, Leaf's twin: Periphina."

"I told you, Vlada had a girl, not twins."

"It would appear," Jovan said, hauling himself to his feet. "That you were wrong."

He took hold of his head and leaned against the counter.

"Are you well enough to walk?" Zin asked.

"My head and side are throbbing," Jovan replied. "But I can walk well enough."

"Good," Zin said, leaning toward the window. "Because there are about twenty soldiers marching down the street. An old lady is pointing in this direction."

"Out the back," Jovan said, as he stumbled past the counter and out into the back garden.

It was a small courtyard, the same size as the shop, and open to the sky. Jovan winced at the bright light, and covered his eyes with both hands.

"Jovan?"

"The light is too bright," Jovan muttered.

"Well, it's not long until sunset. Until then, you'll have to trust me."

"That's a tall order," Jovan said. "How did you escape the inn where I left you?"

"I'll tell you, after we get you over this back wall." He formed his hands into a stirrup and motioned Jovan over with his head.

"City guard!" Jovan heard behind him as he set his foot into Zin's hands and grabbed the top of the wall. He pulled himself over and fell onto the cobbled alley behind. Zin was soon up and over, and crouched beside him.

"Did they see us?" Jovan asked, pressing hard on his eyes.

"No. They were pounding on the door as I came up and over."

Jovan felt Zin's hand on his shoulder.

"Are you going to be all right?"

"Slant hit me between the eyes with some sort of magic. The light really hurts my eyes."

"Then we'll travel by dark," Zin said. "But in which direction?"

"South," Jovan said.

"What is south?"

"That's where Kallidova travels with Leaf, and where Slant and Periphina follow."

"How did you gather that they are traveling south?"

"It's the only direction they'll find allies. If half of what Slant said is true, then he and Kallidova, both Havats, will have allies there. Maybe she's even making her way back to Rightness."

"Let's get you away from here and see if we can make it safely to the south gate." Zin helped Jovan to his feet, pulling Jovan's arm over his shoulder. "Now, lean on me like you're drunk."

"Why are you helping me?" Jovan asked as they hobbled quickly through the alleyways. "You could just as easily have turned on me, or left town on your own."

Jovan felt Zin's hesitation in his shoulders before answering. "Prince Zelmir's father and mine have a long-running vendetta against one another. My father was effectively castrated when the king took the throne, but the king also knows that if he had my father killed, half of Balatar would turn on him. The prince doesn't have the same wisdom not to have that done to me or my father when he takes the throne."

"So? Then leave."

"I could. But where's the fun in that? Maybe my pranks will make it into bards' songs after Zelmir has me killed. I like to think that all this work to make him miserable does something."

"Again I ask: why help me?"

"I'm owed money by Kallidova. So I'll come with you and see if I can't get ahold of that before I go off on some other adventure. Maybe I'll go visit the Kharavadziy caravan cities." Zin sighed. "But also because you're a good man, trying to do something right. It's refreshing. Maybe taking a break from my escapades will provide me some perspective."

"That still doesn't explain why you're helping me."

Zin smiled. "Fine, I'm not sure I know why, either. I'll have to get back to you on that."

Jovan shook his head but decided that was as good an answer as he was likely to get.

They came to a large square. The light of the setting sun flashed against a large yellow building as they crossed.

"Six gods!" Jovan cursed as the light hit his closed eyes.

"The guards we just passed were questioning a bearded old man," Zin said. "And the guards at the next block have stopped a young man with half the length of beard you had. It was smart of you to shave it off."

Jovan reached up and touched his face. "Where are we going?"

"Toward the sea. There are a few places there where I know we can seek refuge."

Suddenly, Jovan felt Zin jerk him sideways into the cool of a dark alley.

"All right," Zin said. "Can you see now?"

Jovan cautiously opened his eyes. The alley ran north to south, with tall windowless walls rising up several stories.

"What is this?"

"They call it Passers Alley. It'll take us down to South Scrounge."

"Is there a street in this town you don't know?" Jovan asked.

"I doubt it. I've gotten into my fair share of trouble since I was a boy."

"Does that have anything to do with how you got out of the inn after I left with the Bear?"

"It may," Zin said with a twinkle in his eyes. "The innkeeper probably would have left me there until tomorrow morning. Fortunately for me, I've known Bilya for some time. After you left, she let me out—probably felt guilty for deceiving me."

"Samov Zin!" a voice shouted from behind them.

Three guards stood at the head of the alley.

"Don't bolt," Zin said.

Jovan reach up and tugged at his ear as the three guards approached.

"Commander Grigg?" Zin asked.

"One and the same," the leader said, smiling.

"Are you still up to the same old tricks?" Zin asked.

"Usually. You?"

"I never stopped."

"Word from the castle is to be watching out for you."

"Me? Why me?"

"The prince misses your company. But we're also on the lookout for a man about as big as your friend here, with a long beard down to his chest."

"I hadn't heard that," Zin said.

"I suppose I didn't hear that either," Grigg said. "But I'd have to be persuaded of that."

"How did you know I'd be taking Passers Alley?" Zin asked.

"I didn't. I saw you enter. Or flee into it, I should say."

"I'd like to move along, if you'll allow."

"I might."

"What will it run me this time?"

The commander turned to the others. "I'll meet you back on the street. These aren't the men we were told to watch for."

The men turned without question and left.

"I want to know how you beat Alvich at bone sticks a year ago. And I heard you know where the prince's copy of *The Edvin Tales* is."

Zin reached into his coat and produced two bone sticks. He handed them to the commander.

"Feel them in your hands," Zin said.

Commander Grigg pursed his lips.

"They're weighted," Zin said.

Realization dawned in the man's face.

"It takes practice to use them right, but I would wager you'll figure it out."

The commander put the bone sticks into his own satchel. "And the book?"

"Try at the top of the second stack of law books. Behind the fourth or fifth volume. I'm sure you'll receive quite a gift from the prince if you turn it in."

The man smiled. "I never saw you. Perhaps I'll never see you again."

"I expect you won't," Zin replied.

Zin turned and began walking. Jovan fell in alongside him.

"Commander Grigg is the most openly corrupt soldier in the empire," Zin muttered as they moved out of earshot.

"What's the catch?" Jovan asked.

"What do you mean?"

"I gather you just cheated him. If only by the huge grin on your face."

"Those were just normal bone sticks. Nothing special about them. But I doubt he'll ever get the chance to find out they aren't any use."

"Why is that?"

"Because I left a note in the prince's book saying that if anyone ever turned it in, that I traded its location for my freedom. It'll expose Grigg as corrupt."

"You're a wicked man," Jovan said.

"I can be. Yes."

"I'm going to regret associating with you, aren't I?"

"No, I don't hold anything against you."

"Not tying you up in a chair and interrogating you?"

"I consider that excusable. I've met your little boy. I'd go to great lengths for him, too, if he was mine."

"I've learned quite a lot today," Jovan said. "What haven't you been fully forthright about?"

"What do you mean?"

"Slant has revised stories he's told, and I've learned some things about him."

"For example?"

"That he and Sephaly Valle-Brons had a relationship with one another, for one."

"I could have told you that," Zin said.

"Or that Kallidova was mistress to the king, and mothered both Prince Zelmir and Sephaly."

"While Zelmir's mother was never publicly named, the king declared him his heir, since his dead wife never mothered one herself. It was the same time I was born—I only know of long-dead court gossip. But Kallidova was the name always thrown around by my mother and her friends."

"I also know that you and Slant have known each other far longer than you first led us to believe at the Blue Tower."

"Ah," Zin said, stopping in his tracks. "He told you that, did he?"

"No. You did."

"I did?"

"You just said that you could have told me that Slant and Sephaly had a relationship. Yet at the Blue Tower you said you only knew Slant by description. How long have you two been working together?"

They came out into another square as the torches were lit.

"Slavint Yunev and I go back to our youth," Zin said.

Jovan replied with a low growl.

"Are you sure you're not a Medved yourself? You growl enough."

"Just continue."

"I knew Slavint as the nephew of Cham Yunev, the king's chamberlain, back in the day. Of course, when King Ihor learned the Yunevs were Havies, he sent the whole lot out of town with stones flying overhead. He has long hated Havies. Most do. But I've heard King Ihor hated them even more after he was seduced and bedded by some Havie girl. Putting two and two together, I'd guess that was Kallidova."

"Havat," Jovan said.

"Yes. I'm referring to the Havats."

"No," Jovan corrected. "Stop calling them 'Havies.' Say Havat."

"Why? Are you one?"

"My grandmother was. I was raised Umernnost. But that's no excuse to disparage them."

"Fine. Havat. I don't know what became of Slant after that. The rumor was he had been admitted to a vedmak school. Nevertheless, a few years later he came back to town with a girl on his arm, and one we all knew well: Sephaly Valle-Brons.

"He was very secretive when it came to his past, but word was he had been kicked out of the school. I'm not very informed about that, as that was about the same time that Vlada was seduced by Zelmir and got with child. Her family disowned her, and Sephaly and Slant became her constant companions."

"Doing what?" Jovan asked.

"As I said, I don't know. I resorted to pettiness and did everything I could to make the prince's life miserable for taking Vlada from me."

The sun had dropped below the horizon, though the sky was still starless. People ducked quickly into inns as guards marched down the middle of the street, eyeing everyone that passed by. Two guards stopped and looked up at a woman beckoning them from a window, as another lit the red candle in her own window nearby.

"You know that little girl, Periphina?"

Jovan's brows rose. "What about her?"

"She was quite the talk in the castle kitchen a few years ago."

"Why is that?"

"Barely able to walk, she was talking and holding full conversations with those who raised her."

"Who did raise her?"

"That's the funny thing: both the cook and Mamm Cillis claim that she's theirs. But that little girl always seemed to do what she wanted and go where she chose. Since I arrived back in town, I've heard that she was acting as the chief scribe's apprentice, mixing up inks."

"But she's four."

"And yet everyone could see her reasoning and often gave her what she wanted. Quite the little manipulator."

"Leaf always seemed wiser than his years to me," Jovan said. "It follows that she would also be intelligent."

"Albeit wicked. She is, after all, the prince's child."

"But so is Leaf."

"Yes, but if that is so, I'd wager he takes after his mother."

"This Vlada you've mentioned. She was kind?"

"Naive perhaps. A smart girl, too. But yes. Kind. And beautiful."

"Is that why you're helping me? Because he reminds you of Vlada?"

"The best part of who she was."

"Is," Jovan said. "I think she's still alive."

"What makes you say that?"

Jovan shrugged. "No one has said she's dead. And for some reason, Kallidova felt that Leaf needed to be raised in Geruz. I have a feeling she is somewhere near there, though I'm not sure where. If we can catch up with Kallidova, perhaps we can find out where Vlada is."

"There," Zin said. A huge grin growing on his face. "That is why I'm going to help you. Not for Leaf. Not even for you. Just for a chance to see her again."

They came to the square in front of the southern gate. It sat in the cleft of a split granite wall several hundred feet high.

"Have you ever gone through the Vhelr Pass?" Zin asked.

"Can't say I have."

"Once we're through the gates, it's a two-mile canyon to the gate at the other end. It's filled with houses and inns too cheap to be in the city proper. Most there support the guards that watch the pass. They'll be more than likely to rat us out."

"We'll be pheasants in an open field," Jovan said.

"Yes, we will. But it's that or find a ship that's willing to smuggle us, yet honorable enough to not sell us out at the first sign of trouble."

"That's not likely to happen." Jovan turned back to the gate and considered his next move. There were ten guards standing out front, all very aware of those that passed by.

Jovan saw a spark of recognition in Zin's eyes as the man eyed the guards at the gate. "Captain Rillen, I believe?"

He broke away and confidently walked toward the gate. The guards all turned and watched him approach. One of them stepped forward, wearing gold stripes on his uniform.

"Samov Zin?"

"Captain Rillen," Zin said formally. Jovan walked up to stand just behind Zin.

"What trouble are you in now, Zin?" Rillen asked.

"Trouble?" Zin said with a smile.

"It's a little late for you to be leaving town, isn't it? Or are you on a mission? Looking out for the smith we're supposed to be watching for?"

Jovan blanched and thanked the gods it was dark out.

"Have you seen him yet?" Zin asked.

"No, but the night is young. Who is this?"

Zin stepped back and slapped Jovan on the shoulder.

"He is a driver from the castle. We're on our way south to Kelnoz to pick up a delivery of ale for the prince's next revelry."

"No dray horse and cart?"

"The two of us are splitting the cost paid to us for the cart down and we'll still have plenty of time to get it back."

"We'll have to log it," one of the guards said.

"If you log it then I'll have to state that I'm bringing back three full barrel's worth of Kelnoz's finest aged ale."

"Yeah, so?" Rillen asked.

"I can't bring you back some additional ale for your own barracks then."

The guards all looked at each other, considering.

"You going to charge us for this one?"

"No," Zin offered. "I'm sure a few pieces of silver won't go missing. I'll pick up a small barrel for you. Maybe they'll have a ham or two to spare."

"I hope you bring back more than that, " Rillen said.

"Why is that?"

"You know the boys in this pass. If this is how you're going to get by me, I suppose you'll be offering the same to every guard captain who stops you. By the time you come back through, will there even be a single barrel left for me?"

Zin laughed. "You're a shrewd man, Rillen. What do you propose?"

"I'll see you through the pass. But any of these excess barrels you bring back make it to my barracks and no one else's."

"I would be obligated to do so," Zin said, holding up his hands in mock defeat.

"I expect more than a single cask."

"You do this for me and my friend here," Zin said, "and I'll see to it that you get an entire wagon full of beer. Then you can sell it to your fellow guard captains for more silver than you paid for it."

"Which is nothing..."

"As you say," Zin said, bowing deeply.

CHAPTER 27 — VHELRAD

"How long do you want to walk?" Zin asked as they came down the long hill leading away from the last gate in the canyon. Full dark had settled overhead and the stars shone bright.

"As long as we can," Jovan said. "If we can find trace of their passing we'll know we're going in the right direction. If we don't, we'll continue on, and hope fate is on our side. The farther we push, the better off we'll be. The girl may be smart beyond her years, but she's still four. She'll need to sleep. And so will Kallidova."

"If they ride by carriage, they can stop and get new ones," Zin said. "With a hired driver they could travel without ceasing."

"They'll have to change carriages at some point. Maybe we'll hit a lucky break."

They walked until morning, and came up a rise that looked down into the Vhelrad lowlands and looked back toward the Vhelr Pass. Dust was kicking up around the gates those many miles behind.

"I'd say the prince has picked up our scent," Zin said.

"We can't keep ahead of him."

"I beg to differ," Zin replied. "There is something you must understand about the prince. He is a juggernaut of peculiarities."

"What do you mean by that?" Jovan asked.

"First, he must have his rest. And he must eat. I've never known someone to be so regimented in that aspect. He will have to stop to rest the horses and eat, and at night he will not travel. So, if we continue to walk without ceasing today, we'll stay ahead of him. We've got twenty miles on him. And his horses, especially if it's a large cavalcade, will not make more than thirty miles themselves. By nightfall, I suspect you and I can walk another twenty to Allyun, a market town, where I expect we'll find signs of Kallidova and the children."

"But if we make twenty miles a day and the prince makes thirty, he's sure to catch up."

"Not if we turn off at Allyun and travel through the forest road. The prince will no doubt slow his pace to be wary of brigands."

"Then let's continue," Jovan said.

"And pray to the Four that Zelmir does as I say."

"Pray to the fifth."

"Vhezin? I pray to him every day," Zin said. "If I could call any god my own, it's the Luck Sable."

"Best beware," Jovan said. "His brother always prowls near."

"I'm aware of that. The thrill of his watching what I've done in spiteful vengeance toward Zelmir since the day he took my love away, is an addiction stronger than any drink, game, or girl."

They passed village after village, finally coming to one where a chatty old man had been awake in the middle of the night when Kallidova had driven through in a carriage. She had been polite but direct in watering the horses, who had worked up a lather, despite the cool night. They hadn't stayed long, but the old man described Kallidova and Slant exactly.

"If the horses were worn to a lather, then they would need to switch within a few villages of here," Zin said.

"That also confirms that Slant and Periphina caught up with Kallidova and Leaf."

"I had assumed as much," Zin replied.

"When is the best time to cut away from our track and go up district?"

"Ten more miles to Allyun," Zin replied. "That is really the best place for her to switch horses, as well. If we press on to that town, we'll catch word and see how hard they left."

Several hours before sundown they came to Allyun. It sat in between two hills to the north and south, with roads running in all four directions, including one that climbed up the southern hill. The work of the day was drawing to an end and the men were making their way to the largest inn for entertainment.

The scents of roasted lamb called to them from a signless tavern. As they entered, a woman proudly wearing Havat orange cut slices from the lamb roasting on the hearth, while her daughter handed rolls to the men who lined up to get their share. The wine they served at the bar near the hearth had been warmed, served in large, wide bowls.

"Know of anyone who will help move these sleek black-hides to a better market?" one man was saying to another.

"I think I got the better deal," the man said. "My plowing was already done, so I could afford to trade my drays to the woman. Then she went and gave me good silver on top of that. If I sell three off for a set of saddled geldings, I can have them on my plow by next year."

"What about the fourth?"

"She lamed him. But that's fine with me," the man said with a chuckle. "I'll stud him. It'll pump some fresh blood into the town horses, I should think."

"I'm a bit of an expert on horses," Zin offered.

The two men spun around.

"Who are you?" one said. "You're new to town."

"Just passing through. Plan to be gone by morning."

"You know horses, though? Where are you from?"

"My friend and I just came down from the capital. It's not often you hear of a horse come from there."

"I never said the horses came from the capital," the man said.

Zin blushed. "I'm always making assumptions that get me into trouble. But you did say they were black and there were four of them. Most carriages in the capital are driven by four black horses."

"I thought you knew you were in the capital because the prince always found you out and spat on you," the man replied sarcastically.

"He can just about spit on anyone in the city from his highest tower," Zin said. The men laughed. "Let me buy you a bowl of wine and tell you about the time I snuck a handful of burrs into the prince's boots."

They took a table together.

"You said you bought the horses from a lady?"

"Lady, maybe, but definitely a shrewd bargainer. She had a man and two children with her."

"Two children?" Jovan asked.

"Now, Jovan," Zin said, changing the subject as the man looked at the two of them in confusion. "About those burrs..."

The morning came too early.

They rose at dawn and made their way to the town center. A few people meandered about their morning chores. Zin had not fared well from his revelry. He closed his eyes and walked blindly at times. The trickle of a spring in the middle of the square washed away most of the noise and seemed to calm the man.

"Shall we head east now?" Jovan asked.

"No," Zin said tersely.

"Yesterday you said..."

"I know what I said. But if we head east, then anyone following us will continue to follow us in that direction. If we leave town from the south and go a mile or two before we cut east, then Zelmir follows in the direction of Kallidova and Slant."

"But that will put Leaf in danger."

"I don't think that Zelmir can catch up with them. But if they catch word that he's on their trail, they'll move with enough urgency to keep their pace up. We know we're following them. Kallidova and Slant don't. So let's keep Kallidova and the Prince both on edge."

Jovan walked away from Zin, who groaned as he worked his way to his feet, holding his head with one hand. The road moved through several easy switchbacks up the hill, and then gently topped the rise. Small brooks bubbled out of the hillside, but did not moisten the raised stone walkway. The entire hill was saturated with life, and in the shade, hidden from the southern sun, the birds and frogs muttered out their calls.

As they approached the crest, the sun shone brightly in their eyes. Zin walked directly behind Jovan, using him as a barrier. At the top, Jovan stopped and looked down into the lands beyond, just making out the sea far to the west. A smoggy smear marked the city of Horodoz many miles to the south. Zin put his hand on Jovan's shoulder and he turned around to look north. Dust was billowing up from the cavalcade halfway to the Vhelr Mountains.

"That will be Zelmir," Zin said. "He's taking his time. Thinks this a game. He'll stop at Allyun tonight."

"And if Kallidova swapped out horses yesterday morning, where do you think that puts her now?"

"She likely had trouble switching out horses again until this morning. So that might put her at that smear of woods halfway from here to Horodoz. That's where I think we'll start cutting her off by going east. Once she reaches Horodoz, she'll be able to switch horses every thirty miles quite easily."

"And she'll be there by sunset?"

"I don't doubt it," Zin said.

"Why not go west now then?"

"We'll be eyed with suspicion by the serfs of Vhelrad. And once we're in the Havoy District we'll be eyed as outsiders."

"Except in the Havoy District, I'm not an outsider, remember?"

"Very well. Then let's cut down this hill at least and make our way west."

"To Rightness."

"Very well. Toward Rightness."

They walked down the hill and along the curves that rounded each hillock. Havat farmers sang in traditional folk songs as they plowed and planted seeds in rows. Young girls ran water between men and the boys chased off birds that brazenly attacked carts of seeds. Each wore a bit of orange on their person openly, bearing their heritage without shame, as it was in towns where they found themselves in the minority.

"I always wonder how it is they've continued to thrive," Zin said. "Every generation they get pushed down and trod upon."

"But Havats always rise," Jovan said. "You can't keep the orange apple down."

"What do you mean?"

"The Havats. They're the orange apple that grew in a grove of red apples. Even though the other trees tried to press in on them, the orange tree never stopped growing.

Pruned and cut back, it always grows, because the roots grow strong. Their heritage is strong."

"So the red apples are?"

"Everyone else."

"We have heritage. The Belkhali have a history of their own."

"Yes," Jovan said. "One of destruction and invasion. You drove out the Ancient Peoples and took their land, and then turned and stole from the Havats of ancient Havv."

"And what have the Havats given?"

Jovan held his hands out in front of him. "This land. Cultivated by the sweat on their backs."

"At least they make pretty girls," Zin said, eyeing a girl stopping for a drink from a water wagon. She blushed and turned away. A large man came over and put his arm protectively over her shoulders.

The small forest Zin had pointed out at Allyun cradled a small lumber mill town. The drinking hall in the center stood beside a taller Havat temple built around a massive tree growing several hundred feet into the sky.

Zin moved ahead of Jovan as he paused to look up the long trunk.

"I hope Leaf got to see this when they passed through."

"If they left Allyun with fresh horses, then I expect they did."

The din of lumberyard workers soaking their palates with ale and their arms with friendship came through the doors. Zin and Jovan strode in and walked toward the counter where two young men, obviously twins, dished out bowls of beer to everyone. They wore orange shirts under black vests and bore broad smiles on their sun-tanned faces. One of them turned to regard them. Jovan saw the smile fade to a more forced one.

"Good evening, sirs," he said.

Jovan nodded, and then reached out and put several coins on the counter. "A couple of bowls for the road-weary?"

Two wide bowls filled with a dark ale soon appeared before them.

"To your health," Jovan said to the innkeeper as he lifted and drank deeply.

"Yes," the man said curtly.

"Did we intrude on something?" Jovan asked. "We only just arrived in town."

"Nothing too big. The last town elder died a month or so back and a new one was just selected. We're drinking to him today."

"Then to the new elder's health and wisdom," Jovan said, lifting his bowl again. "And may your last elder and my grandmother walk the green fields together and look down on their descendants with cheer."

The man seemed to visibly relax when he said this.

"You're Havat?"

"My father was, but he married out."

"Still, you're welcome here. Your friend, though, ought to watch himself." He indicated past his brother to Zin, who was telling a story at the other end of the bar, and the men who listened didn't seem impressed.

"I will see if I can't just move him along. He gets chatty after a bowl or two."

"What brings you through our town?"

"We're actually looking for someone. Did you see a black carriage, like one you might see in the capital, come through here?"

The man leaned forward on the bar, his hands firmly planted. "I'd suggest you leave now and keep walking to wherever you're headed. You won't find a bed to rest your head on."

His brother came and joined him. "Trouble, Ull?"

"This man is asking after a black carriage, Bol."

Bol turned and reached down below the bar and came up holding a stick, with a long sharpened spike sticking out of the side.

Jovan sighed.

"Kallidova is a Havat," he muttered to himself. "Of course she traveled through here and appealed to your better natures to keep anyone asking after her from continuing to do so."

"Chavotz chlai," the first twin shouted.

The entire room went silent and they turned to look at the bar.

"What's the trouble?" Zin said jovially.

"Quiet, Samov," Jovan said. "It is not the time nor the place."

"Chlai!" the other twin shouted.

Whoever wasn't standing, suddenly was. A few drew daggers or pulled out walking sticks from under the table.

"Fifty against two is hardly fair," Zin said as two men grabbed his arms and pinned them behind his back.

"Ull and Bol?" Jovan said, putting out both hands on the bar. "I mean you no harm. I don't even mean the woman I'm pursuing harm. But she took my boy. And I have to get him back."

"Ha!" Ull said. "You are after the boy, but you didn't mention the girl, his sister? He must not belong to you if you don't also claim her."

Jovan shook his head and looked at the floor. "You don't understand."

Rough hands took hold of Jovan's arms. He didn't fight against them. They dragged him over to a table and forced him and Zin onto the bench to sit. Two large mill workers held Jovan's arms. Ull reached into Jovan's coat and pulled out the wroughtwood sword.

"This is a finely crafted piece," he said. "I would have hated to meet the working end of the blade inside."

"Please," Jovan said. "I don't mean you any harm. Just let me go."

"She was very convincing. She said you'd go down fighting, but here you're just letting us sit you down. Was she lying?"

"She wasn't lying," Jovan growled. "But I'm not going to fight you."

"And why is that?" Bol asked, coming up next to his brother.

"Because I know a fight I can't win. And I swore to my grandmother I'd never kill a Havat. Now let me go."

"We can't," Ull said.

"This man, Jovan?" Zin said, indicating with his head. "He's a close friend of the Bear in Khorapesh."

"I doubt that," Bol said.

"And he's fought a vodyanov and lived," Zin continued.

A few of the men let out a mocking laugh.

"And he's boxed the Boyar of the Ring, Zvediz, and won."

Ull's face went flat. "Our father fought in the ring when he was younger. He fought Zvediz and nearly lost his life. There is no way you ever fought, nor beat the unbeaten Zvediz."

"Actually," a voice said from behind Jovan. "It's true. He did."

The man who spoke circled around and came to stand before Jovan and Zin. Slant stood back out of arm's reach, faking his calm while his fear shone in his eyes.

"He also forced one vedmak to give an Oath, and he showed enough mercy to another that the vedmak turned his color and came back to help him out."

"What in the Black Fox's Den are you doing here?" Zin asked.

"Kallidova thinks I stayed behind to make sure you both stay put. But I've spent two very long days on the road with that monster Periphina, and I want to make sure you get to them before it's too late. I think you, Jovan, are the only man who can do the right thing."

CHAPTER 28 — PATHS

The road east from Verin rose gently into the forested Zhorodath district. The undergrowth had been cut back several hundred yards into the trees, though frequently Jovan saw lines of smoke rising up out of the brush, marking woodsmen, or less than legal tradesmen making their living.

Slant and Zin walked ahead, catching up with one another, putting aside the subterfuge they had led for so long.

"What caused you and Zvediz to work together?"

"A job for the Bear a year back," Slant said. "Once that concluded, we continued to do the same thing, from town to town, until we ended up in Righteousness."

"I find it hard to believe you made much money conning conners."

"I made a lot of enemies, sure," Slant said, laughing to himself. "Most of them paid us just to leave town. That's where it helped having Zved with me—most would send someone to rough us up. Needless to say, it was exciting."

"And now you're just smuggling magic children?"

Slant stopped and eyed Jovan, then looked back at Zin. "No. Not any longer. From now on, I think I'll be in the business of helping those children, though I don't know how anyone could help that little monster Periphina."

"What caused you to change your tune?" Jovan asked.

"As I said, traveling with that creature got to me. And led me to other suspicions."

"Such as?" Zin asked.

"I'd rather not go into it right now. Best to wait until nightfall."

They set up a fire back from the road as night descended upon them. Zin was a good shot with the short bow they'd requisitioned from the twin barkeeps, and quickly had three braces of small rabbits over the fire.

As they finished eating, Slant, who'd been uncharacteristically quiet while they ate, turned to Zin.

"Would you mind terribly sleeping apart from Jovan and I?"

"Really?" Zin asked.

"Yes. There are things we need to discuss privately and the information is not mine to share with you."

"Very well," the man said, though Jovan was sure he didn't appreciate being kept in the dark.

He picked up his bed roll and walked off to find a place to sleep, or at least somewhere he could eavesdrop without being detected.

"Let's chat for a bit," Slant said.

Jovan held up a hand. "Before you begin, I want you to understand where the two of us stand."

Slant opened his mouth to speak, and then resigned to just a nod.

"I no longer trust you," Jovan said. "I can't say I ever fully trusted you. I think you're a liar, a cheat, and I suspect you've been working against me since the beginning. I will take little of what you say to heart, but I will hear you out. And when this is all over, I hope never to see your face again, or I just might break it."

"I accept that," Slant said. "Please understand, I have never been against you. I have done everything as Kallidova has asked and now, I do what I do for Leaf, and what I believe he is."

"What does that mean?" Jovan asked.

"I fear that something far darker than just imbuing occurred before the children's birth."

"What do you mean?"

"How many twins have you known?" Slant asked.

"Only a couple, perhaps."

"Well, we Havats have something in our blood that makes them, and often. I grew up with several pairs of twins as distant cousins."

"You mentioned that Kallidova is a Havat," Jovan said, "so it makes sense that she gave birth to Sephaly and Zelmir as twins, and then that the prince sired twins."

"Twins usually run on the mother's side. The Havat have delved deep into the understanding of this. But there's more to it. As I said, I grew up around twins. They tend to not only look alike but have similar mannerisms."

"That makes sense," Jovan said. "They spend enough time with their twin that they begin to emulate one another."

"Yes, but each will have differences as well."

"What's your point?"

"Leaf and Perif have identical mannerisms. And they've not known each other for more than a couple of weeks. Those mannerisms are perfect mirrors of each other. Did you know that Perif can write? She's been trying to teach Leaf to. And he writes with the opposite side. Even when their backs are turned to each other, their reactions to things around them are identical."

"I don't understand what you're getting at," Jovan said.

"Seeing them mirror one another got me thinking. What if they aren't twins?"

"What do you mean 'not twins?'" Jovan asked.

"I seem to recall us talking once about how the Fifth and Sixth came to be."

"Yes. They were once Fate, and the other gods cleft Fate in two to become Luck and Bad Luck."

"Exactly."

Jovan stared into the fire. "You're saying you think that Leaf and Periphina are the product of something similar?"

"I don't think it happened by accident," Slant replied. "You see, when I fled the vedmak school, I took a set of books. They detailed how to imbue. Once Vlada was pregnant, Sephaly was called by the prince and Vlada to help them. I think she helped to imbue them."

"Did those same books also hold the secrets of rivening?" Jovan asked.

"They didn't. There is no given knowledge to how to do it. But I just spent several days with Leaf and Perif. It made me ponder the fact that Sephaly and Zelmir are twins, and I realized how many characteristics they share. They were not raised with one another, either, but as 'cousins.'"

"So you think..."

"I think Kallidova may have riven her own children within her. And perhaps taught it to her daughter."

"Pair that with imbuing..." Jovan left it hanging.

The following day, they could hear the Zhor, the great waterfall that fell from the walls of Zhorod, long before they could see it. Light poured onto the road far ahead, indicating a break in the trees. Zin picked up his speed and took the rise. He stopped and overlooked the meeting of the two great rivers. Jovan came alongside him, though Slant kept back from the view.

The Horod flowed around a hill and into a bowl of water from below, while the Zhor fell for several hundred feet, pouring out of the white stoned city that rose above it. If the castle in Khorapesh scrambled and clung to black cliffs, Zhorod knew its own importance. The entire city focused first around the falls, and then around the tall white tower at its center. With the spray of the waterfall it looked like a city perched on a cloud.

"Are we going to go into Zhorod?" Zin asked.

"I don't think that's advisable," Jovan said. "We'd lose time there."

"Zelmir will, though," Slant said, coming up behind them. He was looking across the river toward the curve of the forest they'd just come from.

Jovan saw movement a mile back down the road. The flash of steel appeared in the shadows.

"We're still a mile to the city gate," Zin said as he turned and started down the road.

"They'll catch up to us before then," Slant replied.

Jovan turned and started to march, then picked up speed and ran.

"There's a road," Slant huffed, "that leads north. If we can get to that before they come in sight of us, we can go up that a ways, and watch to see what happens."

"And if we don't?" Zin asked.

"Then we'll have failed," Jovan said, and picked up his speed.

They came to a bend in the road that curved toward a half-walled causeway running around the cliff edge of the bowl and to the city gate. Slant suddenly turned off and into the brush. Zin followed, and Jovan stopped, looking up at them. Six feet above, they looked back over a ledge.

"Come on!" Slant said, reaching a hand down from the re-taining wall.

Jovan glanced over his shoulder back down the road. He just caught sight of the first soldiers coming into view. He took the man's hand. Slant and Zin hoisted Jovan up into the bushes. Jovan found he'd come up onto a small foot path that led to a smaller second gate to the city.

Slant pulled down on Jovan's shirt, and they all fell to the ground, peeking over the ledge as the prince's cavalcade approached.

Ten soldiers, obviously road-weary, pressed on at a forced march in front of the carriage pulled by four black horses. The prince's personal guard clung to the outside of the carriage. They approached the city gate, which quickly opened and admitted them.

"They didn't slow," Slant said. "So I would hope they didn't see us."

"That means we'll be walking all night again," Jovan replied.

"True," Slant said. "First we have to circle the city, which is not easy. The hills around the bowl are difficult to climb."

"Wouldn't it be easier to just go through Zhorod then?" Zin asked.

"If I wasn't being hunted," Jovan replied. "And if you and Slant weren't so well-known to the prince and his men, then yes."

"We could take horses for a day," Slant offered. "I bet we make it half way to Righteousness."

"I agree with Slant," Zin said. "Let's take a chance and go through the city, and see if we can get some mounts."

"I might know someone who can help us," Slant said.

"Who's that?" Jovan asked.

"She has somewhat of an ill reputation," Slant said.

"Mamm Soscha?" Zin asked, cocking an eyebrow.

"You know her, as well?" Slant asked.

"Yes. I'd bet gold the prince is staying with her, too. Are you on good terms with her?" Zin asked.

"Well enough," Slant replied. "This gives me an idea, actually."

Jovan begrudgingly followed the two of them into the city, built in the same architectural style as Rightness, though on a much larger scale. As they passed Soscha's house, Jovan refused to enter and crossed the street to spend a long, restless hour in a tavern.

When Slant appeared next to his elbow, Jovan almost fell off his stool.

"How did you do that?" Jovan hissed.

"I didn't use any magic, if that's what you're asking."

"What did the two of you do?"

"The prince's stablehand is seeking fresh horses. Soscha let me down into the stables. Zin meted out his own little prank on the prince's carriage, while I may have drugged the stablehand and stolen the four horses he had just requisitioned."

"Will that slow him down?"

"The horses from today will be rested, but we'll have the fresh ones. Can you ride?"

"Well enough."

"Then let's get on the road before Zelmir learns otherwise."

It took some time for Jovan to adjust to the saddle, and the horses didn't appreciate being ridden in the dark. As the dawn began to break, they were riding at an even canter. The road dropped down into a small gully with steep sides.

Zin and Slant slowed at the sight of smoke around the corner. The sound of an old man singing a trail song came to them. Jovan nudged his horse forward and around the corner to a welcome sight. The old trapper crouched over a fire. Next to him sat the skins of several red badgers, while the fatty flesh hung skewered over a heavily smoking fire.

"Greetings," Jovan called out from a hundred feet away, pulling his horse up close.

"Well, what are you doing here?" the old man asked. "And where is the boy?"

He was mostly unchanged, though he had a heavy pack leaning nearby that he hadn't had the autumn before, and his beard was an inch longer.

"I'm returning to him now," Jovan replied. "May we stop and share with you?"

"Not much I can give you, but I'll be here for a day or two drying out this meat for tack."

Jovan dismounted and approached. The other two did likewise.

"These are my travel companions," Jovan said, though he did not offer their names.

"Nice horses you got there," the old man said. "Though it looks like you wore them out."

"Was your winter a success?" Jovan asked, eyeing his pack.

"It wasn't bad," the old man said. "I'm taking the last few hides to the market in Zhorod myself."

"You said you'd be here a while?" Jovan asked.

"I did."

"How much gold would you require to do me a favor?"

"Seeing as how you spared me a great deal of trouble last autumn, I'd say I'd do it for nothing. What did you have in mind?"

They found the trapper's suggested path easily, and it took little persuasion to convince the old man to return the horses to the prince when he came by, declaring he found them farther south of where they had come upon him, rather than the easterly road they now traveled.

As night fell and their feet dragged, they came over a rise looking toward the Red Mountains and their snow-capped peaks. The path they had followed ran parallel to a lesser used road.

"You can just make out the top of the Temple of Negligent Assurance," Slant said, pointing off to the south east.

The setting sun caught the white spire.

"How far would you say?" Jovan asked.

"Probably another thirty miles."

"I can't walk another step," Zin said. "Two days and a night is too long to travel."

"I agree," Slant said. "But Zelmir won't have anywhere to stop tonight."

"He might set up camp," Jovan offered.

"He might. But he might not."

"We'll stop for a couple of hours. Then we'll walk as far as we can and do that again. Come dawn, we can push for Rightness."

Slant agreed to take the first watch. Jovan and Zin found a large tree to lean up against and sought sleep.

The thundering of hoofs jolted Jovan awake.

"Looks like someone is in a hurry to get somewhere," Slant whispered. He crouched next to Jovan and looked past the tree toward the road.

The sound of the carriage and horses pulling up short rang through the woods.

"Why are they stopping?" Jovan hissed.

"I heard them coming a long way off, so I knocked a small tree down onto the road."

"Why?"

"If they are going to catch up, or even get ahead of us, I'd like to stop them for enough time to listen in. Come on. There's a spot ahead that will give us a good view."

Their talk seemed to wake Zin, who stretched his arms and came to. He watched the other two crawling up and over several fallen trees and followed suit.

Four soldiers had disembarked from the top of the prince's carriage and joined the others examining the tree that lay in their way.

"Get it moved!" Prince Zelmir shouted. He was leaning out of the carriage and held his rod in his hand.

"It's not that big," one soldier said, "but it's branchy."

"I don't need your botanical acumen. I wish to be abed."

"Yes, my prince," the man said with a bow.

"If this fresh-looking tree was dropped here, it was done so purposefully," another man said. "It means the old man lied and they are on this road."

"I told you he was lying," the prince whined. "What I don't understand is how they've been able to stay ahead of us for so long."

"My prince," the first soldier said. "As was suggested, they may be traveling long hours. Both day and night."

"Not for this many days," the prince scoffed.

"I was in this area a couple years back," another soldier said. "I think there's an inn not far from here. We could complete the journey into Rightness in the morning."

"Those are words I've longed to hear. Move that tree and get me there. We'll turn out anyone staying and see if they aren't the man the note detailed we should be seeking."

They were able to drag the tree off the road and soon were on their way.

After silence fell over the forest, Zin spoke. "How long were we asleep?"

"An hour, perhaps," Slant said. "I got the idea to start chopping the tree not long after you both started snoring. I had intended to drop it when we left. Then I heard the carriage and finished my work before they were close enough to hear it."

"Looks like that was all the sleep we're going to get," Jovan said.

"We could follow them to this inn and ruin their carriage straps," Slant offered.

"No. If we do that, they'll know we're near. And that they're on the right track."

"I might roll over and catch another hour of sleep," Zin said.

"We have to continue," Jovan said. "We're so close."

"To Righteousness?" Slant said.

"Rightness," Jovan agreed.

CHAPTER 29 — WEAVER

The Umernnosti haven in Rightness had been as hospitable as they were when last Jovan visited, and it was Zin who eagerly urged Slant and Jovan awake before dawn the next morning. His nervousness from the night before had disappeared and was replaced by a cheerfulness Jovan had not seen in him before. Slant disappeared as they came to the street and not long after came back to join them as they passed the remains of what was Kallidova's warehouse. The adjacent buildings still had the black soot on their faces from the fire, while the new timbers going up to rebuild stood out in stark contrast.

"She'll be back here eventually, if she's rebuilding," Slant said.

"Where did you run off to?"

"To check on Zelmir and the humble lodgings he took last night."

"How close to danger were we?"

"Very little, to be honest. The Temple of Negligent Assurance sits like its name," Slant said, "in abandoned silence."

"What do you mean?"

"I mean, the prince stayed there, with us not far from him, right under his nose, and he doesn't have guards out on alert, nor are there stirrings of early risers. I would wager the High Priest threw him a little feast, and they are all still sleeping it off."

"Or they've gone ahead of us while we slept," Jovan said.

"No," Slant replied. "I asked one of the brethren to watch all night. He did so, and happily. The prince never left."

Jovan nodded. "What has Zin so ready to go this morning?"

Zin walked ahead of them with a hop in his step.

"He anticipates seeing Vlada today. He hasn't seen her since she fled on ahead to Geruz."

"I assumed he knew of Periphina being born because he had visited her after."

"No," Slant replied. "He never saw her again. I fear he will not like what he sees."

"Oh?" Jovan asked.

"Kallidova has sent me to check on her a time or two. While I didn't understand what had caused her to become as she now is, when she imbued the children within her, Vlada gave of her mind, her soul, her spirit. There is very little left of her now."

"If we keep up our pace, perhaps we'll cut off Kallidova at Geruz by nightfall," Jovan said as he and Slant matched stride with Zin.

"We aren't going as far as Geruz," Slant said, joining them.

"What do you mean?" Zin asked.

"Vlada has been staying at a forest cabin Kallidova provided for her after Vlada gave birth."

"Where is that?" Jovan asked.

"You know the Borevez Waystop?" Slant asked. "Where we first met?"

"Of course," Jovan said.

"The cabin is half way between Geruz and Borevez."

"You mean the weaver's cottage?"

"I think it was that at one point, yes."

"Vlada is the crazy weaver?" Jovan said, and then bit his tongue as he said it.

Zin scowled.

They stopped for only a short time to see Borev and take a quick meal before continuing on. It wasn't long after when they came out alongside a gentle slope of a hill. Smoke rose from a cottage; four horses grazed freely in the meadow around it.

Zin took off up the hill without hesitation. Jovan sensed Zin's pace gradually slowing, until Jovan came to walk alongside him just short of the meager path that led to the door.

Zin's feet refused to take him up onto the wood porch. Jovan lifted a fist to knock on the door. He felt Slant step up next to him.

"Come in," Kallidova's voice said before his knuckle had met the wood. "No point in pretenses."

Jovan pushed and the door swung open easily into a single room. Kallidova stood by a blazing hearth. A single bed lay against the wall; two blonde children crouched next to it, holding the hands of a golden-haired woman with deathly white skin. Both looked up as he entered.

"Papa Jov!" Leaf exclaimed as he ran toward him, throwing himself into Jovan's arms as the big man crouched down to accept it.

Jovan took a long, deep breath and exhaled.

"You are well?" Jovan asked.

Leaf nodded. "I missed you. Your face is more scratchy now."

"It'll take time to grow back my beard."

Leaf pulled away and looked at his sister. "He's here, like you promised."

Periphina smiled broadly, albeit wickedly.

Leaf took Jovan's hand and pulled him toward the bed.

"What is going on?" Jovan asked.

He approached the bed. The woman who lay there was wavering against death's veil. Cold sweat covered her face and soaked her black hair. Her empty eyes fluttered.

"This is my mama," Leaf said. "I guess she's been here, not far from home, all this time. We have something we have to do for her. I don't want to, but I promised I would if Perif could bring you here. I needed to know you were safe."

"That I was safe?" Jovan asked.

"Yes. I was worried about you. Worried that you had gotten in trouble again. Mamm Kallidova said you hurt Zvediz."

Jovan nodded. "He'll be well, soon enough. What do you and Periphina need to do?"

"Help Mama give Perif a gift."

"No," Jovan said with finality.

His word was echoed from behind as Zin finally gathered enough courage to enter.

"No!" Zin cried out a second time and flew toward the bed. "Vlada!"

The young woman's eyes opened with a start and she took a deep, sharp breath.

"Sammy?" she said weakly, looking up at the man who had lifted her into a sitting position. Samov Zin was kissing her clammy forehead repeatedly.

"I'm sorry," Zin said. "I'm sorry I didn't come to you sooner."

"Don't apologize," Vlada said. "I can die happy now."

"You will do no such thing," Periphina interrupted.

Vlada smiled at the girl and reached out to stroke her hair. Jovan saw the little girl imperceptibly wince, then refrain from pulling back.

"You remind me of myself at your age," Vlada said. "I grew out of that when I met Samov."

"Mother," Periphina said, forcing honey into her voice. "Do you remember what we talked about? The gift?"

"Yes," Vlada said. "You want me to give you more. I don't know if I can, or if I know how."

"Mother," Periphina said, clenching her little jaw. "You gave me something I cannot use."

Vlada pursed her lips. "I gave you something. Yes. I see how smart you are. As full of thought as I am now empty."

"Yes," Periphina smiled. "You gave me your mind. Your intellect. And you also gave Illifan and me a portion of your soul. But you didn't give me any spirit. You gave it all to Illifan. Only he can access the soul-well."

"I don't understand," Vlada said. "I gave Illifan my spirit? But..."

"What would she have left?" Slant asked, standing next to Jovan.

"What do you mean?" Jovan asked.

"If she gave most of her mind, soul, and spirit, it's amazing she can even function anymore, nevertheless the last four years."

"And now Periphina demands she give what is left of her spirit," Jovan said. "What happens if she dies without a spirit?"

"I couldn't tell you," Slant said.

"It is time," Periphina stated ominously. She stood and reached out to touch Leaf's hand. "You will help her do it."

Leaf looked up at her, then to Vlada, then to Jovan.

"Papa Jov?"

Jovan shook his head.

"Yes," Periphina said darkly. "You cannot keep it from me."

"You have what you need," Kallidova said. "Jovan is right. This cannot be."

"What do you mean? You cannot turn on me!" the little girl screeched. "Not after traveling all this way!"

"You can learn," Kallidova said, "as anyone else does, to reach down into the well."

"I do not wish to wait," Periphina said with spite.

"Periphina," Vlada said weakly from the bed. "I don't think I have the strength to do what you ask. I don't remember how."

"That's why Illifan is here. He can help."

"You said she was sick and what I did was going to help her," Leaf said.

"Illifan," Periphina said with condescension in her voice. "Illifan, if you help me do this, we can turn our power back and save her. Strengthen her."

"If she survives," Slant said. "She will be more broken than she is. If she dies, neither of you have the strength to pull her back."

"We could give her strength," Periphina offered. "From the two of us." She glanced around the room, and quickly looked away from Jovan when they made eye contact.

"You intend to force Leaf to do it all," Jovan said. "It will break him."

"It will not kill Illifan," Periphina said, not denying his accusation.

"Why are you allowing this to continue?" Jovan whispered to Kallidova, moving next to her. "Because you hope this will distract her from your daughter?"

Kallidova shot him a look, then looked back at the children.

Jovan shook his head and then took a step forward. "This has gone on long enough," he said, placing a hand on Periphina's shoulder. "It's time you leave your mother alone. She has given enough, and had enough taken from her."

The girl turned and looked up at Jovan. He saw the anger rising in her, a reflection of his own rage he knew too well. He took hold of her and lifted her up, his hand clamping over her mouth as she began to scream. Her arms began to flail as she tried to get at him. He turned and walked from the cabin and out into the sunlight. He held her as she continued to fight and rage at him, powerless to do anything. She slowly calmed down and began to whimper. He placed her on the ground, but kept a firm grip on her.

"Are you calm now?" he asked.

She nodded, wiping tears from her eyes.

"That was uncalled for," he said.

She laughed and then yawned. Then she looked up into his eyes. "I'd like to go back inside now."

He took her hand in his and turned to walk back into the cabin. Looking to the north, he saw the dust of the prince's cavalcade a few miles off, and shook his head, knowing he had little time.

"Is everything all right?" Slant asked as they came in.

"Yes, I think so," Jovan said. "I would guess today is the first time she's been told 'no' and she took it as any child her age would."

Vlada slept now in Zin's arms, her breath coming in quick successions. Periphina went and crouched next to the bed, then looked back.

"Why is she breathing like this?" she asked.

"You know why," Jovan said softly.

"No," Periphina said, frowning at Vlada. "This can't be."

Vlada's hand gripped Zin's in squeezes that came fewer and farther between.

Then, they stopped. The wind outside seemed to stop with Vlada's final breath.

"Illifan," Periphina said, looking over at her brother. "Help her! She doesn't need her spirit now. Take what you can and give it to me!"

"I can't," Leaf replied. "She's gone." Quiet tears fell from his eyes. "But she said to say that she loves you."

Periphina spun on the room. Her eyes fell on Kallidova.

"Then you can give me some of your spirit," she said. The anger burned in her eyes. "Since we are blood."

"It won't work," Slant said. "You have to be close blood. A mother, a father, a twin..."

Periphina spun to look at Leaf, who now had his head lowered. Vlada slipped away, her face relaxing. Zin cried quietly over her as he cradled her.

"Illifan," Periphina said, "you could give me some of it."

Jovan stepped forward and took hold of the little girl's shoulder.

"No, Periphina," Jovan said. "You need to stop."

"No! I want what is owed me!"

"Nothing is owed you," Jovan said. "Don't you understand? You've already been given a gift, and early enough that it's part of who you are. Use that gift. If you were given more, without having earned it, where would it stop?"

Periphina turned and buried her head into Jovan's shoulder as he knelt. She began to sob quietly. "I planned this day to be such a good one. And now it's ruined. Why did she die? We just arrived..."

"Her love, Zin, returned to her. Her children live. She knew she could die happy."

"And leave me with nothing."

Kallidova came and knelt behind her. "Periphina. We can find a teacher. Someone who can help you unlock your potential."

"No," Periphina said in defeat. "No, that won't work."

"Why not?" Kallidova asked.

The little girl spun, a small knife in her hand. She plunged it into her grandmother's chest. Kallidova fell back, surprise caught on her face.

"You can give me yours. I need father to keep his, so I can inherit his authority. I need Illifan to keep the soul-well strong. But now you have nothing else to live for. So give me what is owed!"

Jovan took hold of the little girl's wrist and squeezed until she dropped the knife.

"No," Kallidova said, coughing. A thin line of blood ran quickly down her chin. "If this is what you have already become, then I will let the gods judge me for my sins, and hope they do the same to you, you little monster."

She slipped downward into the pool of blood forming under her, and began to rasp slower and shallower breaths.

Periphina turned and ran from the cottage, half crying, half screaming.

"We have to keep her from succeeding," Zin said, setting Vlada back down onto her pillow.

"We have," Jovan said. "She said she needs Leaf and Prince Zelmir left unharmed."

"Yes," Zin said. "That leaves Sephaly."

Kallidova began shaking her head, violently, coughing up more blood. "Don't let her hurt my baby," she rasped.

"You split her from the prince in a rivening," Jovan said to Kallidova, dropping to her side. "Didn't you?"

She nodded.

"How?" Slant asked.

"There is a group of Havats," Kallidova said. "They hold the secret. I made the king promise to give me one of the children."

"And you told Sephaly how it was done?"

"My own children were born prematurely," she said, coughing, "before we could imbue them. Vlada's were the same. What choice did I have?"

"Then this was always part of the plan," Jovan said. "To place an imbued ruler on the throne."

"Instead," Slant said, "it created a cruel, evil prince, and a fair and kind Sephaly. And now history repeats itself."

Kallidova clutched at Slant's shirt.

"Save Sephaly," she said, as she fell to the ground, lifeless.

"We don't have much time," Jovan said.

Slant and Zin looked at him quizzically.

"The prince's cavalcade is not far away. I saw them when I stepped outside. We ought to leave this place and see if we can get to Geruz before they can."

"Perif has seen them," Leaf said, walking up and placing a hand on Jovan's shoulder. "I can feel her running to them."

"Let her go," Jovan said. "The prince won't harm her."

"I'll stay here," Zin said. "To see to the bodies."

Jovan nodded and took Leaf's hand in his. "I think we can cut over the hills to Geruz and hopefully beat them there."

Slant peeked out of the cabin. "The cavalcade has stopped on the road, and Periphina is standing next to the coach. Let's go now."

Jovan, Slant, and Leaf slipped out the door and around the corner, then ran down the back side of the hill toward the woods. As they turned to look back, the smoke from the chimney was met by smoke pouring from the door.

"He's setting fire to the place," Slant said with a laugh. "I hope he makes it out himself."

"I don't think he cares," Jovan said.

"Will Periphina be all right?" Leaf asked Jovan, who hefted him up onto his shoulders.

"Yes. I expect she'll explain much to the prince, and they'll come riding into town in style. The prince has been on our trail every step of the way, almost as though he knew we were headed here from the beginning. We expected them to follow Kallidova's trail."

"Periphina left a message for Zelmir before they left Khorapesh," Leaf said.

"That little girl had everything planned to the letter," Jovan said.

CHAPTER 30 — END

They came over the top of a bald rise and could see back down the road that curved the long way round toward the town. The prince's coach raced along a road below them, curving around the same hill, guards forced to march alongside it in full regalia. Down the other side of the hill, Geruz had no clue that anyone was approaching.

"We run," Jovan said. "And we'll still have trouble beating them to the motte and bailey."

Jovan picked the boy up and vaulted down the hill, the black-clad Slant just behind them. They came to the flat stretch and raced toward the gate. A figure stepped out.

"Halt!" Gostis said. Then he startled in surprise. "Jovan! What are you doing back?"

"I don't have time to explain. I have to get to Lord Valle-Brons."

"I can't let you in," Gostis said. "You were exiled."

"Gostis," Jovan said, stepping up to the man, breathing heavily, "Sephaly is in danger. I need you to stall the entourage approaching. Don't ask me questions. I know you can't stop them. Just make it difficult for them to get to Gull Stone as long as you can."

"Jovan," Gostis said, "I..."

"Gostis. Have I ever lied to you?"

Gostis sighed. "Go on up. Tell the Smytt brothers I need them down here at the gate."

Jovan smiled. "I owe you."

"Yes, you do."

Jovan ran through the small town and to the gate leading up to the gray castle above. The Smytt brothers were lazily watching their approach.

"Gostis wants you down at the main gate, quickly," Jovan barked.

They didn't even stop to question him. They picked up their spears and ran down into the town. Jovan turned to see a commotion starting at the gate, and knew it wouldn't be long.

Jovan led the way up the steep hill, as he felt the first drops of rain hit his face. No one stood guard at the main entrance, so Jovan pushed through the doors and entered. Two men sat by the fire playing cheques. One of them was Lord Valle-Brons's steward. He rose as he saw Jovan approach and opened his mouth in protest as they started up the stairs.

"You had best see things straightened up," Jovan said. "Prince Zelmir Valle is entering town as we speak. I expect he'll want hospitality shown to him."

The steward froze and then spun to begin putting the place in order.

They came to the top of the stairs and Jovan pushed the door open.

Verth Valle-Brons stood at the window, his back to the door. Slant slipped in behind Jovan and slinked away to the curtain across the room as Jovan put Leaf down on the ground.

"What is this?" the lord asked, turning from the window. "Jovan. What are you doing here?"

"I'm here because Prince Zelmir Valle is coming."

"To see you dead?"

"I'm sure he'd like that. But no. I expect he comes to see Sephaly."

"No!" Verth roared. "He will not touch my daughter again!"

"Touch your daughter?" Jovan asked.

"He took her innocence. It drove her mad."

"I'm afraid I don't think that is what happened," Jovan said. "Much has occurred since I left. And I'm hoping to learn a truth or two before the prince arrives. I need to see Sephaly."

The curtain moved aside and Slant emerged with the frail form of Sephaly in his arms. She looked up at Slant, smiling simply and fondly.

"You," Verth hissed.

Slant shrugged.

"You started this," the lord said.

"I may have," Slant said. "But it goes back even further. To your wife, I'm afraid."

"What?"

Jovan walked over and knelt beside Sephaly, who now sat in her father's chair, Slant at her shoulder. Leaf brought a blanket over to her, and she took it, smiling at the boy.

"You've grown, Illifan," she said wanly.

"Sephaly?" Jovan asked.

She looked away from Leaf and over at the man next to her.

"Are you his protector?" she asked, a deeper look of confusion in her eyes than the last time they had met.

"I've tried," Jovan said.

"And he is a good little boy?"

"Never one better."

She sighed and relaxed.

"Sephaly, I need to know what happened."

"What do you mean?"

"To make Leaf. I need to know."

She looked over at Slant, guiltily, then looked back.

"I learned many things from Slavint," she said. "Things I shouldn't know. When Zelmir asked I come to Khorapesh to help him with something...how was I supposed to know what he wanted?"

She stared into nothingness as she fell silent.

Jovan took a breath to ask her to continue, when she spoke again.

"When he told me what he wanted me to do with that girl who carried his child, the pieces fell together for me. I knew the truth of what I was. And I knew what I needed to do to save everyone."

"What did you do?"

She smiled and touched Jovan's face. "You might not understand, dear man."

"Tell me anyway. In simple words."

She took a deep breath and sat up, a strength seeming to enter into her.

"I convinced Vlada to let me help when it was time for her to imbue the child. I told her I would give the child some of my soul and spirit, while she would give her soul and mind."

"But you did something else."

"Yes. My mother split me from Zelmir. And so, without the girl knowing, I performed a rivening and split Illifan from his sister. Vlada gave her mind and I gave my spirit. But we gave of our souls to the two of them. I just hoped I gave the right one the spirit."

"What do you mean, the right one?"

"You know how Prince Zelmir is. He has some goodness in him, but not much. It could have been that Periphina got the spirit, unlocking the power of her soul. But instead, it was innocent little Illifan."

A commotion rose from the hall below.

"It gives me peace to know I succeeded. Perhaps the sins of my mother can be washed away yet."

She stood cautiously and walked back to her seat at the window overlooking the sea.

Footsteps pounded outside before the door burst open. The little girl, Periphina, marched in, taking in the room and the people within quickly.

"Where is she?" she asked.

She saw the woman by the window and ran over to her, composing herself on the way.

"Hello, dear Sephaly," she said with no emotion in her voice.

"You do not hide your spite well," Sephaly said weakly, turning to look at her.

Several men fumbled to carry Prince Zelmir in. They placed the box litter on the table, and then opened it, revealing the evilly grinning man.

Verth stepped forward. "You are not welcome here," Lord Valle-Brons quavered.

Zelmir shot out with his rod, just missing the man. Two guards grabbed Verth and pulled him away. Verth's shoulders dropped in defeat and he fell silent.

"Well," Zelmir said, looking around the room, "here we are."

He saw the little boy and then Jovan. He scowled, but Jovan could make out hesitation in his eyes. Then he turned to Sephaly.

"Hello, cousin," he said with emphasized venom on his tongue. "Although, given the interesting conversation with this little girl this past hour, perhaps I ought to call you 'sister.' It also seems you kept the success of our little venture from me. You told me Vlada was dead, and the child with her. Periphina, here, is under the impression that you went a little further than we had ever discussed."

He looked over at Leaf.

"Aren't you a good little boy?" Zelmir asked.

At that moment, Jovan could see Sephaly's smile in Zelmir. They were the same. With the two of them in the same room they felt like two halves of a whole, somehow.

"Do you know why I'm here?" the prince asked Sephaly, without taking his eyes off Leaf.

Sephaly shook her head.

"I'm here to help this little girl fulfill her destiny. See, your little subterfuge creating the boy has kept something from her that she needs."

"I did not keep anything from her. I gave something to the boy so she could not have it in the first place."

"That is what I said!" Zelmir roared. "And I intend to see to it that you give her what she needs."

"Why don't you give it to her?" Slant said to the prince.

"Who?" the prince said, turning. "Ah. The Havat mongrel. I suppose we owe you much for what you stole from the ved-mak school. See he dies after this," he said to the guards.

"He did ask a valid question," Jovan said.

"And I still owe you an excruciating death," the prince said, pointing his rod at Jovan.

Jovan smiled. "I don't think so."

"What is it you need me to do?" Sephaly asked. "I need you to say it."

"Give me the means to accessing the well," Periphina said.

"I cannot," Sephaly said, smiling wanly.

"Why not?" the little girl screeched.

"You see, your mother did not give you her mind and spirit. Only her mind. She had plenty of spirit to give, but with her mind lost, she had no way to access it. I gave more spirit than I should have. Together, Vlada and I gave too much of our souls. We compromised them. It took all of our strength just to keep back a portion of my spirit and a portion of Vlada's mind. There is nothing left to us. You both have it all."

"We could have a vedmak come," Periphina said thoughtfully to the prince. "Pay him to excise the last vestige of spirit from her."

"No. I don't think so," Sephaly said. "I have succeeded in my goal. The power lies in the innocent Illifan. Now, I think it is time I take away any hope you have of suffering me to give you such."

She looked around the room and smiled at each person in turn. Lord Valle-Brons approached her and took her hand as she offered it to him. She stood from her seat and smiled at him gently.

"I'm sorry you got mixed up in all of this," she said, taking her hand from his and placing it on his cheek. "But I do this for the soul of the world."

She took a step toward the window, and disappeared to the collective gasp of the room.

Verth threw himself across the room first to look out the window. "I can't see her!" he cried. Then he turned and raced out the door. "Sephaly!"

The guards followed after him.

"Pick me up! Pick me up!" the prince shouted. The guards hoisted the litter and they all spilled out of the room.

Jovan crossed to the window. Slant and Leaf stood next to him. Slant had tears rimming his eyes. "It was better that way. For her."

"She's not gone yet," Leaf said solemnly.

"What?" Jovan said. He looked out the window, but he couldn't see her. "How do you know, Leaf?"

"I can just tell. Like with Perif. Once I met her again, it was like we could feel each other. Like we always could. It was how I knew you were going to be alright, before you found me again."

He heard a rip and Slant had a tapestry in his hand. "Go. See if you can steal her away before they get to her. That little monster will find a way to take a portion from her if you don't."

"They'll kill you and me for this. You ought to leave."

"I'll go to Gordilah, I think."

"See Leaf gets out of town safely; send him on to Miller's Hollow. I'll meet him there."

"Are you and I square now?" Slant asked, a bit of hope in his eyes.

"I still don't trust you," Jovan said. "But I am no longer angry with you."

He knelt next to Leaf, held both of his shoulders, and nodded. Leaf threw his arms around Jovan's neck.

After a moment, Jovan stood, took the tapestry from Slant, and leapt from the window, the tapestry slowing his fall. He came to the end with another twenty feet still to go and fell the rest of the way to the turf, rolling down the hill a ways before stopping. It was sheer and all but inaccessible by a small sheep path. He scrambled around until he found the still form of Sephaly.

"Who is it?" she whimpered.

"Jovan."

He lifted her onto his lap, trying to make her more comfortable.

"My protector. Again."

"I will help you get out of here."

"No. Don't bother," she said in a voice weaker than before. "I can't feel my body."

"They'll come for you. And somehow force you to do what they want."

"Then we'll take that from them. I knew what I did was wrong even as I was doing it. But I had to. Zelmir wanted it."

"You can't change the past."

"I can't. But you can see the debt paid for all of our mistakes. Take what I have to offer. You can use my last strength better than I can, anyway, if only for a short time."

A puff of white fire came out of her mouth. Jovan felt the rush of her strength leaving her and entering him. Her eyes went glassy and she was gone.

He heard the scrambling of a soldier behind him, trying to move along the wet rocks above. He laid Sephaly down softly and turned. As he stood, he felt the imbued strength coursing through his muscles.

The soldier drew a sword and took a hesitant step toward Jovan, then swung, his balance on the steep hill providing him no help. Jovan took hold of the man's wrist and pulled.

The man cried out as he fell head over heel and rolled, disappearing over the escarpment into the crashing waves below.

The color of the world drained to gray, and a pulsing beat pounded in Jovan's head as anger surged. Jovan walked up to the wall as two more men came around the corner. They had no time to react as Jovan dove into them. He took hold of their sword arms and twisted them sharply, with a crack. They cried out, and then fell silent as he brought their helmeted heads together. Their still forms and indented helmets told Jovan they would not rise again.

The footing became easier as he rounded the edge of the bailey. He could see the prince fleeing down the hill in his litter between his four personal guards. Five more of the prince's guards looked up at Jovan, pole arms in hand, turning away from the form of Lord Valle-Brons, curled up and whimpering on the ground.

They charged Jovan, holding their pole arms low, their roaring battle cry empty compared to Jovan's louder fury. He moved more quickly than they could as he spent the unnatural energy that bled off him in puffs of white smoke from his mouth.

He took hold of the first spear and pulled so hard the man fell down at Jovan's feet. Jovan tossed the spear away and stepped on the man, kicking his other heel out into the chest of the next.

The other three hesitated for a moment, but it was all Jovan needed. He took hold of the third and pulled down so hard the man's knees buckled in two different unnatural directions. The man screamed.

Jovan was surprised to realize he had taken the wrought-wood stiletto from his coat. He grinned wickedly and swung the scabbard around, taking the fourth across the side of the neck. Jovan felt the crumple of bone under the strength he bore down on the soldier.

The fifth lost his courage and turned to run. Jovan burst forward with an uncanny speed and overtook the man, shoving the end of the stiletto into his back with a swift in and out. He fell with a weak whimper.

Jovan turned and looked back at the scene for a moment. He could tell the strength Sephaly had given him was quickly bleeding off—but it would be enough. He burst down the hill and toward the town.

The town guard stopped in their tracks as they marched up toward the motte and bailey. Gostis held a hand for the others to stop and let the bloody juggernaut surge past them. The people of the town now stood outside their homes. Some looked toward the edge of town where the four guards bearing the litter ran to escape. The others looked on as Jovan raced past them.

Two of the prince's guards had stopped and were trying frantically to put a chain in place on the gate. The prince's carriage leaned nearby, one of the wheels off its axle. Jovan smiled to himself, knowing Gostis had done more than enough to ensure the prince was stalled. The girl Periphina watched from inside the carriage. She screamed at the two guards to hurry with their work to stop Jovan.

Jovan ignored her and rushed toward the gate. The impact of Jovan hit the first man, crushing him against the gate.

The other tried to draw his sword, but the pommel of Jovan's stiletto took him in the forehead, and he fell to the ground.

Jovan turned to the gate. The guards had succeeded in securing the chain. He sheathed and dropped the wrought-wood sword and took hold of the gate in both hands. Drawing a deep breath, he exhaled as he lifted. White smoke poured from his mouth. The gate lurched and tore free from the posts.

The gate suddenly became heavy in his arms and he dropped it to the side with a crash. He could hear the collective gasp of the town, but paid them little heed. He took up his sword and ran off down the road.

The roar of his rage filled his mind, but the strength Sephaly had given him had been spent with the crashing of the gate. He closed the distance to the prince and the two guards trying to do the work of four with the litter between them. The prince looked back over their shoulders and screamed at them frantically to hurry. Jovan pulled his stiletto from its scabbard and threw it in a long arc. It spun through the air and stuck in the road just ahead of the first soldier. His toe caught the edge of the blade, forfeiting his balance.

The soldiers and litter went down in a tangle of legs and cries as Jovan fell upon them. He pulled up the sword and shoved it into one soldier and then the other. Then he stood over the prince, now spilled out on the side of the road, lying in the same ditch as he had four years prior.

Jovan dropped the sword and slowly lowered himself over the prince, placing his thumbs against his throat. The prince's screams of rage and defiance pierced through the gray of the world with a splash of red, matching Jovan's anger. A wave of clarity broke over him, and he stopped.

The prince continued to holler in gasps before realizing he was not dead. He looked up with the eyes of an embarrassed child at the blood-covered man who straddled him.

"Thrice," Jovan said. "Thrice I have held you in my hands. Thrice I could have killed you. Yet you still will not see reason. I could have left you for dead that day and saved the whole world a hurt. If you had not been a presence to fear, those children would have each been raised by a loving mother, instead of being hidden away. Instead, the world has been smeared with the vile decay of forbidden magic."

"You will reap what you sow."

"No. You have reaped what you have sown. You will now take the girl. I think, if she does not have you assassinated, the gods will see to it that your kingdom falls to waste from her machinations."

"But the boy..."

"He is mine."

"I will not relent."

"Then I will kill you now."

The prince winced.

"You will not seek us out. If you do, I will hunt you down, and I will kill you. It will not be done quickly, either. Do you agree?"

The prince nodded.

Jovan rose and began to walk away.

"You'll reap what you sow, as well!" the prince shouted defiantly.

And Jovan ignored him.

EPILOGUE

The long, uphill walk on the winding path to the Miller's Hollow drained what little energy he had left in him. The small cottage was built over the milling floor, which hung out over the surface of a half-empty hole of water, a hundred feet below. The wheel turned slightly with the trickle from the depleted brook that fed the pool below.

He walked under the trickle and stuck his head in it for a while, letting the cold water wash away the last bits of strength along with the blood that stuck to his face. He walked up to the threshold and stepped within.

A fire burned in the hearth. Leaf was pulling a cloth over the table, a slab of dried meat and cheese on the board ready. He looked up and smiled.

Leaf climbed up onto Jovan as he slumped down on a chair, nestling his golden head onto Jovan's shoulder.

"Papa Jov?"

"Yes?"

"What do we do now?"

"I think we'll go explore the world. I owe you that debt."

"What about me?"

"What do you mean?"

"Do I owe a debt?"

"No, boy. But I think you'll end up paying it one day, anyway."

"Pay for what?"

"The sins of your ancestors. But if anyone is able to do so, it's you."

"Can I just be a boy for a while, though?"

Jovan looked down. Wisdom far surpassing any person he had ever met looked up at him through a four-year-old's eyes.

"Yes. I think you deserve that much."

The End

Photo by Renae Meredith

About the Author

Andrew D Meredith's journey has taken him to many fantastical places. From selling books in the wilds of western Washington to designing and publishing board games in the great white midwest. He's now committed to the quest he was called to so long ago: the telling of fantastical tales, and bringing to life underestimated characters willing to take on the responsibilities no one else will.

For all the latest updates, you can follow him as @andrewdmth on Instagram, Facebook, Twitter, and Goodreads or visit his website at AndrewDMeredith.com.

CPSIA information can be obtained
at www.ICGtesting.com
Printed in the USA
FSHW011128201021
85555FS